VERNON SCANNELL, born in 1922, served with the Gordon Highlanders in the Middle East and in the D-Day landings in Normandy (see his autobiographical *Argument of Kings*). In his youth he boxed both as amateur and professional and subsequently taught English in a prep school, but he has been a full-time writer since the early 1960s, publishing novels, criticism and four autobiographical prose books as well as over a dozen volumes of poetry. An early collection, *The Masks of Love* (1960) won the Heinemann Award, *The Loving Game* (1975) was a Poetry Book Society Choice and he has been awarded the Cholmondeley Poetry Prize and a Society of Authors Travelling Scholarship. In 1980 he was granted a Civil List Pension for services to Literature and he is an honorary Fellow of The Royal Society of Literature.

# VERNON SCANNELL

## *Feminine Endings*

London
ENITHARMON PRESS
2000

First published in 2000
by the Enitharmon Press
36 St George's Avenue
London N7 0HD

Distributed in Europe
by Littlehampton Book Services
through Signature Book Representation
2 Little Peter Street
Manchester M15 4PS

Distributed in the USA and Canada
by Dufour Editions Inc.
PO Box 7, Chester Springs
PA 19425, USA

ISBN 1 900564 07 6

British Library Cataloguing-in-Publication Data.
A catalogue record for this book is available
from the British Library.

Set in Sabon by Sutchinda Rangsi Thompson
and printed in Great Britain by
The Cromwell Press, Wiltshire

To Alan Benson

*with gratitude for his
hard work and word-processor
wizardry*

# SUNDAY

'IT'S NOT WORKING, Chris,' Serena said. 'It's all been a big mistake.'

She was standing in the open doorway of the administrative office of Crackenthorpe Hall, one of the four centres for the teaching of creative writing established by the Bendover Trust. This worthy foundation had been endowed in 1974 by the now deceased Arthur Bendover, multimillionaire, cybernetics wizard and poetry lover.

Serena Burton was quite small with a sharp-featured, pretty if now petulant face and a feathery cap of dark hair. She wore tight faded blue jeans and a large woollen sweater which looked more than big enough for the man she was talking to and did, indeed, belong to him.

Chris Haynes, her partner and co-warden and director of studies at Crackenthorpe Hall was a tall gangling man with glasses and already thinning pale hair although, at thirty-one, he was only five years older than Serena.

He looked up from behind the littered desk at which he was sitting and, still holding the official-looking letter he had been frowning over, he made a vague murmuring noise of interrogation: 'Errr . . . ah . . . hermmm . . .?' Working?' His mouth was slightly open and Serena thought that he looked maddeningly stupid. 'Mistake did you say? What do you mean? What's not working? What's a mistake?'

'Us,' Serena said. 'The whole set-up. You and me. This bloody place. I thought we were going to be fine here. Plenty of time for our own work. You painting, me writing. But it's not been like that at all. I haven't written anything, not a bloody line in the last month or more. Not a line worth keeping anyway. And I know damn well I'm not going to. I'm dried up. Blocked. And you know why as well as I do. Running these courses is like running a Brownie Camp. They're like kids. The last lot *were* bloody kids. We only got rid of them yesterday and there's another lot coming today. I really don't think I can face it.'

'Hey now, wait a minute.' Chris dropped the letter he had been holding on to the desk. 'This one's different. These aren't kids. I admit the last bunch were a bit of a pain. We should've known. Schoolkids don't come to a place like this to work. It was just a skive for them and their teachers weren't much better. But this one's an open course. All grown-ups. They'll be serious committed people or they wouldn't pay good money to come here. Adults, not kids. And it's all poetry. No prose, short stories or whatever that guy Ellis was supposed to be doing with the kids. Believe me, sweetheart, you'll get started again on your own work. I bet you'll be stimulated. It's a pity about MacDuff letting us down at the last minute. That was bad luck, him getting 'flu. But you've got hold of a good bloke to take his place . . . haven't you? I mean he'll be all right, won't he? This chap Napier. He seemed keen enough to come, even at such short notice. He'll be okay, won't he?'

'Don't know. Should be all right I suppose.'

'Yeah. I'm sure he will be. Must admit I'd never heard of him. What kind of poet is he? Didn't you say he's getting on a bit?'

'You've never heard of anybody. He's very well known. At least he used to be.'

'How old is he?'

'I don't know. Sixty something.'

'Would he be in the thingummy book?' Chris left his seat and reached for *The Oxford Companion to Twentieth-Century Poetry* from a shelf which held a *Chambers English Dictionary*, *Roget's Thesaurus*, a *London A to Z* and a few other works of reference. Still standing he flicked through the pages; then he stopped and began to read, almost to himself, his muttering barely audible.

Serena leaned against the doorpost, her arms folded, looking at him, eyes narrowed with resentment.

'Listen to this,' he said. 'Gordon Napier – that's the bloke, isn't it? Here he is. Born 1934. Educated Uppingham and Merton College, Oxford, where he took a First in Greats . . . What's that mean?'

'It means he's got brains.'

'Yeah, . . . well, he seems to have published a lot of stuff. Let's see

. . . one, two, three . . . ah, six, seven – no, eight. Eight volumes of poetry and something called *The Rape of Euterpe*.' He pronounced the last word 'U-Turp'. 'That's critical essays, it says here. He's done National Service in the army and worked as a schoolmaster and as a copywriter in a London advertising agency. There's more. I'll read what it says – Napier's first collection, *Made to Measure*, anticipated the work of the Movement Poets, with whom he has never been officially associated, and it attracted much favourable notice. His subsequent work, however, never quite fulfilled his early promise and his reputation had faded in recent years.'

Chris snapped the book shut and replaced it on the shelf. 'Sounds like he's a bit of an old has-been, doesn't it? Have you ever read any of his stuff?'

It seemed at first that Serena could not be bothered to answer but then she appeared to change her mind and said, 'Yes, I've read a few things. Matter of fact we had a poem of his in our O Level anthology.'

'Christ, he must be old!'

'Thank *you*,' she said and went out of the office, backheeling the door behind her.


'My God, I feel old,' Gordon Napier said to himself as he slowly and painfully unfolded his legs and heaved himself out of his seat while the train jerked and shuddered to a halt. He peered out of the window to make sure that he had read the name of the station correctly. It was Ancliffe all right. He pulled his case and old overcoat down from the luggage rack and hesitated a moment before he decided not to pick up the *Observer* with its half-completed crossword puzzle. He sidled and shuffled his way to the end of the carriage where he stopped outside the toilets to put on his coat before taking up his case again and descending to the platform.

In the bleak, wind-shaken half-light of the late November afternoon he saw that half a dozen other passengers had left the train, among them the awful young woman he had encountered early on the journey. At King's Cross, a few moments before the train had left the station, she had taken the only available seat in the carriage, which was the one opposite to his own, her arrival first signalled by a heady waftage of scent. Before sitting down she had said in an unnecessarily loud and what he thought aggressive voice, 'Do you *mind*?'

He had looked up and seen her handsome but not at all friendly dark eyes on his *Observer* which he had quickly removed from the table between them with a muttered 'Sorry'. She had then promptly dumped an enormous leather shoulder-bag on to the table and extracted two glossy magazines, a newspaper, a box of tissues and a Filofax, all of which she spread over at least half of the table's surface.

When the train had stopped at Doncaster, where a lot of passengers alighted, the young woman had gathered up her belongings and moved to another seat and table, giving Gordon what had seemed to him a look of something like contemptuous distaste. Now, as he watched her teetering on high heels along the platform with a large suitcase as well as the shoulder-bag, a terrible thought occurred to him: could she be Gabriella Cornwell, the poet who was to be his fellow-tutor on the course?

The other passengers who were making their way to the exit looked unlikely candidates for the role. They were all at least middle-aged, two men and three women, all carrying bags or suitcases. Picking up his own bag he thought, 'Well, I'll soon find out.'

A moment later a young man with spectacles, wearing jeans and an anorak, appeared on the platform and greeted the travellers, including and with greatest warmth, Gabriella Cornwell, if that was who she was. Then Gordon saw the young man look in his direction, raise a hand in salute and hurry towards him.

'You must be Gordon. Am I right? I'm Chris Haynes.' They shook hands. 'Here, let me take that.'

The little group was waiting at the station exit as Chris and Gordon joined them. 'Do you two know each other?' Chris said. 'Gabriella . . . Gordon. The rest of you can introduce yourselves in the bus. It's too cold to hang about out here.'

He took Gabriella's case as well as Gordon's and set off, followed by his charges, one of whom, the frailer of two elderly ladies, seemed to be having trouble lifting her case.

Gordon said, 'Let me help you with that.'

'You're very kind. I'm Maureen Symes and that's my friend Eileen Davidson. We both belong to the Barkestone Writers' Circle.'

Gordon made a vague sound of interested acknowledgement and went out of the station to where Chris had parked the Cracken-thorpe Hall minibus. When the passengers and their luggage were all aboard Gordon found that he was sitting in the front with Gabriella Cornwell and Chris who was, of course, driving. Behind him the two men were introducing themselves. 'I'm Arthur Kirk.' The voice was quite old and carried a small note of doubt as if the speaker were not quite sure of the truth of his claim.

'Oh, how d'you do. I'm Bernard Hanson. I think this is going to be fun, don't you?' This voice was probably as old but chirpier.

Before Arthur Kirk could respond a younger woman's voice spoke: 'My name's Margaret Baker. Have you gentlemen been on courses like this before?'

Neither had. 'What about you?' Bernard said.

'Oh yes lots. I love them. You meet such interesting people. I've made lots of friends. And I enjoy the practical side as well. I mean taking my turn in the kitchen, thinking up meals, getting them ready. You'd think I'd get enough of that at home but it's different somehow.'

'Are you married?' Arthur Kirk asked. Then added quickly, 'If you don't mind my asking.'

'Course I don't mind. Yes, I'm married. Two boys, seventeen and twenty. They are happy looking after themselves for the odd week. Jim, my husband, isn't much of a one for culture but he doesn't mind me going on courses. I think he enjoys the change now and then. Says he appreciates me more when I get back.'

As they drove away from the station yard Chris said, 'So you two've never met. I got the idea all you poets knew each other.'

Gabriella said, 'Most of us do. Brian MacDuff's an old friend. What happened? Why isn't he here? Why wasn't I told?'

'He's got a bad dose of 'flu. We didn't know ourselves till yester-day. Serena tried to ring you but couldn't get through or you were out or something. The poor darling was going spare. She must have phoned nearly all the poets in the UK before we got hold of Gordon and he agreed to save the day.'

'Do the people on the course know Brian's not coming?'

Chris cleared his throat. 'Ah, er, no. Not yet.'

Then he half-turned in his seat addressing the passengers behind him. 'Brian MacDuff's ill. Got 'flu. So Gordon Napier here is taking his place. We've been lucky to get him at such short notice. Very lucky. A proper announcement will be made to everybody at dinner.'

From the rear of the bus Gordon heard whispering and thought he heard the single word 'Who?' and then his name repeated. He was beginning to regret having accepted the previous day's invitation. At the time he had thought only of the welcome fee and had even felt a tiny stirring of hope that his reputation might be due for one of those inexplicable resuscitations that sometimes occurred with almost forgotten older writers. A moment's reflection should have told him that the invitation had reached him only after it had been declined by almost everyone else in the country who had ever published a volume of verse and that revivals of reputations did not happen to poets who wrote intelligibly and mainly in recognisable traditional forms.

Gabriella said to Chris, 'You haven't been long at Crackenthorpe Hall, have you? Last time I taught on a course here there was a couple called Ian and Julia running things. That wasn't all that long ago. About last Spring if I remember rightly.'

'Yeah, you're right. We've been here only since August. That's me and Serena. Do you know her? I mean know of her. Serena Burton?'

'I don't think so. Should I?'

'Well, I just thought you might. I mean she's a poet. Maybe not very well known. Not like you, Gabriella.'

'Call me Gaby. Everyone calls me Gaby.'

'Okay. Gaby.'

'And what about you? Are you a poet too?'

'Not me. No. Tell you the truth I'm not really into poetry. I mean I like it all right but a lot of it – well, I just don't get it. I mean it doesn't seem to make any sense. I expect it's my fault. I'm a painter. I do the admin, most of the organising, chauffeuring and that stuff. Serena does the lit bit. Picks the tutors, arranges courses and all that.'

Gordon, who was becoming uncomfortably conscious of his non-participation in the conversation, said, 'Has your – what's her name? Selima? – '

'Serena.'

'Sorry. Serena. Has she published? You said the second name was Burton, I think?'

'That's right. Serena Burton. Yes, she's published a book – well, it's more what you'd call a pamphlet I suppose. About twenty pages. It's called *By Owl Light*.'

'Ah. Do you know the publisher?'

'Yeah. They're called The Slow Motion Press. You heard of them? They operate somewhere in Yorkshire I think. Huddersfield, Halifax, somewhere like that.'

'I don't think I have,' Gordon said, 'but I'm not really very much in touch these days with little presses, magazines and so on.'

'What about you, Gaby,' Chris said, 'you heard of them?'

'What are they called again?'

'Slow Motion Press.'

'Never.'

'Oh well . . . You might kind of let her think you've heard of her. She's been a bit fed up lately. It'd buck her up no end if she thought her name meant something to you. She certainly knows your stuff, Gordon. Did you for O Level, she says.'

Before Gordon could respond to this doubtfully welcome information Chris announced, 'There it is folks! Over there, see. To the left, up there on the hill. Crackenthorpe Hall, the ancient pile itself.'

Peering through the minibus window Gordon saw, high on the distant wooded hills, the looming mass of masonry against the heavy pewter sky. A few yellow lozenges of light were bright against the dark stone in both upper and lower parts of the building. Crackenthorpe Hall was a gothic-looking structure, its great height and castellated upper regions causing Gordon to think of some tall man o' war of long ago riding the undulations of the hills like ocean waves.

He said, 'What period is it, do you know?'

'Not sure. Supposed to be about two hundred years old, I think.' Then he added, 'It's got a ghost, or so they reckon.'

Either Maureen or Eileen gave a little squeak.

'What kind of ghost?' one of the men in the back of the vehicle asked. 'Man or woman?'

'Don't know. A woman, I think. Sludgens – that's the gardener and odd-job man – he says he's seen it but he's not the most reliable witness in the world. Serena's the one to ask about it. She's more into psychic stuff than me.'

The minibus turned off the road into a narrow and pot-holed lane with low dry-stone walls on either side and began to climb.

'We'll be there in a few minutes,' Chris said.


In the long spacious kitchen Serena was preparing a separate sauce for the vegetarians who would not find acceptable the bolognese which was already simmering on the stove. Two of the students, or 'punters' as Chris usually called them, had arrived together by car and been directed to the bedroom allotted them. Once she had got rid of them Serena, back in the kitchen, had pulled from her jeans rear-pocket a ball-point pen and a folded sheet of paper on which the course-members' names were written. She flattened out the paper, found the names of the two arrivals – Carol Lumsden and Freda Jones – and scribbled in the margin next to them, 'schoolteachers, one fair, one darkish going grey, both from Manchester'.

Ten minutes later she heard from the courtyard the splutter and roar of a motorcycle's engine and then its being abruptly silenced. She went out of the kitchen and through the imposing entrance hall to the main front door to see who could be arriving on the kind of transport she associated with either old movies of the Sixties or present day neo-fascists in black leather, whose round, denuded skulls were scarcely distinguishable from their shining helmets. But the young man who was walking towards her, though dressed in the expected leathers, did not in the least resemble the crop-headed National Front thug she had imagined. He had a kind of rucksack slung over one shoulder and was carrying his helmet, swinging it by the chinstrap, and he was smiling pleasantly. His head, far from being shaven, was an untidy but distinctly decorative mass of dark wavy hair and he moved, despite his heavy clothing, with something of a dancer's grace.

'Hullo,' he said, 'I'm Tony Frame.'

Serena introduced herself and pulled out her list of students.

'Ah, let's see. Yes. You're sharing with Howard Simpson. I'll show you where your room is.'

She led him inside the building and up the main stairs to the first floor. 'This is the one,' she said. 'Howard's not arrived yet. I expect he'll be here soon. He's coming by car.'

It was a pleasant enough room though austerely furnished with one large wardrobe, a chest of drawers, two single beds and a wash basin. The only picture on the walls was a large unframed reproduction of Picasso's *Harlequin and his Partner*. Under the window which overlooked the courtyard was a table and two straight-backed chairs.

'There are two bathrooms and loos on this floor,' she said. 'Just along the corridor on your left.'

Tony Frame was looking at the Picasso.

'Chris, my partner, put that up,' Serena said.

'Nice,' he said. 'A bit odd somehow, for this place, but all right.'

He dropped his rucksack and helmet on to one of the beds. 'Who's this – what did you say his name was? The one I'm sharing with?'

'Howard Simpson. He's some kind of businessman. Don't know exactly what he does. I think he's pretty well-off.'

'That's surprising, a businessman on a poetry course. Mammon and the Muses.'

'Oh, I don't know. You get all kinds. You won your place here, didn't you? First prize in a poetry competition wasn't it?'

Tony grinned self-consciously. 'Christ, it sounds awful, doesn't it? Pathetic in a way.'

'No! Not at all. There's nothing wrong with poetry competitions. Specially if you win them. I've gone in for a few but never won one.'

'You write poetry yourself?'

Serena nodded and was mildly relieved, but also a little disappointed, when he did not ask her if she had published anything.

She said, 'Dinner, if that's not too posh a word for it, is at seven. The dining room's at the back of the house on the ground floor. I expect you'll find your way. I hope you enjoy the course. Oh, I almost forgot. Brian MacDuff's not coming. He had to cancel. A bad dose of 'flu. But we've got Gordon Napier to take his place. I think we're quite lucky. You know his work?'

Tony smiled, rather ambiguously Serena thought, and nodded. 'A little,' he said.

'Right. I must get on with the dinner. I'm afraid it's spaghetti.'

Still smiling Tony said, 'I'm sure it will be lovely.'

Serena returned to the kitchen but she did not write anything next to Tony's name on her list. She knew that she would have no difficulty remembering which of the students Tony Frame was.

It was not long before, within minutes of each other, two sharply contrasting motor cars pulled into the yard. One was a large and imposing machine that contrived in its design to suggest both opulence and a sleek almost menacing sense of power. Serena took scarcely any interest at all in cars yet even she knew that it was a Mercedes Benz. The other was a small, self-effacing vehicle of the kind that Serena thought of as a District Nurse's car. She had no idea of its make but guessed that it was the most inexpensive of an out-of-date range produced by one of the famous firms like Ford or Rover. Its driver, though, was not in the least self-effacing and looked as though she should have been in the Mercedes in place of the man who climbed out of it. He was rather stout, dressed soberly in a dark suit and the kind of striped shirt that Serena had seen only on Conservative politicians being interviewed on television.

The Mercedes owner was, as Serena immediately guessed, the businessman, Howard Simpson. The girl, who was quite tall with wonderful dark auburn hair and a face of unusual, slightly un-nerving beauty, was, she said as she came into the hall, 'Viv Marshall and I'm dying for a cup of tea.'

That monosyllable 'Viv' suggested to Serena vividness and vivacity, a liveliness and brilliance of colouring that seemed wholly appropriate to its owner.

Serena said, 'I'll show you where you're sleeping and you can take your stuff up and then come down here to the kitchen – that door over there – and we'll have a cuppa.'

Howard Simpson had carried an expensive-looking leather suitcase into the hall and was waiting to be directed to his own accommodation. Serena noticed, with mild irritation, that when she spoke to him his eyes did not leave Viv on whom they were fixed with a canine look of brown devotion to which its object seemed entirely oblivious.

As they climbed the stairs Serena said, 'Viv, you're sharing with Joan Palmer. She hasn't arrived yet. And Howard, you're with Tony Frame who you'll meet in a minute. Wait there a sec while I show Viv to her room.'

As she returned to conduct him to his room she heard the sound of the station-party arriving in the hall and Chris's cheerful voice imparting information and issuing instructions.

Suddenly she realised that her earlier mood of depression had evaporated and that she was quite looking forward to meeting the rest of the students and especially to making the acquaintance of the two poets.


Gordon Napier opened his suitcase which he had dumped on the bed when Chris had shown him into his room and brought out from beneath a protective layer of shirts and underwear an unopened bottle of *Famous Grouse* whisky. He had already noticed that there was a glass tumbler on the shelf above the wash-basin mirror. He rinsed this under the tap, then poured a fairly generous measure of whisky into it and added a roughly equal amount of water. He drank with one swallow about half of the mixture, released an appreciative sigh and, still holding the glass, crossed to the window.

The twilight had now deepened into an uncompromising darkness, starless and obliterating, so that Gordon could see nothing of the valley that his room overlooked. What he could see was his own reflection in the smooth black depths of the window pane. For two or three seconds he gazed with gloomy recognition at the rather heavy-jowled, broad face with its bushy eyebrows and untidy mass of grey hair, the time-worn, crumpled mask that now concealed the once quite handsome young poet's features. With one hand he drew the curtain, then took another swig of his drink and turned back to face the lamplit room. He put the glass down on top of the chest of drawers and began to unpack.

At seven o'clock he was lying on the bed, dozing, with an Elmore Leonard thriller open on his chest when the deep vibrant boom of the dinner-gong sounded from somewhere below. He swung his legs off the bed and put on his shoes. Then he gave his hair a quick, perfunctory brushing, slipped on his jacket and went down to the dining-room.

It was, with its dark panelled walls and high ceiling, an impressive place and it seemed that most of the students were already seated at the long oak table at the head of which, side by side, sat Chris Haynes and Serena Burton. In the great room the table looked agreeably festive with its shining cutlery and glassware and, Gordon observed with interest, half a dozen or so bottles of wine distributed among the glasses, plates and dishes.

Chris stood up and called, 'Ah, Gordon! Come over here and sit next to Colonel Barnes. Just here, look, between the Colonel – or George as he'd rather be called – and Kirsty.' Then, as Gordon took the vacant seat, Chris said to his immediate neighbours, 'This is one of our tutors, Gordon Napier. I'm sure you know his work. And two of your students, Gordon, George Barnes and Kirsty Black.'

Kirsty Black was young, probably no more than twenty-one or two, and, although she was sitting down, Gordon could tell that she was not tall. Her hair, which was straight, short and boyish, was an improbable yellow and, although her features were neat and attractively symmetrical and her eyes of an almost infantile blue clarity, her look was, in some way difficult to define, disconcertingly pugnacious. Perhaps it was something about the set of the chin, the slight furrow between those childishly candid blue eyes. Certainly she did not seem particularly pleased to meet Gordon.

George Barnes was much more affable. He looked to be in his late fifties and, whether or not Chris had been in earnest when he called him 'Colonel', or was merely making a joking reference to his appearance, the man certainly bore the aspect of the stereotypical ex-military man. He was dressed in an old-fashioned Harris tweed suit, check shirt and woollen tie and his hair and small moustache were neatly clipped.

Chris, who was still standing, said, 'I think everybody's here now.'

'No they're not.' Serena, sitting at his side, was consulting her list. 'One to come.'

'Who's that?'

'Just a minute. I'm looking. . . Yes, here we are. John Stamper. He's coming by car. I think he's got quite a long journey. Comes from High Wycombe or somewhere. Let's hope he hasn't broken down.'

Chris said briskly, 'Well, we can't wait for him. I'll just make one announcement before we eat. As most of you already know, Brian MacDuff can't be with us. He's ill, bad dose of 'flu. But we've been lucky to get Gordon Napier – here he is – to take Brian's place. So he and Gaby – that is Gabriella Cornwell, sitting over there at the end of the table – he and Gaby are your tutors for the course and they'll be saying a few words – sort of setting up their stalls – after we've eaten. Serena and I will have a few things to say as well, mainly about the logistics, how things are run here. But that'll do for now. Okay Serena, start dishing out . . . Oh, I nearly forgot. Vegetarians, please raise your hands . . . Okay, thank you.'

As Serena filled the plates with spaghetti and sauce and they were handed down the table, George Barnes said to Gordon, 'Can I interest you in a drop of plonk?'

'You most certainly can,' Gordon said. Then he added, 'Where did you get it from?'

'The office. What's-his-name – the chap who's running the show – he told us earlier. They've got a stack of the stuff for sale. Not much choice, I'm afraid. Spanish red or white. Franco's revenge. Better than nothing though.'

'Let me go halves on it.'

George shook his head. 'No, no.' Then he said, 'Perhaps we can take turn about, if you'd like to. You get one tomorrow. How would that be?'

'Fine.'

The wine was, Gordon thought, far more palatable than he had expected it to be. 'It's not bad, is it?'

George sipped and nodded. 'If you've got to drink cheap stuff go for Spanish red every time. Cheap French is ghastly. Italian undrinkable. Ah, here's the grub. Smells all right.'

The spaghetti bolognese was excellent and Gordon ate with enjoyment for he had not eaten since a noon sandwich. On his left Kirsty Black, who had chosen the vegetarian sauce, was pushing the spaghetti around her plate but eating very little of it.

Gordon said, 'Not to your taste? You don't seem to be eating much.'

At first he thought she was not going to answer him at all. Then she said, 'It's all right I suppose. I'm not hungry. In fact I'm fed up. I wouldn't have come if I'd known Brian wasn't going to be here.'

'Brian?' It took him a couple of seconds to realise that she was referring to the absent MacDuff. 'Oh, Brian MacDuff. Do you know him?'

'Yes . . . well, I've met him. He came to our college and gave a reading. It was great. He was lovely. Very sexy.'

Gordon thought glumly that he must be a very poor substitute for lovely and sexy MacDuff. 'Which college are you at?'

'I'm not at college *now*.' She sounded irritated, as if he had said something foolish or insulting, or both.

'Oh, I'm sorry. I thought . . . are you? I mean what kind of work . . . ?'

'Advertising. Copywriter – well, trainee copywriter actually.'

'And you write poetry?'

'Of course.'

It was Gordon's turn to feel a twinge of irritation but he tried to dismiss it. 'Yes. Silly of me. You wouldn't be here otherwise.'

'I told you. I only came because I thought Brian would be the tutor. That's what the brochure said. Brian MacDuff and Gabriella Cornwell.'

This time he did not try to hide his annoyance. 'I'm very sorry,' he said, 'I can see I must be a dreadful disappointment.'

If he had expected her to show contrition or embarrassment not a trace of either was displayed.

She said, 'Can I have some of that?' pointing to the bottle of wine.

'You'd better ask George. He bought it.'

It was at that moment that everyone's attention was directed towards the dining-room door which had suddenly opened to permit the entry of a tall man wearing a tweed cap and belted raincoat and carrying in his right hand a valise. Gordon guessed that he was in his late thirties. He was quite good-looking in the strong, firm-featured style of old-fashioned boys' adventure story heroes. He might have been a soldier in mufti but not, like George Barnes, an officer. A senior N.C.O. or perhaps a warrant-officer, efficient, rather stern, dependable.

He said, 'I'm sorry I'm so late. I'm John Stamper. Got held up on the motorway. Roadworks. I should have allowed for them.'

Chris stood up and waved towards the empty seat at the end of the table next to Gaby. 'Come and sit down. We haven't eaten everything. Not quite. Just leave your things there. Come and sit next to Gaby – Gabriella Cornwell, one of the tutors. You're not vegetarian, are you?'

John Stamper shook his head. 'No, strictly carnivore.'

He took off his cap and raincoat, placed them on top of his valise, and took his place at the table.


The meal was over. A fresh fruit salad and cream had been enjoyed and this was followed by an assortment of cheeses, a mild and a strong Cheddar, a good Stilton, and a nicely ripe Camembert, eaten with either crackers or bread. Conversation, which had been slow to start and, for a long time, subdued, was now lively.

Serena rose to her feet and Chris, seated at her side, banged on the table and shouted, 'Attention please! Everybody quiet please!'

The chatter flickered, guttered and died.

Serena spoke: 'Now we're all here, the first thing we're going to do is introduce ourselves. You've all met – well, that is except John who's only just got here – you've all met Chris and me. For John's benefit, I'm Serena Burton and this is my partner, Chris Haynes. Now, what we've always found valuable is for each student to intro-duce himself or herself. So what I'm going to ask you all to do, one at a time, is stand up and just say a few words about yourself. You know the kind of thing – My name is Billy Blake, or whatever, and then say briefly why you've come on the course and what you expect from it. You might like to say what kind of experience you've already had of courses like this – if any – and what you think is valuable or a waste of time. It might be useful for the tutors to know how advanced you are, whether you've ever published anything and so on.

'Gaby and Gordon – it might be a good idea for you to make a few notes. Could come in useful later when you're planning your sessions. Have you both got something to write on and with?'

Gaby already had a notebook open on the table and was scribbling in it.

Gordon said, 'I think I've got a pen. Yes, I've got one here. But . . . '

Chris passed over a sheet of plain A4 paper. 'Use that. Should be big enough. I've got more if you need it.'

'All right,' Serena said, 'if you're all ready. Let's start with Tony, here on my right, and go round the table from there. You ready Tony? Just stand up and say I'm Tony Frame and I'm blah-blah-blah . . . Okay?' She sat down.

Tony pushed back his chair and stood smiling, evidently at ease. He said, 'I'm Tony Frame and I'm here because I won a poetry competition run by a little magazine called *Calliope*. This course was first prize. Frankly, I'd rather have had the money, but here I am and I mean to make the most of it.'

Chris said, 'Have you published anything, apart from the one that won the competition?'

'Not much. One or two things in the little mags, that's all. I'm looking forward to working with a real pro like Gaby. And Gordon, of course.'

He sat down. A solitary pair of hands began to clap but stopped abruptly when no others joined in.

Serena said, 'That's fine. Thank you Tony . . . Carol, you're next.'

The fair, bespectacled woman on Tony's right rose and said, 'I'm Carol Lumsden and I teach English in a Manchester comprehensive. I've been on a few educational courses but nothing like this one. I think creative writing is, or should be, very important in English studies and I've never been too confident about my own attempts at writing. Certainly not at writing poetry. So that's why I'm here. I hope to learn a bit about the craft and maybe get a bit of inspiration from real poets.'

Next to speak was Bernard Hanson, one of the elderly men who had travelled to Crackenthorpe Hall from the station in the back of the minibus. He said that he had always loved poetry, ever since he was a small boy, and now that he'd retired from the bank he'd like to try his hand at it. Not, he added with a twinkle, that he expected to win the Nobel prize. Someone tittered politely and he sat down and murmured something, perhaps encouragement, to the woman next to him, who was sitting directly opposite to Gordon.

She stood up and spoke rather quickly in a pleasant voice with a very slight northern accent: 'My name's Joan Palmer. Like – er – Carol, I'd like to know more about the craft of poetry. I read quite a lot but I'm not always sure either of the meaning or of the quality of what I'm reading. I've often wondered if I might learn more about the art if I tried to write some myself but I've never had the confidence to start. I suppose that what I'm looking for on the course is stimulation as well as instruction.'

She sat down quickly, her head slightly lowered. Gordon looked at her with interest and sympathy. He had noticed her while they were eating and had thought she looked nice. It was not easy to estimate her age; somewhere around the mid thirties, he guessed, and she was good-looking in an unemphatic, almost tranquil way. He hoped she would be one of his students.

Arthur Kirk and Eileen Davidson, who had sat in the minibus with Bernard Hanson, spoke next, neither saying anything in the least memorable, and then John Stamper, the late arrival, rose to his feet.

'I'm John Stamper and my work hasn't got much to do with poetry or any of the arts.' His voice was surprisingly light for such a solid-looking man and he spoke without any easily recognised accent. 'I'm not going to say what that work is because I've got a week off from it and I want to forget all about it while I'm here. Just take it from me that it involves quite a lot of the seamier side of life. I've always been a great reader and, like lots of people, I've had the feeling for quite a while now that I might be able to write something interesting. Trouble is, I've never known exactly what. I've tried the odd short story but they never came out the way I'd sort of seen them in my head before I wrote them down. In fact they seemed boring and, if they bored me, I couldn't see them interesting anybody else.

'Then, about six months ago, I read some poems by an American called Frost, Robert Frost. You've probably heard of him but I hadn't, not at the time. Anyway, I thought they were tremendous. It started me reading poetry and I've read a few other poets since them but no one as good as him. Well, to cut a long story a bit longer, I got the idea that I'd like to try my hand at writing it, poetry I mean. Of course, I know the chances are I'll be no good at it. Obviously it's a gift and, more likely than not, it isn't one I'm lucky enough to be born with. But I'm looking forward to trying all the same.'

Gordon began to scribble on the paper Chris had given him. He was aware that the businessman, Howard Simpson, was introducing himself but he did not take in much of what was said. Then Margaret Baker, whom he recognised as a minibus passenger, spoke.

She elaborated a little on what she had said on the journey from the station, assuring everyone that she was happy working in the kitchen and, although she said it herself, she was rather a good cook and she would always be willing to give advice and practical help if needed. As for poetry, she was not what they would call a highbrow, and she found Modern Art of all kinds very difficult to understand. For her, poetry had to have rhythm and rhyme or, as far as she was concerned, it wasn't poetry. But she was here to learn and she hoped that she would make lots of new friends.

Next, it was George Barnes's turn to speak. He stood up, cleared his throat and began: 'I'm George Barnes, retired professional soldier. I think it's a fairly common idea that all soldiers are philistines who don't give a damn for the arts. Not true. Old chum of mine played the piano like Paderewski and my adjutant painted some really splendid landscapes. As for poetry, Archie Wavell was a fine soldier and he brought out a rather good anthology called *Other Men's Flowers*. General Hackett was a classicist, visiting professor at King's College, London. And what about the great soldier-poets of the past, Chaucer, Sidney, Surrey, lots more? So we're not all numb-skulls. I admit I'm not really a scholar myself, but I've liked to read poetry, among other things, since I was a schoolboy. Never had a serious crack at it though, so when I heard about this place I thought here's my chance. So here I am.'

When he sat down, to vague murmurs of approval, Kirsty, on Gordon's left, whose turn it was next, did not move. There was a sudden, oddly watchful silence.

Gordon muttered, 'I think they're waiting for you.' Kirsty ignored him.

Then Serena called, 'Kirsty: We're waiting for you!'

'I've nothing to say,' Kirsty announced, without rising, 'except I came here because Brian MacDuff was supposed to be a tutor on the course and it seems like I've wasted my time and my money.'

That silence again, its texture very slightly changed, now holding a thin thread of excitement.

Serena, a little flushed with either embarrassment or annoyance, spoke in a louder voice than she normally used. 'Chris has already told you. Brian went down with 'flu at the last moment. It just wasn't possible to let you know – to let anyone know. Nobody else has complained and neither should they. We've found a jolly good replacement in Gordon Napier and I think we're very lucky to have him. I suppose if you really want to make an issue of it you could leave, though it's getting a bit late for trains – oh no, you came by car didn't you? Well, it's late for a long drive then. As for your money, you could probably get it back if you applied to the Trust's offices in Manchester and lodged a complaint. But I'd have thought, if you want a week's intensive study of poetry and to learn something about the secrets of the art, and maybe improve your own work, you couldn't do better than study with either of our tutors who're both highly praised and established poets.'

From around the table came a muttering of what might have been endorsement.

Then Gaby Cornwell, who was sitting opposite to Kirsty, said, speaking quite softly, as if they were alone, 'I know you're disappointed about Brian, but don't desert us. After all, you're here to write your own poetry, like everyone else. And, no matter who the tutor is, it's you that has to produce the goods at the end of the day. I, for one, would like to see what those goods are like. Come on, Kirsty. You're young. Young and bright. We need you here. So stay.'

Another mutter from the audience, this time of encouragement.

'Oh, all right,' Kirsty said, 'I'll stay.'

Gaby smiled. 'Good. I'm sure you'll enjoy it.'

'Right,' Serena said briskly, 'who's next? Ah yes, Viv, perhaps you'd say your piece. And keep it nice and short.'

Vivienne Marshall, on Kirsty's other side, stood without hurry, and seemed to be gazing steadily at Gaby. After a rather disconcerting pause she said, 'My partner, Dave Mottram, went on a poetry course at the Dorset place – what's it called? – Oaklands. That was in August. Perhaps you remember him Gaby? You were one of the tutors. The other one was James somebody – Solway, or something like that.' It appeared that she expected Gaby to answer.

A few seconds passed then Gaby said, 'Oh . . . ah, no. No, I don't think I do. What did you say his name was?'

'Dave Mottram.'

'No, I'm afraid not. I must have met at least a hundred new people since the Dorset course. I mean at readings, workshops, festivals and so on. No, I'm sorry. I can't put a face to that name.'

'*You* made a big impression on *him*. He talked about you a lot. Still does.'

Gaby smiled. 'Well, that's nice to hear.'

'So that's why I'm here. I came to see for myself the wonderful Gabriella Cornwell.'

A brief, rather taut silence. Then Gaby said, 'Not just to have a look, I hope. You intend to do some writing I imagine.'

'Possibly.' Viv did not sit down at once but stayed on her feet, staring at Gaby with what could have been an alarming intensity, though Gaby did not seem particularly troubled by it.

'Next please!' Serena called, consulting her list. 'That's Maureen. Then Freda Jones and that's everybody.'

Viv, in the same slow way that she had risen, resumed her seat, still staring across the table at Gaby. Then Maureen Symes, the other elderly lady from the minibus, rose and said she was looking forward to the week and she was hoping to improve her verbal skills and learn, not only from the tutors but from her fellow pupils. She had published only one poem after years of trying and, admittedly, her one success was in the little, privately printed anthology produced by her Writers' Circle. Still, she would keep trying.

Freda Jones said that, like her friend Carol, she was a teacher, though not at the same school, and she too believed poetry to be very important, not only in English lessons but in life itself, because it enriched the imagination and acted as a custodian of the language. 'At least,' she added, looking rather pink and defiant, 'that's what it *should* do, though a lot of what passes for poetry nowadays doesn't seem to me to do much in those directions.'

A man's voice, probably Arthur Kirk's, grunted 'Hear, hear!' and, as Freda sat down, Chris stood up and said, 'Thank you folks for that. I'll get the next part over as quickly as I can but you'll all want to know roughly the way the week's going to go. Tonight, when Gaby and Gordon have said their pieces we'll get the washing up done and then down to the pub. That's The Shepherd's Crook in Maldenwick, only a mile or so away. I can squeeze quite a few in the minibus but it would help for those with cars to use them. Of course there's no compulsion. You don't *have* to go to the pub, but I expect most of us'll want to. I know I shall.

'Now, tomorrow and in fact every day. Breakfast and lunch are both informal. In other words you help yourselves. You'll find plenty of tea, coffee, milk, cereals and so on in the kitchen. Lots of bread, butter, marmalade, eggs, stuff like that. I think I'm right in saying there's ham and pâté in the fridge. I know there's loads of cheese. You'll find plenty of tins, too, beans, soup, that kind of thing.'

'And fresh fruit,' Serena prompted him.

'Oh yes, and fresh fruit. The evening meal's at seven, like tonight. Three students will be responsible for this each day. I'll put up a rota in the kitchen but this is flexible. I mean if anyone wants to work with somebody else it can always be arranged. The cooks – or their spokesperson – hands me a shopping-list each morning and I take the minibus into Ancliffe and do the shopping. So whoever's on kitchen duty doesn't have to miss any of the morning sessions. And Margaret Baker, who's hot stuff in the cooking department, has very kindly offered to be around every day to give help and advice.

'Now for the business of why you're all here, the poetry. We'll have two groups working every morning, one in the library and one in the recital-room. Both are great places for working. These sessions will start at ten and finish at half past twelve with a short break for coffee. When you've heard Gordon and Gaby set out their stalls you'll have a better idea about which group you'll want to join. Of course, you're not bound to stay with one group. You can switch tutors, or stay with one, whatever you like.

'Now for the way the whole week's going to be arranged. I'll put all this up on the notice-board in the hall, but I'll mention each thing briefly now. Every day you have a session in the morning with the tutor. In the afternoon, if you're not on kitchen duty, you're free to do pretty well what you like. You might like to go for a walk, get some inspiration from nature. You might want to work quietly somewhere on your own or you might like a one-to-one with Gaby or Gordon. They're there to talk about your work, any problems you come up against. If you've brought poems with you give them to one or other of the tutors to read at their leisure and they'll get back to you and fix a time for a chat.

'Monday evening, after dinner, Gaby gives a reading in the library and you have the opportunity to ask questions. Okay? Tuesday, the same routine in the day, groups in the morning, free in the afternoon. Then, in the evening, Gordon gives a reading followed by questions. Goes without saying, we end up at the pub after the readings.

'Wednesday evening is students' choice. Each of you chooses a poem you really like and maybe tell us why you like it so much before, or after, you've read it to us. *Not* a poem of your own. There's a whole pile of poetry books in the library so you ought to be able to find one that takes your fancy.

'Thursday's the night for the visit from our guest-poet. As you know that's going to be Zak Fairbrass. I'm sure he'll give us a great reading and you'll be able to talk to him afterwards.

'Friday night is the final one of the course and it's then you'll all have your chance to read the best bit of work you've done during the week. One poem – or two at the most – from each student. Saturday, of course, we pack up. Everybody to be off the premises by noon.'

Chris half lowered himself to his seat then straightened up again. 'Oh, yes. Gaby, Perhaps you'd say a few words about the way you mean to work with your students. Tell 'em what's on offer.'

He sat down and Gaby stood up. She said, 'I won't take up a lot of time that could be more happily spent in the pub but I'll just make a few points about my views on poetry and poetry-workshops. I'm not all that interested in technique. In fact I think there's a lot of pretentious waffle talked and written about poetic technique. What I'm interested in is the exploring of the psyche, the imagery of our dreams and our subconscious minds. I believe that these can be sources of a wisdom and beauty that can't be tapped by the rational intelligence. So my workshops – horrible word! – will be closer to seances or transcendental meditation than lessons in the classroom. Not that I'm blind to the importance of artistic form and careful use of language. These will be dealt with, of course, but not as ends in themselves. They are the means by which we capture the fleeting moments of vision of the eternal. So I hope to be able to help students to get rid of their inhibitions, those hidden fears that can prevent access to their inner longings, and cleanse their vision so that, in Blake's words, they can see the world in a grain of sand.'

Gaby sat down.

'Gordon?' Chris said, and Gordon rose to his feet.

'Well,' he said, 'that's one view of poetry and I think Gaby expressed it pretty well. Up to a point I agree with her. Poetic technique – I mean a knowledge of and maybe a certain skill in handling the various prescribed metres, stanza forms and so on that our poetic ancestors have handed down to us – technique like this isn't enough in itself. Any moderately intelligent and literate person can learn to write verse which is technically correct, but this doesn't mean that he or she can write poetry. On the other hand I can't think of any real poet of the past or present who doesn't show a thorough mastery of his craft. In fact all the poets I most enjoy and admire make use of the traditional ways of writing verse, however much they might modify and adapt them. Frankly, I've no idea how the divine spark that blazes into poetry can be kindled. But having read and studied and tried to write the stuff for about half a century I think I do know a bit about English verse, and that bit of knowledge is what I can offer you. I'll try to avoid pretentious waffle though.'

'Okay,' said Chris. 'Thanks Gaby and Gordon. Now let's get this lot cleared away, then off to the boozer. If we get a move on, we'll be there well before ten.'


The Shepherd's Crook revealed itself as the kind of pub that Gordon had not seen since, as an undergraduate, he had occasionally been able to afford jaunts out to remote Thames Valley inns. There was no canned music and the fire, glowing and flickering in the hearth, was a real one made of burning coals. On a shelf above the mantelpiece stood the room's only incongruent furnishing, a television-set but, though images moved and grimaced on its screen, they did so in complete silence for the sound had been turned down to zero.

The Crackenthorpe Hall party had been able to seat themselves round two tables which they had pulled together and the other customers, an elderly couple sitting at one of the other tables and three men standing at the bar, took little notice of them.

Chris saw with relief that Kirsty, who was between Viv Marshall and Tony Frame, seemed to have recovered from her disappointment over MacDuff's absence and was now in high spirits. All who had wished to to go the pub had been able to squeeze into the minibus, except for Howard Simpson and Viv, whom he had quite easily persuaded to accept a ride in his grand Mercedes.

Chris was a little worried about Serena's decision not to come, though he thought she had recovered from what he regarded as her earlier sulks. By the time his second pint of bitter was half-finished his vestigial concern had disappeared and he was conversing cheerfully with John Stamper and Gaby.

He said, 'It's a great little pub, it really is. Cyril – that's the landlord – doesn't bother too much about licensing-hours. He doesn't like to open too early on Sunday evenings but he'll keep serving for pretty well as long as you want to keep drinking. And it's a great pint too. What do you think of it, John?'

'The beer? Pretty good.'

Tony, sitting opposite to Stamper, said to him, 'You're keen on Robert Frost, then. Which are the ones you like best? Any favourites?'

'I like nearly all the ones I've read so far. There's one called *The Road Not Taken*, that seemed very good. And one called *The Sound of Trees*. I liked that one too. I wouldn't mind learning it by heart. Oh yes, there's *Stopping By Woods on a Snowy Evening*. That's a great one.'

Tony nodded slowly; then, almost as if to himself, he recited:

> 'The woods are lovely, dark, and deep,
> But I have promises to keep,
> And miles to go before I sleep,
> And miles to go before I sleep.'

John's serious, strong, heavy-browed face lit up for a moment in a transforming smile of recognition that was surprisingly charming. Gaby, sitting next to John, said, 'Oh, that old chestnut. Nursery stuff. It makes it worse that Frost was such a bastard to his wife and kids and then he goes and writes these pretty little poems about trees and flowers and birds and things.'

John's face had quickly settled back into its look of stern watchfulness.

Tony said lightly, 'Pretty little poems like *Home Burial*, Gaby? *Fire and Ice*? I wouldn't expect him to be the feminist's favourite fella, but you have to admit he wasn't a bad poet.'

Kirsty, perhaps thinking she might avert a possibly acrimonious exchange, said brightly, 'Brian MacDuff wrote a poem called *The Ice Cream Man Cometh*. It was brilliant. He read it at a gig at that place near Swiss Cottage where they do jazz and poetry.'

'Sorry I missed it,' Tony smiled.

'It's in one of his books, *Noughts and Kisses*.'

'Ah, I must see if I can get it.'

Howard Simpson was talking in a low voice to Viv, who was sitting between him and Kirsty, but his words were not, it seemed, engaging her attention, and her infrequent, small nods were probably less a response to what he was saying than an unconscious gesture of assent to some private reflections of her own.

Then the door opened and a man came in and crossed to the bar where the three drinkers, who were standing there, greeted him with verbal salutations that were incomprehensible to Gordon and the rest of the Crackenthorpe party, except for Chris who called out his own greeting, which was probably a rough translation of the native form: 'All right then, Harold?' Then he added, 'Bit late on parade tonight, aren't you?'

Harold came across to the table with his pint but he did not attempt to take a seat. He was a man in his late fifties, very lean and hard-looking, gnarled like an old tree. His face was long, equine and lugubrious, with a sprinkling of bristles like iron-filings on the chin and jaws. What little hair he possessed was grey and cropped very short.

Chris announced, 'This is Harold Sludgens. He's gardener and odd-job man at the Hall. How d'you get here, Harold? On your bike?'

'Gnaw. Bluddy pooncher. Cum on shanks pawny dinta.'

'Had a puncture and had to walk, eh,' Chris said helpfully. 'Well, I expect we'll be able to squeeze you into the bus.'

'Druther wark.'

'Okay, suit yourself. Let me get you a drink then.'

No objection was made to this suggestion and Chris went with him to the bar and bought him another pint of bitter although he had taken no more than an inch from the top of his first one.

Back at the table Chris said, 'He's a good worker. Not got a very good reputation in the village though. I don't quite know what he got up to but there was a bit of trouble with the law. That was some time back and he seems to have settled down all right now.'

'Does he live in the Hall?' Tony asked.

'No. In the Lodge. You probably saw it on the left just after you come into the drive. It's not a bad little house and there's a decent-sized garden. They keep a few hens – him and his wife, Ivy. She's our cleaner and general help. They're probably happy enough, though happiness isn't the first thing you think of about either of them.'

'I thought he was rather sweet,' Kirsty said.

Tony nodded. 'I suppose he was. In a Neanderthal sort of way.'

'You're just jealous.'

'I admit it. Of course I'm jealous. But let me get you another drink. What about you, John? Same again?'

As Tony went to the bar, Gordon finished his own pint and said to George, 'I think I'm going to switch to something else. What about a scotch?' Then to Joan Palmer: 'Sorry, I should have asked you first. Would you like another gin and tonic? Or something else?'

Joan shook her head. 'No, thank you. Nothing for me. I've still got quite a lot of this left. I don't drink much anyway.'

As he left the table for the bar Gordon heard Viv saying to Howard Simpson, with a small note of asperity in her voice, 'No, I *don't* want another drink any more than I did two minutes ago,' and he was glad that luck had elected Joan as his neighbour rather than the glamorous but, to him, rather alarming Viv.

When he returned with the whiskies George and Gaby were talking about Kipling.

'. . . quite a clever versifier,' she was saying, 'but all that patriotic drum-beating and flag-waving gets very boring. And of course he glorifies soldiers and war – I suppose you, as a soldier or ex-soldier, have to agree with that stuff but it doesn't do much for me.'

'No, I suppose it wouldn't,' George conceded.

Gordon sat down with the drinks. 'Actually,' he said, 'I don't think Kipling's nearly as jingoistic as he's made out to be. *Danny Deever*'s hardly a jingoistic poem, is it? Eliot said he thought it was a remarkable piece of work, and I agree with him.'

Gaby sniffed. 'Eliot's very old hat now. Your generation – if you don't mind me saying so – thought everything he said about poetry was holy writ and it was something like blasphemy to question it. We see him a bit different from that. We see him for what he was – an anti-semitic, racist plagiarist in fact. I suppose it's natural enough that someone like that wouldn't object to Kipling's imperialistic rant.'

Gordon did not think it would be diplomatic to argue too forcibly with his co-tutor yet he could not stifle all protest. 'I wouldn't call any of it rant,' he said, 'and poems like *Harp Song of the Dane Women* and quite a few others can't be called anything but fine poetry.'

Rather to his surprise, Joan Palmer said, 'The Kipling poem I've always liked is *The Way Through the Woods*. I must have been about fourteen – maybe younger – when I first read it and I like it just as much now as I did then.' Then she surprised Gordon again by quoting, without any sign of self-consciousness:

> 'You will hear the beat of a horse's feet,
> And the swish of a skirt in the dew,
> Steadily cantering through
> The misty solitudes . . .'

Then Gordon astonished himself by joining her in the last lines:

> 'As though they perfectly knew
> The old lost road through the woods . . .
> But there is no road through the woods.'

For a couple of seconds they smiled at each other in a fleeting confederacy of pleasure and then, at the other end of the joined tables, there was a sudden commotion as John Stamper pushed back his chair and crossed the room quickly, calling to the landlord as he moved, 'Do you mind? The news . . . something I want to . . . ' He turned up the sound on the television above the mantelpiece and everyone looked towards the screen.

The newscaster, a well-groomed young man in a dark suit, was saying, with the tone of voice and seriousness of facial expression reserved for the announcements of graver items of interest, that the body of the young woman who had been discovered on the previous day in a wood near Amersham in Buckinghamshire had now been identified as Clare Deacon from Chesham and the police were treating the death as murder. This latest brutal attack could be related to the two earlier killings of young women which had occurred in different regions of the country, the first in Cumbria and the other in Derbyshire. The police believed that the culprit might be someone who regularly travelled up and down the country, possibly a lorry-driver, and all young women were warned not to accept lifts from strangers driving either commercial vehicles or private cars.

Howard Simpson said to no one in particular, 'Oh, switch that damned thing off. We're here to get away from all that kind of thing.'

For the first time since they had arrived at the pub Viv looked at him with all of her attention. 'From all what kind of thing? Women being raped and murdered?'

He laughed artificially and uneasily. 'You know what I mean. Mundane things. The news, politics, scandal. Material things. I thought we'd be able to get away from all that for a few days.'

Viv was still looking at him steadily, but she did not respond to his affected laugh with even the vestige of a smile. She said, 'Did you hear? The police say women shouldn't accept lifts from strangers. I did, didn't I? I accepted a lift from you.'

On the television screen, now silent again, an American politician with an overfed face and big, mirthless white grin was waving from the boarding steps of an aircraft. John Stamper had returned to his seat.

Howard said, 'Yes, you took a big chance getting into the Merc.' It was meant to sound flippant.

'Did I?' Viv looked entirely serious.

'Oh, come on: You can't really think . . . I mean look at me! Do I look like a murderer?'

From the other side of the table, Gaby, whose attention had been attracted by their talk, said, 'What *do* murderers look like? Nobody knows. They all look different. Hardly any of them look like horror-movie baddies. The ones you see in the papers look like timid little book-keepers or merry-faced quiz-masters. You just can't tell.'

John Stamper was saying to Chris, 'Have we got time for another?'

'I should think so.' Chris gestured towards Cyril, the landlord, tipping an imaginary glass to his lips and raising his eyebrows in enquiry.

Cyril nodded and shouted, 'Last orders, please! One more and that's your lot!'

John stood up and said, 'What are we having? Kirsty? . . . Chris?
. . . Tony?'

Then he went to the bar to order their drinks.

Back from The Shepherd's Crook the minibus passengers, now
joined by Viv whose escort and driver had left in his Merc and a huff,
alighted with varying degrees of agility and noise and headed, in
little groups, back to the great house. Tony and Chris were talking
animatedly about David Hockney's paintings, with Kirsty skipping
along beside them trying, with little chirping inanities, to divert
Tony's attention to herself. Gordon, walking behind them with
George Barnes and John Stamper, thought without rancour that she
seemed to have found someone to rival Brian MacDuff for sexiness,
though he rather doubted that she would find fulfilment with the
object of her desire. He could hear Joan Palmer close behind talking
with Gaby and he guessed that Viv would be with them.

Inside, some of the party decided to go into the kitchen and make
hot drinks but Gordon and his two companions climbed to the
first floor where, wheezing quite audibly from the ascent, Gordon
managed to say, 'Either of you feel like a nightcap? I've got some
scotch in my room.'

George assented at once and John hesitated only a moment before
he, too, accepted the invitation.

'You'll have to get glasses though,' Gordon said. 'I use my tooth
mug. There'll be glasses in the kitchen but it'd be easier to get them
from your room. You two are sharing aren't you?'

A few minutes later the three men were in Gordon's room with
their tumblers of whisky and water. John, who was straddling one of
the two upright chairs said, 'Listen to that wind. It's getting really
wild.'

George, perched with Gordon on the side of the bed, nodded.
'There were forecasts of gales on the news this morning.'

Gordon took a sip of his drink. Then he said, 'What do you
think of the set-up here so far? Think you're going to enjoy the
week?'

John frowned. 'Can't tell yet. That woman – what's her name? –
the poet . . . '

'Gaby?'

'Yes, that's her. I can't imagine getting on very well with her. She said something about Robert Frost writing nursery stuff. What the hell's she mean by that? That young chap Tony told her off, though. He didn't agree with her at all and he seems to know a thing or two.'

'She was the same when I mentioned Kipling,' George said. 'She called his poems rant – you heard her, didn't you Gordon? We all know Kipling's a bit old -fashioned but he strikes me as a damn good poet all the same. Certainly knew a bit about soldiering. Not only that, though. He knew a lot about ships and the sea. Then there's one about the old remedies, herbs and things, and I seem to remember the Plague came into it too. Wish I could remember it. Jolly good poem, I thought.'

Didn't he write that one *If*?' John asked. 'I know people – I mean intellectuals – sneer at it, but I always thought it was very good. It makes good sense and it sounds good too.'

Gordon nodded. 'You're quite right. That's exactly what it sets out to do and exactly what it does.'

'Quite agree,' George said. 'Absolutely.'

'But . . . ' Gordon paused, then went on, '. . . we mustn't forget there are other kinds of poetry which don't have the same aims as Kipling's, but in their own way are just as successful. Once you've got your ear tuned into them, and got your head round what they're trying to do, as they say nowadays, they can be just as enjoyable.'

John and George looked at him quizzically, perhaps a little suspiciously, Gordon took another sip of his whisky. 'George, I think you mentioned Chaucer and Sidney earlier this evening, at dinner time, when you were saying your little piece. Well, they're both wonderful poets and we can still read them with a lot of pleasure today. We can still learn from them too. But we can't write like them. I'm not talking about the quality of what we might be able to write. I mean we can't use quite the same forms of expression, for all sorts of reasons. The language has changed so much since then. That's obvious in Chaucer's case, maybe not quite so obvious with Sidney, and when we get to our more recent ancestors, a lot less so. But in fact our language has changed quite a bit since Kipling was writing, and so has the world we live in, and the changes must affect the way we write. Not just a matter of change in language – idioms, vocabulary, rhythm, syntax, all that stuff – but changes in society, religious and philosophical beliefs, science and technology. There's a huge gulf between Tennyson, say, and Kipling, though they were both alive at the same time. And God knows what Kipling would have made of Dylan Thomas who was certainly writing and publishing before Kipling died.' Gordon drained his glass. 'Sorry,' he said, 'you didn't come here for a seminar. Drink up and have a drop more of the celebrated beef.'

He held up the bottle of *Famous Grouse* but his pun, such as it was, seemed to be lost on both of his companions who held out their glasses to be recharged.

As he was pouring whisky into John's tumbler a sudden snorting noise came from George, followed by a throaty chuckle. 'Got it!' he exclaimed. 'Famous grouse – celebrated beef. Jolly good. Very witty.'

John Stamper looked from one to the other, his face serious, not so much puzzled as watchful, uncommitted.

'Cheers,' Gordon said. 'We'll make these the last. It's past midnight. Don't want hangovers tomorrow.'

The other two raised their glasses with murmured salutations and all three drank.


In the self-contained flat on the third floor occupied by the co-directors of studies, Chris switched off the light in the living-room and carefully opened the bedroom door, hoping he would not disturb Serena's sleep; but his caution was wasted for she was sitting up in bed reading by the light of a bedside lamp.

'What you reading, love?' he said.

She lowered the book and then put it down on top of the duvet.

'Melissa Hull. Gaby recommended her, said she was marvellous, and I remembered we'd got her last book for the library so I dug it out.'

'What's it called?'

'*The T Bone Psalms.*'

'T Bone?'

'That's right.'

'What's it mean, T Bone Psalms?'

'I couldn't say. But I haven't read all the poems yet. I must say they're a bit weird.'

Chris sat on the bed and picked up the book. He flicked over a few pages and then he stopped and read for a minute or so.

'Listen to this,' he said. 'I'll read it to you. It's called *Bomb Outrage*. Listen:

> The conference of pink ducks has ended.
> Votes of thanks settle in their sugary nests.
> Next year will be different.
> I shall have married the dumb constable by then
> and he will be bubbling softly
> in his blue oven.
> The moon's tonsils will have to come out
> and we all know who will operate,
> the General himself and his
> tambourine-rattling lassies.
> They will be there with swabs and sherbet
> dancing attention in the snowy theatre
> Where the dead anaesthetist
> begins to stink.

'What does it mean? What's it got to do with a bomb outrage? Pink ducks and taking out the moon's tonsils and the anaesthetist stinking – decomposing, I suppose. What can it possibly mean?'

'I don't know. You can't just read one like that. You have to read them all. You've got to get to know this other world she's creating where nothing's like it is here in the ordinary world. A kind of surrealist world.'

Chris turned the page and read for a few seconds then dropped the book. 'Do you really like this stuff?'

'I don't know. It's the first time I've read her. I'm too tired to take them in. I'll look at them tomorrow when I'm feeling brighter. If I get the chance.'

He took both of her hands in his own. 'You feeling all right?' he said. 'It's been a long day. Of course you're tired. I'll see to it you get a good rest tomorrow, I promise . . . ' She looked at him without much expression. He went on, 'Listen love, this morning – you know, when you said it's not working. You didn't mean it, did you? You didn't really mean we're not all right together, did you?'

Serena looked at him thoughtfully; then a faint smile moved on her lips and in her eyes. 'Perhaps not. We'll have to see, won't we?'

He leaned forward and kissed her.

She said, 'You stink of beer,' but her voice was not unfriendly.

'I'll go and brush my teeth.'

'Hurry up and come to bed.' She slid down and pulled the duvet up to her chin.

He stood and shrugged off his sweater. As he unbuttoned his shirt he said, 'It was a funny old evening in the Crook tonight. I'm a bit worried about that bloke Stamper.'

'Mmm? What you say about Stamper?' Serena's words were blurred and soft with imminent sleep.

'I don't know. You may think I'm crazy but I've got an uneasy feeling about him. I'll tell you what happened. You know the way Cyril always has the telly on but never turns the sound up? Well, it was same as usual tonight. Nobody taking any notice of it. Then suddenly, at eleven o'clock, our friend Stamper jumps out of his seat and tears across the room and turns up the sound. It's the eleven o'clock News. And what's he so interested in? I'll tell you. That girl that's been murdered, that's what he wants to know about.'

'What?' Serena's eyes opened and her head was raised just a little from the pillow. 'Murdered? What girl? What are you talking about?'

'You know, the one we heard about on the radio this morning. Don't you remember? A girl found strangled in some woods in Buckinghamshire somewhere. They seem to be linking it with those other murders up here in the north. Well, one was up in the Lakes and the other further down in the Midlands. They reckon it could be a lorry driver or a rep, somebody who travels up and down the country a lot.'

'What's all this got to do with Stamper?'

'Well, if you'd been there you'd have seen the way he acted, the way he looked. Obviously he'd kept an eye on the telly all night and as soon as the News came on with the report about the murder he was over there in a flash to turn the sound up. Nobody else would've bothered. And that's all he was interested in. Nothing else. Just the stuff about the murder. Once he'd heard that he turned the sound off and sat down again.'

'What are you trying to say? Okay, he wanted to hear the News so he turned the sound up. What's wrong with that?'

'No, that's not what he did. It wasn't the News he wanted, it was just that one special item, the murder of the girl. He didn't want to see or hear anything else. Just that, just the girl's murder.'

'Well, I don't know . . . So what? He's interested in the murder. Lots of people are. That's why it'll be all over tomorrow's tabloids.'

Chris finished undressing and slipped under the duvet with Serena.

He said, 'Earlier on, this evening, you said where he came from, didn't you? Somewhere down that way wasn't it?'

'High Wycombe.'

'That's right, Buckinghamshire, isn't it? And that's where the murder was.'

'Oh, don't be silly Chris. Just because he lives in the county where it happened. Thousands of people live in Buckinghamshire. If something like that happens on your doorstep you're bound to be interested. Now, for heaven's sake put the light out and let's get some sleep.'

Chris switched off the bedside lamp. In the darkness he said, almost as if addressing himself, 'But his interest didn't seem natural. It was like he had a special reason for wanting to hear about it. When that bit of the News came on I'm sure he wasn't aware of anything else. I bet he didn't even know where he was or who he was with. It was weird. And another thing. What was all that stuff he said at dinner-time about wanting to get away from his job? But he wouldn't say what the job was, would he? Something about seeing the seamier side of life. I thought then that there was some-thing a bit fishy about him.'

'Good . . . night,' Serena said, spacing the words carefully and emphasising each with finality, 'and go to sleep, or at least let me go to sleep. I don't think Mr Stamper will be murdering anyone tonight.'

For a moment it seemed that Chris might not be deterred from expatiating on his suspicions of John Stamper but, instead, he returned Serena's goodnight and in a very few minutes they were both sleeping soundly.


Alone now, Gordon looked thoughtfully at the whisky bottle, noting that slightly more than half of its contents had been consumed. The temptation to pour himself one more measure was abruptly dismissed, and he opened the wardrobe, from one shelf of which he took the rubber hot-water bottle which he had placed there when unpacking. He would not have wished anyone to know that his wife, Susan, had insisted on his taking it with him because, to him, its possession and use seemed either childish or spinsterish, yet, all the same, he was grateful for her care and foresight. Then he remembered that he had promised to telephone her on his arrival and he had failed to keep his promise. He offered her a quick mental apology and told himself that he would call her the next day.

He filled the rubber bottle from the basin tap, which gushed with comfortingly hot water; then he carefully screwed tight the stopper and placed the bottle in his bed. He began to undress.

The wind that John Stamper had commented on was now, if anything, wilder than ever. It swished and sighed and ululated in the night, and Gordon again thought of Crackenthorpe Hall as a great old sailing-ship, riding out the tempest with its miscellaneous crew of crackpots and poseurs, poetasters and pupils, young and old, dreamers of dreams, seekers of grails, tellers of tales, the lost and the lonely, the strong and the frail. 'And who was at the helm of the vessel?' Gordon asked himself as he climbed into bed and, after the briefest time of reflection, answered that there was no one there at all.

There was an electric switch cord hanging from the ceiling above the headboard of his bed but he did not pull it at once, but lay there with the light on, his feet warming on the bottle, listening to the blind tantrums of the wind. He wondered idly which of the students would choose him as their tutor when the first practical session started in the morning. He was fairly sure that George Barnes and John Stamper would elect to work under his tutelage and was hopeful about Joan Palmer. He was uncertain about the older ladies, Maureen and Eileen, as he was about Bernard and Arthur, though all of these, he guessed, might be rather intimidated by Gaby's youthful assertiveness and what they no doubt would regard as her 'modernity'.

Howard Simpson, with whom he had not yet exchanged a word, and whose presence on the course puzzled him, had obviously been offended by Viv in the pub and she would surely be one of Gaby's students for her own mysterious reasons. As for Tony and Kirsty, the two teachers, Carol and Freda, and the happily domestic Margaret Baker, he had no idea what their choice would be, except that he would take a bet that Kirsty would follow wherever Tony led.

Gordon reached up and pulled the light-cord. In the darkness he snuggled down beneath the duvet and closed his eyes. The wind soughed and moaned against the window. He thought of de la Mare's lines:

> When I lie where shades of darkness
> Shall no more assail mine eyes,
> Nor the rain make lamentation
> When the wind sighs . . .

How did it go after that? Oh yes, got it:

> How will fare the world whose wonder
> Was the very proof of me?
> Memory fades, must the remembered
> Perishing be?

He tried to recall the beginning of the next stanza but, although tantalising echoes from it hovered just beyond memory's reach – something about *dust surrendering to dust* and *rusting harvest hedgerows* – the lines eluded him. The ability to summon vast tracts of verse to mind, that was once the envy of his peers, was now deserting him. *Memory fades*: certainly his was fading fast.

He had first read the de la Mare poem, *Fare Well*, when he was at his prep school and had at once been enchanted by its melancholy cadences and imagery. That kind of thrill, sharpened and deepened by imperfect understanding, so that the lines were more mysterious than they would have been had he encountered them at a later age, was something that could be experienced only in childhood or youth. The pleasure he gained now from reading an unfamiliar poem was qualitatively different. In growing old, he had not become wise but analytical, sceptical, emotionally defensive. Perhaps he should not have accepted the invitation to come to Crackenthorpe Hall, for – at least, at the moment – he felt no eagerness to try to bring sweetness and light to the benighted.

He turned on his side. How *did* those lines go? *Hand, foot,* . . . *lip to dust again* . . . something like that . . . *hand* . . . *foot* . . . *lip* . . . *dust* . . . *dust* . . .

The darkness deepened; it assailed his eyes, and Gordon slept. But not for long.

He awoke suddenly and, for a second or so, he experienced a small panic in the unfamiliar and narrow bed, missing the warm and comforting presence of Susan at his side. Then he remembered where he was and, for a moment as brief as his disorientation had been, he felt calm; but this relative tranquillity was then disturbed by a flickering sense of unease at whatever it was that had awakened him. He was sure he had heard a noise in the room.

He lay, now on his back, eyes wide but sightless, staring into the impenetrable blackness, his head slightly raised from the pillow. He held his breath for as long as he could, listening. Then he heard, or was almost sure that he heard, the sound of breathing, not his own and not far away, perhaps at the foot of his bed.

He said, 'Who's there?' fumbling above his head for the light-cord which his scrabbling fingers failed to encounter.

'Who is it?' he said again, his right hand still frantically searching the wall overhead and hearing in his own voice a peculiar and shaming high-pitched note.

Then, as his hand fastened on the light-cord and pulled, and the room leapt into briefly dazzling brightness, he saw the door closing and heard it click shut. Instantly he scrambled out of bed and, as his bare feet made contact with the skimpy woven rug which slithered beneath them on the polished floor, he overbalanced backwards, breaking his fall with his right hand. Quickly back on his feet, he sprang to the door, swung it open and peered out, up and down the dimly lit corridor. No one was there, not a movement, not a sound. The shadowed emptiness seemed to be watching him. The silence itself listened to his own heavy breathing.

Gordon turned back into the bedroom and closed the door. He

bent and straightened the rug on which he had slipped and, as he stood erect again, he remained quite still and began to sniff the air. Again he sniffed, deeper this time, and peered around him as if he might perceive the source of the strange odour that had not been in the room before. At first he could not positively identify the smell; he knew only that it was familiar, but not recently experienced. He sniffed and sniffed, baffled: it was like trying to recall a melody from the distant past, once known well but not heard for many years. Then, in the mind's misty darkness, recognition flared: it was the smell of celery, pleasant, slightly pungent, vaguely nostalgic with a certain bitter-sweetness.

He climbed back into bed but he did not extinguish the light which was still burning when, at last, weariness overcame perplexity and mild, unfocused apprehension, and he slept a deep dreamless sleep.

# MONDAY

GORDON SAT AT THE HEAD of the table in the library and looked at his group of students who were seated around him and he felt for them a kind of affectionate gratitude that they were applying themselves so seriously to the work that he had set them. Heads were bent over writing-pads, notebooks or the sheets of lined A4 of which Chris had left a pile to be distributed among students who had not brought their own paper. Suddenly someone's head would be raised to stare with blind, questioning intensity towards distant and mysterious prospects before ducking down again as laborious or frantic writing was resumed.

It was, he thought, curiously touching to see them working like this, George Barnes who had led men in perilous predicaments and places; Carol Lumsden and Freda Jones, both accustomed to being in charge of and deferred to by their own students; John Stamper, saturnine and sternly watchful; Joan Palmer coolly and gently self-contained; Margaret Baker, on her own assertion happiest in the kitchen baking bread or preparing tasty sauces, and Howard Simpson, like George and the two teachers, far more used to telling subordinates what to do than obeying instructions from someone who, in other circumstances, would not be likely to gain his respect; all of them absorbed in their tasks with the seriousness of children at play.

Chris had been delighted to find that the fourteen students had, without any prompting from him or Serena, spontaneously divided themselves into two groups, exactly half of them choosing one tutor and half the other. Gordon too was pleased, as well as relieved, when he found so many waiting for him in the library at ten o'clock that morning. Now he was wondering whether the exercise he had set them was the kind of thing they would be able to profit from or find any satisfaction in working at.

He had begun the morning's session by announcing that he intended starting with something quite elementary and he hoped that those for whom the projected exercise seemed too simple would nevertheless get on with it and maybe even get some pleasure from it. Then he had talked about free verse and blank verse, giving examples of iambic pentameters and lines from D. H. Lawrence, Pound and Whitman to illustrate free verse, and was gratified to see his students writing them down to his dictation. Then he had said, 'Now I'd like you all to write a bit of strict blank verse as a kind of limbering-up exercise and I suggest you all write on the same topic. I'm sure you all noticed what a wild night it was last night, that great howling wind that made you thankful you weren't out there in it. Well, that's going to be our topic. Just a few lines, say a dozen or so, on the subject of a windy night. I know it sounds like a fourth-form essay but don't be put off. I want it in blank verse – you've got clear examples there – and remember what I said about poetry *enacting* experience, not simply talking about it. Aim at making it happen, a gale of words. In strict iambic pentameters. I know it's an impossible thing to ask of anyone at ten o'clock on a Monday morning, or any other time for that matter – so get on with it.'

Soon after they had begun writing Gordon decided they had earned a coffee-break so they wandered off in twos and threes to the kitchen where they helped themselves to coffee or tea, chattering animatedly and, as Gordon was pleased to observe, mainly about the work he had set them. Things, he told himself, were going quite well.

Back in the library the students returned to their tasks and, after a while, Gordon moved round the table to see how they were getting on. Howard Simpson, he saw with surprise, had covered one sheet of paper and was half-way down a second.

'May I have a look?' Gordon said.

Howard finished the line, or sentence, that he was writing, leaned back and replaced the top of his expensive-looking fountain-pen with what seemed to Gordon an air of considerable self-satisfaction. 'By all means,' he said.

Gordon picked up the sheets of paper and began to read. The handwriting was even and perfectly legible with no alterations or crossings-out. The title, *A Windy Night*, had been inscribed at the top of the first page and below it was written a reasonably accurate account of the previous night's weather in serviceable but undistinguished prose with little or no use of figurative language and, as far as Gordon could see, no attempt whatsoever at writing in metre.

'Ah . . . er . . . yes . . . I see,' Gordon said. He glanced down at the table and saw that Howard had dutifully written out the examples of blank verse that had been dictated. 'That's a fairly good first draft. Now, what about seeing if you can get it into verse. Like those Wallace Stevens lines for instance . . . ' He quoted, slowly and with weighty emphasis on each stressed syllable:

> 'The mules that angels ride come slowly down
> The blazing passes, from beyond the sun . . .'

Howard was looking up from his seat at the table with an expression of total incomprehension.

' . . . or maybe you should leave it as it is if you think it's better like that,' Gordon added and returned the composition to its author, moving away, conscious of his own duplicity and cowardice.

He said, addressing the whole group, 'I think the best thing would be for me to collect your Windy Nights so I'll be able to take my time over looking at them and then we can talk about them tomorrow before we tackle something else. As Chris said, anyone's welcome to come and have a chat about their work or anything they think I might be able to help with.'

As he began to collect their exercises, Carol Lumsden said, 'Before you take them away could you clear up one little point that's worrying me?'

'Of course.' Gordon moved round the table to where she was sitting next to her friend Freda Jones. 'What's the problem?'

Carol tore out a page from her spiral-bound notebook and said, 'You told us that we had to write in blank verse, that's in iambic pentameters, like Shakespeare – well, maybe not very much like Shakespeare, but you know what I mean. Five iambic feet in each line, yes?'

'Yes, that's right.'

'Then there should be ten syllables in each line?'

Gordon nodded. 'Yes . . . well, there could be an extra syllable at the end of the line or you could drop one at the beginning. But these can't be *stressed* syllables. You've still got your five stresses.'

Carol nodded slowly, looking at the page she had torn out. Then she handed it to Gordon. 'The ninth line,' she said. 'It's got eleven syllables but I think it sounds all right.' Everyone round the table was listening attentively.

Gordon saw that she had written twenty lines in a neat rounded hand, a fair copy taken from many untidy drafts. He read the lines through before going back to the one she had mentioned, which he then read aloud:

'The same that gently lullabied in summer . . . ' He repeated it, then said, 'That's fine. In fact I like the whole thing very much. The contrasts with remembered summer winds are fine and you've brought off some nice images. The line you mentioned is perfectly all right. Metrically I mean. That extra unstressed syllable in *summer* at the end of the line is what's called a feminine ending.'

Joan Palmer, who was sitting opposite to Carol, said, 'Why feminine?' Her smile was amiably mischievous.

Gordon looked across the table at her. 'Eh?' He sounded absent-minded because he was still going over Carol's lines.

'I said why *feminine* ending?'

'Oh, because it's a weaker, softer sound, it's . . . oh dear. I see what you mean. Yes, not at all politically correct.'

'I don't think Gaby would approve.'

Gordon resisted the momentary temptation to say that Gaby had probably never heard the expression, or any other prosodic term for that matter.

He said, 'It's gentler, less emphatic. It's often used to vary the regular beat of the pentameter that can get a bit mechanical, a bit monotonous. And poets might use it to suggest or hint at uncertainty. I suppose the famous example is Hamlet's *To be or not to be*. Line after line with feminine endings . . . that is the *question* . . . nobler in the mind to *suffer* . . . outrageous *fortune* . . . those endings sort of echo the tentativeness, the wavering uncertainty in Hamlet's mind. I don't know who first called the endings feminine. Obviously way back when women were the weaker sex.'

The members of the group began to collect their possessions together and leave for lunch, each handing Gordon his or her work. Only John Stamper stayed seated and still seemed to be brooding over what he had written.

Gordon said, 'It doesn't matter if it's not finished, John. Let's have what you've done.'

John looked up and nodded. Then he separated one sheet of paper from a few other sheets and handed it to Gordon. He crumpled up the others in his large fist and tossed them into the waste-paper basket.

'I don't suppose it's much good,' he said as he rose and left the room.

Before adding John's work to the rest, Gordon, his curiosity roused, read it through. He did not know what he should have expected but he was agreeably surprised. Clearly, handling of the metre had presented no difficulties or, if it had, they had been satisfactorily solved. The lines were classically correct, perhaps a little too much so for full effectiveness, but the content was a different matter. There was nothing predictable about the imagery which managed to carry a dark vein of menace, a sense of malign destructiveness without resorting to the kind of Grand Guignol language that an inexperienced writer might employ. John's night wind was a blind, bullying and brutal force that, he seemed to be suggesting, was the material manifestation of something dark and murderous in the human psyche.

Gordon was now alone in the library. He looked at the waste-paper basket where John had thrown the crumpled sheets of paper. If he felt a flicker of uncertainty about the propriety of inspecting the discarded sheets he ignored it and retrieved them from where they had been thrown. He straightened them out and read. As he had guessed, two of them were filled with disconnected words and phrases and a few of the images that would appear in the final version, and another sheet showed, with many alterations, the shaping of that version from the inchoate sketches and scribblings on the rough drafts. The remaining sheet, though, was different from the others. It carried nothing that resembled verse or imaginative writing of any kind. Instead there was what looked like a rather crudely drawn map with cryptic signs scrawled at various places on it and, underneath the map, in a rough frame, were written three names, each with a different but fairly recent date inscribed at the side. The names were Jenny Clarke, Tina Arthurson and Clare Deacon. They meant nothing to Gordon who re-crumpled the sheets of paper and returned them to the basket.

Gaby's group had, so far that morning, done no actual writing. They had been busy, though, in what she called consciousness-raising exercises. One of these involved Gaby saying the word 'cat' and each member of the group saying, with absolutely no premeditation, the first word that sprang to mind. Eileen, one of the Barkestone Writing Circle ladies, had said 'Pussy' and Tony had giggled and been quite sharply reprimanded by Gaby. After some discussion about the possible unconscious impulses behind the choices of associative words the group was given the word 'Yellow' which produced 'coward', 'peril', 'custard', 'daffodils', 'line', 'fever', and 'lemon'.

'Now,' said Gaby, 'here we've got a mixed bag of words, all of them in some way – however obscure – related to 'yellow' and to 'cat'. What I'm going to ask you to do is to take all of the fourteen words we've so far got and put together a piece of writing – I won't call it a poem – a piece of writing, using all of the words in any order you like. Don't bother about verse or rhyme or anything like that. Try to let your imagination flow freely. It doesn't matter how odd or even ridiculous the result might seem. Of course you can use any other words you like but for heaven's sake don't try laboriously to make sense. The last thing we want's a logical narrative or discourse. I know that most of you will be in the habit of using language to express already formulated coherent ideas. It won't be easy but I want you to get away from that. I want to see you sparking words off one another in ways the rational intelligence wouldn't allow them to. Here are the words for those who haven't already got them down. Pussy, Tiger, Milk, Spit, Tail, Whiskers, Howl, Coward, Peril, Custard, Daffodils, Line, Fever and Lemon.

'Okay? You all got those down all right? Good . . . Anyone wanting paper, there's plenty here. Just help yourselves.'

The students exchanged looks, puzzled, aghast or amused. There was some muttering between Bernard and Arthur who both seemed to be unconvinced of the value of this exercise.

Gaby smiled at them encouragingly. 'Don't worry. You've got the words there in front of you. Let them get together, collide with each other, mate with each other. Treat it as a game. Don't worry about making sense. The words will make their own wild music. Trust the words. Trust your unconscious mind.'

Tony Frame was already scribbling away, looking relaxed,

leaning back from the paper he was writing on, head slightly to one side, smiling faintly. Kirsty, sitting next to him, looked worried and kept peering over to see what he was writing. Maureen and Eileen, both old hands at writing-workshops, were beavering away conscientiously. Viv, too, seemed to be getting the words down without difficulty.

Gaby moved among her students looking at their efforts. After a while she said, 'Anyone who's finished like to read theirs out?'

After a short pause Tony raised one forefinger.

'All right Tony. Let's hear yours.'

He recited in a sing-song voice:

> 'Milk the tiger at your peril.
> Daffodils and custard howl.
> Coward pussy in a fever
> Spits from whiskers, waves its tail.
> The little lemon, tiny lion,
> Lies down on the yellow line.'

Some of the other students made little noises of admiring approval and some of them looked at each other, nodding or grimacing, communicating dismayed knowledge of the inferiority of their own efforts.

Gaby, however, seemed less favourably impressed. 'Very neat, Tony,' she said, 'but admit it. It's doggerel, isn't it? That kind of tumpti tumpti tumpti rhythm's okay for nursery rhymes and maybe kids' light verse but you can do better than that.'

Tony's smile did not for a second fade or waver. 'Well, Gaby, as you said, treat it as a game. That's the kind of game I chose to play.'

'Ah yes, but what I was after was more of a releasing of unconscious associations, an altogether darker flow. I mean, when you're using regular metre like that and trying to find rhymes or half-rhymes or whatever, the whole process becomes too intellectual, too *conscious*. See what I mean? There isn't space for the magic to get in.'

Tony nodded amiably, 'Yes, I see what you mean. Maybe I'll have another shot at it.'

'Anyone else like to read what you've done?' Gaby said.

At first no one seemed eager to volunteer and she was about to go on with the session when Viv said, with almost a challenging note in her voice, 'I'll read you mine if you like.'

'Oh good. Listen everybody. Viv's going to read us hers.' They listened and Viv began, speaking quite slowly and deliberately:

'The coward thought only of her poetic pussy.
In my fever of rage I wanted to spit and howl
"Cowardy cowardy custard!" He was mild as milk,
harmless as a daffodil, the man I had once
thought was a tiger. I could pull his tail
and tweak his whiskers and he would not protest.
Betrayal stung in my mouth, sour as raw lemon.
Someone was in my line of fire and in grave peril.'

In the brief, slightly shocked silence, Arthur coughed and muttered something inaudible to Bernard. Then Tony said, 'That's terrific stuff, Viv. Really brilliant. Don't you think so, Gaby?'

Gaby was looking steadily at Viv and she was smiling faintly, her eyes quizzical, perhaps a little surprised. She said, 'I do indeed. May I look?' Viv let her take the sheet of paper which she read, nodding slowly to herself. 'It really is a very strong piece of writing, Viv. There's a lovely ambiguity about *coward*. Is the coward a woman or a man? There's passion here and mystery. And that's what poetry is all about. I find it very interesting indeed.'

Viv was staring back at her. 'I thought you would,' she said, and the words seemed to be loaded with more than the obvious meaning.

Gaby, her eyes again running over the words on the paper, did not appear in the least disconcerted by what might have been a note of menace in Viv's voice.

'Yes, very interesting indeed. Perhaps we'll have a talk about it some time in private. But now, everybody. Please listen. We're going to think about your first *real* go at a poem. I'd like all of you to produce something by the morning session tomorrow, something on what I'm going to suggest to you now. The theme, ladies and gentlemen, is murder. Yes, yes, I know. Melodramatic stuff, you're thinking. But is it? Or isn't it the stuff of everyday life?'

'Not *my* life,' Arthur Kirk said, just loudly enough to be heard.

'Oh? Not *your* life Bernard?' Gaby said, her eyebrows raised.

'Arthur.'

'What?'

'My name's Arthur, not Bernard.'

'Oh, sorry. Arthur. You think murder's something quite remote from your life and I'm sure it is, in the sense that you haven't yourself committed murder – at least not literally, not physically. But no man is an island. You can't be unaffected by the murders that go on – not just now and then, but every few seconds, all over the world. Not that I want you to think about the subject in that way. I mean I don't want a dissertation on the incidence of murder in so-called civilised societies all over the world, interesting though that might be. That's the business of the prose writer or sociologist or journalist, the historian. We're poets. We must become the murderer or the victim or perhaps both. I expect you've heard about those recent murders, three I think, all of them young women, raped and then horribly done away with, strangled. The terror of those last conscious moments, knowing after the unspeakably hideous violation by the brute male that he – that *it* – is going to kill you! And what must it be like to be *him*, the killer, the destroyer, the rapist. What hell – or could it be paradise for him – what heaven or hell does he spend his days and nights in? What terrible and irresistible force compels him to do what he does?

'Choose your viewpoint. You can be the poor frightened, doomed victim or you can be the ruthless predator, the killer. Or you can be God. You can look into the consciousness of both murderer and murdered. This is the power of the poetic imagination. It can confront the intolerable and shape it into some kind of terrible beauty . . . ' Gaby paused for a moment. 'Yes, Maureen. It *is* Maureen, isn't it? I see you're looking at your watch. And you're quite right to. I've run way over coffee-break time and I'm sorry. I'll let you go in a couple of minutes. In fact we can call it a day. I just want to say this. You've got your theme. Murder. It's up to you what you do with it. You could choose non-physical murder, the killing of another person's dreams and aspirations through insensitivity or deliberate cruelty. The murder of trust, faith, love. I leave it to you. I hope you all will have finished at least first drafts by the time we meet tomorrow. I mean when we meet for our morning workshop. We'll be meeting, of course, this evening for my reading. And if anyone wants to come and see me for a one-to-one, you know where I live.'

There was a small silence before the group began to talk among themselves, at first exchanging brief, low-voiced remarks and questions while Gaby collected together her belongings. As soon as she had left the room, the talk grew louder and more sustained. Someone, probably Tony, made a comment which drew from Kirsty a wild, high shout of laughter. Gaby, on her way to her room, heard it and smiled a little grimly.

The night gale, which had provided a subject for Gordon's group of tyro poets, had subsided into a snivelling, rain-filled wind which kept everyone indoors that afternoon except for Chris, who drove into Ancliffe to shop for the supplies requested by Margaret Baker who, with Carol Lumsden and Bernard Hanson as her assistants, had appointed herself Head Cook for that evening's meal. When Chris returned he found Serena in the kitchen drinking tea with Margaret.

He dumped the large cardboard box containing groceries on to the long work-surface and said, 'There you go, Margaret. I think I've got everything you wanted.'

'What's that?' Serena asked him, pointing at two newspapers which rested on top of the box's contents.

'Oh those, the *Telegraph* and the *Mirror*. John Stamper asked me to get them. I told him it was policy not to encourage newspapers on courses here but he said he had good reason for wanting to see them and if I didn't get them for him he'd drive into Ancliffe himself and get them. So I got them, as you see.'

Margaret said, 'Perhaps he wants to see the Sports pages. He looks like somebody who'd be interested in sport.'

'I don't think that's what he's interested in,' Chris said in a tone freighted with darker meaning.

Serena made a little noise of exasperation. 'Oh, Chris, don't start on about that again! I expect Margaret's quite right. He wants to see how Rangers or Spurs or whatever they're called are getting on in the Milk Cup, whatever that is.'

Margaret, puzzled but sensing the possibility of an ill-tempered argument, interceded quickly: 'Cup of tea, Chris? Kettle boiled a second ago. Won't take a minute.'

Chris shook his head. 'No thanks. I'll put this stuff away and go and see if Sludgens has fixed that washer I told him about.'

While he was storing away the boxes and packages into the cupboards and fridge Margaret said to Serena, 'I think Gordon's workshop went very well this morning, considering. I mean it always takes a bit of time for things to sort of warm up. Has anyone said anything about Gaby's lot?'

'No one's said anything to me. I hope I can find time to look in on both groups tomorrow. At least I'll be able to get to Gaby's reading tonight.'

'Oh yes, Gaby's reading. That's something to look forward to. I'm sure we'll all enjoy it.'


'Gaby's reading her own poetry this evening,' Arthur Kirk said. 'That should be interesting.'

Bernard Hanson, who was sitting on the side of his bed reading over what he had written on a sheet of lined A4, looked up at his room-mate who stood at the window watching the rain sweeping across the valley.

'You don't sound very enthusiastic.'

'No. Are you? I mean are you really looking forward to it?'

'Well, perhaps a bit more than you are. I'm curious to see what her stuff's like. I meant to get something of hers out of the library before I came here but somehow I never got around to it.'

'I did.'

'You've read something of hers then? What did you make of it?'

'Tell you the truth, I couldn't understand a word of it. Or maybe that's not quite accurate. I suppose I could tell you the meaning of most of the words if you just put them in front of me, out of context as it were. But I couldn't get any idea of what she was trying to say when she'd strung them together. And look, Arthur. Like you I'm a reasonably intelligent man, wouldn't you say? Not badly educated, decent grammar school, nothing spectacular but respectable marks all the way through. Professional exams and all that. Right? Then why is it that Gabriella Cornwell's poetry left me utterly bewildered?'

Arthur left his place at the window and sat down on the edge of his own bed, facing Bernard. 'I get your drift' he said. 'I must admit I find her hard to follow sometimes, even when she's just *talking* about poetry. But I do think that old chaps like you and me have to make an effort to get tuned-in, as they say, to what the young 'uns are up to. I mean that young fellow Tony doesn't seem to have any problems with Gaby's ideas and I thought that bit of poetry he came up with – and it took him about as long as it takes to tie your boot-laces – I thought it was jolly good. Of course it was light stuff, a bit like Lewis Carroll I thought, but he'd finished before I'd used up half a dozen of those words.'

Bernard nodded. 'Oh yes, he's a clever young chap all right and I agree he came up with a clever bit of verse. But that's not what I'm interested in. As I said last night, I've loved poetry since I was a schoolboy. What I like is beautiful language like "Season of mists and mellow fruitfulness" or "The lowing herd winds slowly o'er the lea". That's what I call poetry. Why can't these modern people write things like that? Why write ugly meaningless gibberish?'

'Dunno,' Arthur said. 'Because we're living in a different world I suppose. Everything changes doesn't it? Poetry, like everything else's got to keep up with the times. Look at painting. Picasso and all those women with eyes where their ears should be and two noses. And music. Things they play nowadays on the wireless, supposed to be symphonies or tone-poems or something, and they sound like people kicking over dustbins or feeding-time at the zoo. And what about that fellow Damien somebody? A dead sheep, wasn't it? And the critics said it was marvellous. Put it in the Tate. But it's no good saying why can't they do it the way their great-grandfathers did it. Might as well say why doesn't Richard what's-his-name – Branston? Branson? – why doesn't he make railway engines like Stephenson's *Rocket*?'

Bernard frowned. 'But you're talking about two different things. Railways, technology, science, things like that aren't the same as the arts surely. I mean the great music and painting and poetry of two or three centuries ago is just as beautiful today as it was the day it was created. A poem isn't something functional that has to be scrapped when a better one's been produced.'

'That's true. I can't say I like modern art any more than you do. But I can't believe they're all frauds and hoaxsters. I mean a lot of the things we think are great – things in music and painting and literature – things nobody would argue about today, well, they were thought terrible when they were first written or played or performed. I don't know all that much about it but I think it's true that painters like the Impressionists, that everybody likes nowadays, came in for a lot of stick when their work first went on show. And Stravinsky. He's the obvious example. *The Rite of Spring*, that was the piece, wasn't it? Nobody liked it. First time it was played everybody yelled and booed and screamed abuse at it. But now it's always played at the Proms and everybody likes it. I like it myself.'

'So do I,' Bernard said, 'but I can't believe anybody's going to like some of the modern cacophonous stuff you hear on Radio Three.'

'But that's exactly the way people felt about Stravinsky. Taste changes. We ought to be glad if we can take in the new as well as the old. The fact we can enjoy Stravinsky as well as, say, Mozart or Brahms is something to be thankful for, isn't it?'

Bernard nodded, rather dismally. 'I suppose you're right.' Then he said, 'So you think Gaby might be the Stravinsky of the poetry world eh?'

'You never know,' Arthur said, and they both laughed. Then he went on: 'I suppose we could try old Gordon's lot, couldn't we? I'm sure Chris said we hadn't got to stick with one tutor, didn't he? Maybe we could switch. I think Gordon might be more on our wavelength.'

'Probably. But what would Gaby think? Might seem to her like a vote of no confidence. Even a bit insulting perhaps.'

'Perhaps . . . maybe we should give it another day or so.'

'Maybe we should . . . that means we'd better get on with murder.'

'Get away with it?'

'I doubt if Gaby Stravinsky would allow that.'


Tony Frame lay on the top of his bed reading a copy of Ted Hughes's *Birthday Letters* which he had found in the Crackenthorpe Hall library. Every now and again he smiled and, once, he gave a little chuckle. When Howard Simpson came into the room Tony lowered the book and said, 'Hullo. Had a busy morning? How did your session with Gordon go?'

'All right, I suppose. I haven't had any previous experiences of this kind of thing so it's hard to say whether it's up to scratch or not. What about you and Gaby's lot?'

'Rather fun, in a way.'

'That's hardly the way I'd describe our morning.' Howard crossed to the window and sat down on one of the two upright chairs at the small table. 'What do you make of that woman, Viv? She was there wasn't she? In Gaby's group?'

'Viv? Yes, she was there. In fact she wrote a rather good piece, I thought. Very violent and strange. A bit like her really.'

'What d'you mean, like her?'

Tony swung off the bed and sat on its edge, feeling with his feet for his shoes. 'I mean she strikes me as a woman of strong passions, moody, difficult, maybe violent. Potentially. Very attractive in a way, but dangerous, possibly. You've seen her. You must know what I mean.'

'What was this thing about? The thing she wrote.'

'About? It was a poem, Howard. Poems aren't *about* things. They simply *are*. Or that's what dear old Jumbo, our English master at Radley, used to say. I've always thought it one of those things that *sounds* true but when you begin to think about it loses its first shine of truth.'

'I don't know what you mean. The only poems I know *are* about something. The *Charge of the Light Brigade*'s about the Charge of the Light Brigade.'

'Yes, but you could argue it's not *about* the Charge but it's a verbal equivalent of the Charge, it's the Charge transposed into language. I mean the answer to the question "What was the Charge of the Light Brigade?" could be "A poem by Alfred, Lord Tennyson."'

'That's all too deep for me. All I asked was what did she write about? Nobody can use words without saying something, so what was she saying?'

'Ah, I think that's a bit too deep for *me*.'

'You mean it was rubbish? Nonsense? What's she want to write nonsense for? Anyway, you said yourself it was good. How could you say it was good if you didn't understand it?

Tony left the bed and took the other chair. 'I said it was good, Howard, because it had the sound of authentic passion. The authority of true feeling. The exact nature of that feeling I can't really claim to know and I'm not at all sure that Viv herself would be able to tell me. Her poem was an expression of emotion and emotions aren't often simple, unambiguous, single-stranded. Take your own feelings about Viv for instance.'

'What do you mean, my feelings? They're simple enough. I can't stand the bloody woman.'

'At the risk of sounding impertinent I don't think your feelings are as simple as you say. Be honest, Howard. Isn't your – whatever it is – distaste, hatred, disapproval, isn't it true that you feel other things at the same time? Desire, for instance? A wish for her respect? Admiration? A bit of love even?'

'Certainly not: I told you. I can't stand the woman. I'm not saying I didn't fancy her a bit when I first saw her. But last night she was bloody rude and insulting and the only feeling I've got now as far as she's concerned is good old-fashioned hatred.'

Tony's eyebrows lifted fractionally. 'Not a tiny scrap left of what you felt at first? Can you truly say that? Not the faintest feeling of desire?'

'The only desire I've got is to give her arse a good spanking.'

'Do you think you'd like to kill her?'

'What!'

'I mean if circumstances were right. Not the faintest possibility of ever being found out.'

'Of course I wouldn't! What the hell d'you think I am? I'm not one of your fancy intellectuals. I say what I mean, nothing more and nothing less. I said I'd like to spank her arse and that's exactly what I mean. Not strangle her or stick a knife in her. Just a bloody good spanking.'

'Yes, I see. I only wondered because Gaby set us our prep on the subject of murder. We've got to write about it as the murderer or victim or both. It just occurred to me, if you had just the teeniest sort of feeling you'd like to do away with Viv you might have been able to give me a little insight into the way a killer's mind works.'

'Well, I bloody well can't.'

'No, of course not. I see that now.'

'Anyway, what's she want to get you to write about murder for? Hardly a poetic subject I'd have thought.'

Tony seemed to be pondering this last remark. Then he said, 'Tell me to mind my own business if you like, Howard, but I can't help wondering why you came on this course. I think it's true to say you're not mad about the arts in general or poetry in particular, are you? Please don't think for a second I'm criticising you. I can see you're a person with great gifts of your own kind but I wouldn't have thought . . . ' He shrugged. 'I see I'm being too inquisitive. Forgive me.'

'No. no you're not. It's all right, Tony. I don't mind. You're quite right. I'm not a great man for the arts. Quite true. On the other hand you mustn't think I'm a thickie. You don't get to be Sales Manager of Eddington-Black Pharmaceuticals unless you've got something going for you up here.' He tapped his forehead. 'And you mustn't think I've got no feelings for the finer things either. I like good music. I've taken clients three times to *Les Misérables*. I bought Vicki – that's my wife – all the Classic FM *Great Tunes from the Operas* for her last birthday. An extra of course. I got her a Honda Civic for her main present. We go to the theatre quite a lot too. Maybe not Shakespeare but serious stuff all the same.

'As you can imagine, I don't get much time for reading. That's partly why I thought poetry would be a good thing to get into. I mean because it's shorter and it's got what you might call cachet. I'm not just a soulless business man you know. I heard about this place from Tish, my daughter. Somebody at her college, a girl friend of hers, had either been here herself or a friend of hers had done a course here. Anyway, she got the details for me and I thought I needed a break from everything – business, family, wife, the whole soul-destroying grind. You know what I mean? A complete change. Meet new people. New experiences. Recharge the batteries.'

Tony looked at Howard with an expression of wondering compassion. 'I don't think,' he said carefully, 'Crackenthorpe Hall is quite the place for life-changing experiences or battery-recharging. Wouldn't you have done better to take a plane to somewhere warm and sunny with palm trees and whatever you fancy in the dusky maiden line for a few days? Poetry workshops are about as glamorous and life-enhancing as carpentry workshops. But you weren't to know that, I suppose.' He looked at his watch. 'Well, I'd better see what I can do for Gaby in the way of murder. I think I'll go down to the library or somewhere and find a quiet corner.'

Howard said, as if Tony had not spoken, 'Did you see that play on telly a few weeks ago? Maybe a month or so. I think it was on BBC 2 or maybe it was Channel 4. About a writing course. I can't remember the actors' names but there was a rather thick-set chap with greying hair. And there were a couple of very shaggable girls, one was dark and the other was sort of gingerish, a bit older but not bad at all. Well, they all seemed to be at it, if you follow me. More like a poetry knocking-shop than a poetry workshop.'

'Ah, I see. And that's what you expected to find at Crackenthorpe.'

'No, not really. not to that extent. But these plays are supposed to be based on real life, aren't they? And I've heard of similar goings-on at Summer Schools, and I've been to a few weekend conferences myself where rumpy-pumpy hasn't been entirely unknown. Speaking of which, I think that Kirsty girl's got her beady little eye on you.'

Tony stood up. 'Do you really think so? Well, Howard, I'm afraid I must leave you for an hour or two. Go and squeeze out a few deathless lines about violent death. I'll see you later. It's Gaby's reading tonight, isn't it? See you at that if not before.' And Tony, with his yellow folder marked in elaborate script *T. Frame's Poetical Effusions* went out of the room leaving Howard to stare out through the rain-smeared window at the bleak landscape of the unloving North.


Gaby's poetry reading was due to begin at eight o'clock but there was a short delay while the kitchen team for the day finished washing up the dinner things. At a quarter past, everyone was settled in the recital-room and Gaby was seated at the far end behind a table on which some books and papers rested next to a jug of water and a glass tumbler. She was faced by four rows of chairs on which the audience sat. Serena, who was to introduce the speaker, had placed herself with Gaby at the table but, when the performance began, she would remove herself to a chair at the side.

She said, 'All right. Everybody settled? Margaret . . .? Carol . . .? Bernard . . .?' These were the three latecomers from the kitchen. 'Good. We're a little late starting but I'm sure what we're going to hear will be well worth waiting for. I know you're not here to listen to me so I'll be brief.

'Gabriella Cornwell – Gaby to all of us – doesn't really need any introduction. She's one of Britain's leading younger poets and she's just published her fourth volume of poetry, *The Colour of Stillness*.

It's been very widely praised and it's been awarded the Blackstone
Poetry Prize for 1999. As I'm sure you all know, she's read her
work on television and radio and performed at virtually every major
literary festival in the country. I won't go on, but leave Gaby herself
to tell us what she's going to read. Oh, one other thing. Gaby will be
happy to answer any questions you might like to ask at the end of
the reading. Gaby . . . all yours.'

Serena withdrew to her seat and Gaby stood up. 'Thank you,
Serena. And thank you all for waiting so patiently. I'm going to read
mainly from my latest book, *The Colour of Stillness*. I'll say just a
few words by way of introduction. I think you'll find the poems
themselves are fairly self-explanatory but it might be helpful if I
explained that the book consists of a sequence of interrelated poems
which are concerned with a particular woman's life and history. The
woman, who's never named, is in her early thirties. She's had a
fairly long relationship with a man – also not named – and it's just
come to a traumatic end when the sequence begins. After he's left her
she discovers that she's pregnant.' There was a little intake of breath
and sympathetic murmur from some parts of the audience.

Gaby went on: 'The poems explore her feelings of desertion and
betrayal and the gradual coming to terms with motherhood, or
should I say imminent motherhood. Incidentally, this is her first
pregnancy. As you will see – I hope – she *does* come to terms with
her new self and she accepts with joy her pregnancy. But then – and
here is the black centre of the sequence – she has a miscarriage
and she's left, forlorn, forsaken, damaged and traumatised.

'The rest of the poems deal with her gradual and painful recovery
and the growing realisation that only other women, or another
woman, can help her to heal and survive. I've given you this short,
kind of synopsis because, of course, I can't read the complete
sequence. It would take more time than we've got. But I can read a
few poems from each key episode and I think you won't have any
difficulty in following the whole drama.'

Gordon, sitting at the back of the room with George Barnes and
John Stamper, thought that he would probably have a great deal of
difficulty, but he resolved to listen as carefully as he could. After all,
quite sensible reviewers had found things to praise in her work.

Kirsty, sitting just in front of Gordon, whispered audibly to her
neighbour, 'Do you think she's attractive, Tony?'

'We must concentrate on the words,' Tony answered.

'But *do* you?'

'Devastatingly. Now please keep quiet.'

Gaby was reading in a strong but unmelodious voice, that varied very little in tone and pitch, with a slight rising inflection at the end of every line, a curious delivery that had little or nothing to do with the sense, as far as Gordon could detect any sense at all. Quite soon his attention began to stray and he was aware only of the monotonous, vaguely hectoring voice droning on as a sonic background to his thoughts of other things.

He wondered whether there had been any mail for him at home that morning. Although, these days, he rarely received invitations to broadcast, lecture or give readings, and even more rarely, letters from admiring readers and requests from editors or publishers to write articles or books, he still listened for the morning postal delivery with a tiny but living flicker of hope and anticipation. You never knew.

Once, out of the blue, he had received a letter from 10 Downing Street, signed by the then Prime Minister's Private Secretary telling him that the PM wished to offer him a grant of £300 from a sum given by an anonymous donor to encourage the arts in Great Britain. That was nearly thirty years ago when such a sum, though not munificent, was very welcome to a freelance writer with a young family. Susan had given up her teaching job because June had just been born and Pauline and Anthony were only five and eight. Gordon had been freelancing for only four years and, while he was doing quite well, better in fact than ever before or since, the money had given them much pleasure, almost as much for its unexpectedness and the implicit recognition of literary status as for its purchasing power.

Dear Susan, she'd always been a staunch supporter and believer in the importance of his work. Indeed, he sometimes thought she was more convinced of its merit than he himself was. In his darker moments of self-doubt and despondency she was always there to cheer him up with ribald remarks about his more ludicrously inept younger rivals and to remind him of the praise that he had, in the past, received from the more discerning reviewers. And when, six years ago, Guy Lockwood, the new editorial boss at Fadden and Lewis, had written a letter telling him that the firm was cutting back

on its poetry list and the sales and critical reception of his last book
had forced them to ask him to look elsewhere for a publisher, Susan's
indignation was so much greater than his own that his efforts to
calm her rage were mercifully therapeutic.

Dear Susan, he said to himself again, and thought he must not forget to give her a call that night.

In the room there was a small atmospheric change, a rustle of
relaxed attention perhaps, recalling him to the reading, and he
realised that Gaby had reached the end of a poem or group of poems.
Then she began to read again. At first the hard, insistent and monotonous voice was little more than an abstract noise but, with an effort,
he brought the words into focus and tried to hold their meaning.

She droned:

> '. . . a far noise eating the edge of darkness,
> a thin splinter of sound, not music or song.
> She tastes its coppery bitterness
> and spits it out, a small serpent,
> a mottled reprimand. He has not called.
> His broken umbrella has no more tears to shed,
> the pale letter-box gorges itself on blood,
> it has not danced since yesterdeath . . . '

Gordon's mind floated away with 'yesterdeath', turned it over,
looked at it and discarded it. This was the kind of stuff sympathetic
reviewers called 'mysterious'. Wallace Stevens had written somewhere that a poem should almost resist the intelligence. There
was something in that, but surely Gaby's kind of writing didn't
*almost* resist the intelligence, it refused with monstrous vanity and
arrogance to engage with it at all. He wondered what odd activities
her students were called on to perform. And then he began to think
about his own group's work of that morning.

They hadn't done at all badly, he reflected. Apart from Howard
Simpson's lump of plain prose, everybody had produced something
readable and, although not all of them had been able to write
regular iambic pentameters, he was pretty sure they would be able to
before the week was over. John Stamper's piece had been one of the
most interesting and George Barnes, he was glad to find, had handled the metre well and written a very creditable piece of blank verse,
marred only by an occasional archaism. Tomorrow, Gordon

thought, he would talk about diction and then, perhaps, about rhyme, and possibly put them to work on a sonnet or some other rhyming form.

He slyly glanced at his watch. Gaby had been at it for more than three-quarters of an hour and showed no sign of flagging. Unlike some of us, he thought, and instantly had to bite hard on a wide, importunate yawn. He and George had shared a bottle of Franco's Revenge over dinner and drowsiness was buzzing softly in his head and pressing gently on his eyelids. Gaby's voice went on and on:

'Buy me what you never will,'

she intoned,

'black dumplings under the jub-jub trees,
a pudding of anodynes. Pour the wine,
let it shout its colour through the window
of its existence. It is the colour of stillness,
the colour of death in derelict motels.
Spread your savoury despair
in sandwiches of flesh, call
for the robin and the hoard of dreams,
cry nocturnal pendulums . . .'

Gordon's head sank, his eyelids closed and he slept.


'Poor Gordon fell asleep,' Joan Palmer said. 'I don't think Gaby's going to put him on her list of favourite people.'

Viv was taking from her handbag two miniatures of gin and a bottle of tonic and putting them on the table beneath the window.

She said, 'Bring the glasses over.'

They had just returned from The Shepherd's Crook where they, with the other non-teetotal members of Gaby's audience, had spent a convivial hour or so with the poet herself.

'Yes, I saw him snoozing away,' Viv said when they were seated with their glasses filled, 'and I can't say I blamed him. I thought her stuff was incredibly difficult to follow. Didn't you?'

Joan sipped and nodded. 'Impossible. I gave up after the first ten minutes and thought about other things.'

'Such as?'

'Oh, I don't know. The usual. How my mother was getting on. How would I feel when she dies, which could be soon. People at work. What would they make of this set-up? Friends. Other people on the course. Cabbages and kings . . . you know . . . '

'What sort of work do you do? You've never said.'

'Very dull. Civil Service.'

'Oh? Doesn't that cover a lot of things? The treasury, things like that? Or is that something else? What part of it are you? I can't imagine you behind the Post Office counter.'

'I don't usually talk about it.'

'Official secrets? Intelligence? M.I.5? Is that Civil Service?'

Joan laughed. 'Nothing like that. I told you. Very dull.'

'What then? I'm intrigued. It can't be anything to be ashamed of.'

'Well, not ashamed exactly. Just something I'd rather people didn't know about.'

'What? Tell. I won't tell anyone else. I promise.'

'All right. Inland Revenue. I'm Assistant Inspector of Taxes in Bradford. That dull enough for you?'

Viv thought for a moment. 'I don't know. Don't know enough about it. I'd have taken you for something different. University lecturer, something like that.'

'Something dull.'

'Not at all. There's nothing dull about you. Quiet perhaps. But clever. Deep.'

Joan smiled. 'I think you're the deep one, Viv.'

Viv, who had lost much of her guarded, uncommunicative manner during the pub session, suddenly looked withdrawn, secretive, even perhaps a little dangerous. 'What do you mean, deep?'

'I don't know. What *you* meant I suppose. A little bit mysterious perhaps. Not giving much away. You're not much like the others but then, most of us are different from each other, I suppose. Except the teachers and those two old boys, Arthur and Bernard.'

Viv swallowed a little of her gin and tonic. Then she said, 'You're not married are you? Or divorced?'

Joan shook her head. 'No.'

'I'm a bit surprised. You're very attractive in a quiet way.'

'Dull.'

'Not a bit! You shouldn't keep saying that. I bet there are hundreds of men who'd fancy you a lot. I bet you've had a few proposals.'

'One or two.'

'No one you fancied?'

'No. Well, not enough. In any case I met my lover – my *demon* lover . . . ' Joan giggled uncharacteristically, the unaccustomed extra gin doing its work . . . 'and we set up home. A love nest. Well, some kind of a nest. Not all that much love, come to think of it, though we had our moments I suppose. It's funny. Looking back I don't remember much passion. In fact I don't really remember much about those years I spent with Paul. That was his name. Paul.'

'Years! How many years?'

'Nearly seven. It seems unbelievable now, I remember so little. I suppose we got into a kind of routine pretty quickly and one day, week, month was very like another. We didn't even have rows very often. Seamless weeks, months, years – gone before you knew they'd passed. I feel as if I've been robbed.'

'Why did you move in with him if it was such a dreary affair?'

'I didn't. He moved in with me. And I don't think it was dreary to begin with. I know it wasn't. But it's so hard to remember the undreary times. I know there was excitement, and maybe even love, but when I try to remember those times all I'm able to do is run a kind of video in my mind of him and me doing certain things, going to certain places. But the *feelings* aren't there. I can't recapture them. I know I was in love, or thought I was, and I know I was hurt when he left, but I wasn't hurt all *that* much and the pain soon went away. And, though I wouldn't have admitted it at the time, it wasn't all pain. There was a bit of relief there as well. I was on my own again and it wasn't long before I knew that this was something I'd been wanting for quite a long time.'

'Why did he go? Someone else?'

'Yes, someone in his office. A young girl.' Joan took another sip. 'I can see now, even that was predictable. He was a very conventional man. The seven-year itch, male menopause, whatever they call it, had to be conformed to, like all the other masculine rites. I know he was beginning to be frightened of growing old. He was only three years older than me. Barely forty when he went. But he'd already started reading the obituaries as if he was checking on how long he'd got left.'

'And didn't you miss him at all?'

'Not a bit. There were one or two moments when I'd wake up and wonder where he was. I mean my body missed him for a second or two. But no. I was glad he'd gone.'

'He and this girl. Are they together now?'

'Well, no. I don't think they ever actually lived together. He got himself a flat. Not difficult for him, as he worked for the Housing Association. Actually he wanted to come back. Just over six months after he'd gone he came over and said he'd made an awful mistake, he'd always loved me, could I possibly forgive him and have him back. So I said, "No, not possibly." And the odd thing was that he took an awful lot of convincing that I meant it. I think he really expected me to welcome him back with tears of joy.'

'Men,' Viv said, and they both took a sip.

'What about you? I see you wear a wedding ring.'

'Oh that. Yes, that's been over for a long time. Well, we split up five years ago. I got married too young. Too young and to the wrong guy.' Viv paused and smiled, secretively, dreamily.

Joan said, 'What was wrong with him?'

'Nothing, except he was just about the most boring man in the world. Boring and sentimental, a terrible mix. He worked for one of the big car dealers in Leicester. He called himself the Sales Promotion Manager but he was just a car salesman. And cars were about all he was interested in. Cars and Leicester City Football Club. He had no taste at all. In anything. Size was what excited him. Size in all things. He wanted a big house, a big car, a big salary, a big cock – that's what he really could have done with . . . '

Joan's eyes widened and she gave a faint gasp and then they both laughed.

'I mean it,' Viv said. 'Size was everything. His favourite music – the only music he ever listened to – was Big Band stuff. Oh yes, and he loved Sinatra. That dreadful, loud, *big* voice, bawling about his own personality. He loved that.

'On Valentine's Day he'd give me the biggest Valentine Card in the world, all great satiny heart and roses. I swear to you that he'd never voluntarily read a book in his life. So why did I marry him? I don't know. I was living at home. Wanted to get away. I thought he was smart and, God help me, sophisticated. Shows what I was like at twenty-one. I thought he'd give me a nice easy life. I was a silly young idiot.

'Anyway, after nearly five years I met Dave Mottram. He worked on the local paper but always said he was heading for higher things. He wrote poetry, or rather he talked a lot about writing poetry. He never showed me any of it, if it existed. If he'd written anything that was any good I'm sure he'd have shown it me. He's not a modest guy, our Dave. He was just about everything that Charles wasn't. He wasn't sentimental, at least not about me. Last thing he would have done would be zap me Valentine Cards the size and subtlety of *The Sun*. Or any other kind of Valentine for that matter. He never remembered my birthday and more often than not he was late for any date we had. Never gave me flowers in his life. He drank too much and often got all tearful about his terrible childhood. But he wasn't a bore. Sometimes maddening, even nasty, but I was never bored. And sometimes, no special reason, he'd take me out to the best place in town and we'd wine and dine like lords, and we'd go back home and make love like I'd never dreamt of in the days with Charles. I was crazy about him.'

'Did you get married?'

'No. Never arose. I got a divorce in 1996 but Dave and I had been together then for nearly two years and he never suggested marriage. I probably thought of it but it didn't seem important. We had our ups and downs but on the whole it was a good relationship. We always had things to talk about and we were always great in bed. And then, last summer, he decided to go on a poetry course, similar thing to this one, at a place in Dorset called Oaklands.'

'The one Gaby was teaching on.'

'That's right, the one Gaby was teaching on. And when he got back he'd changed. I was sure something had happened. He talked about Gaby all the time. Gaby thought this, Gaby said that. Gaby told me so-and-so. I tried to show interest, asked him what he'd written, asked if I could see it. But he said it wasn't ready to be looked at yet. He'd only done rough drafts. I thought he must have got something finished in a whole week of writing so why wouldn't he show me? I said, "Did Gaby see what you'd written?" and he said, "Of course. She was my tutor."

'And this is what really got my suspicions going. He'd gone off me. In bed I mean. I won't say he wasn't interested, but the old magic had gone. It wasn't there any more. And suddenly I saw what had happened. This superwoman, Gaby, had taught him more than poetry writing. She'd had him in the sack. She'd seduced him and he was besotted.

'I went crazy. I'd never felt jealousy before, not like this. It was mad, obsessive, there all the time, never letting up for a second. I'd go through Dave's pockets. I'd watch him looking out for the morning mail and we'd both rush for it. I was sure he was in touch with her, phoning her, writing letters. But I never found a scrap of real proof. What I *did* find though was his poems. In between the pages of one of his books – something about Civil Rights in Northern Ireland and Black America – a book he thought I'd never look at in a million years. He never guessed I'd go through every bloody book in the place, sneezing and coughing from all the dust. And there they were. His poems.'

'And what were they like?'

'Well, I couldn't make a lot of sense of them. They were like Gaby's I suppose. Clumps of words, all in a mad conspiracy not to mean anything. Except for one thing, and that was there all right. Sex. You couldn't mistake the symbols or images or whatever they call them. They were sexual all right. Plump, soft juiciness, quivering, warm, velvety-skinned. Lots of fierce thrustings. A lot of fruit – plums and peaches and apples but not the kind you'd see in the supermarket, I'm sure of that. One thing I did know for sure. I had to see this woman he was so mad about. I had to see her face to face. That's why I'm here.'

'What did he say when you told him you were coming here?'

'I didn't tell him. He thinks I'm at my sister's in Banbury.' They both picked up their glasses and drained them.

Then Joan said, 'But what are you going to do, Viv? I can understand your jealousy, up to a point. But it must have occurred to you that it's possible you're wrong. That what's-his-name – Dave – he could have been simply impressed by her as a poet and teacher, sort of hero-worship. I mean you've no reason to suppose they've been to bed together, have you? Didn't Gaby say she couldn't even remember which of the students on that Dorset course he was?'

'That's what she *said*. Dave's not the kind of man you'd be likely not to remember. Her saying she didn't remember him was near enough proof she remembered him very well indeed. And for good reason.'

Joan shook her head slowly, doubtfully. 'Well, true or not, she'll say the same thing if you ask her again. What will you do then?'

Viv's smile was brilliant, 'I shall kill her,' she said and, after a few moments, Joan joined in with her wild laughter, but Joan's mirth was puzzled, wondering, almost aghast.

At almost the same time that Viv and Joan were taking their first sips of gin and tonic, Gordon and George Barnes were seated opposite each other in the poet's room.

George raised his glass. 'Good health,' he said and drank; then, looking at the bottle which stood between them, he remarked, 'Looks as if the old Celebrated Beef is nearly finished.'

Gordon nodded. 'Not quite dead. There's at least a decent dram each left. I'll get more tomorrow.'

'No. No, absolutely not. My turn. I'll pop into Ancliffe in the afternoon. Or I expect Chris'll be going in for supplies. He'll be quite happy to get me a bottle.'

'Tell you what,' Gordon said. 'We'll both get one. A couple should see us through to the end of the week. Be more than enough, particularly if John Stamper isn't going to be joining us.'

'I don't know where he's got to tonight. He wasn't in the room when I went in to get my glass. I don't suppose . . . '

'Don't suppose what?'

'Well, he seemed to be getting on very well with Gaby in the pub. I don't suppose he's . . . no, I shouldn't think so.'

'You mean . . . ?'

'No . . . I don't know. He's probably in the kitchen drinking coffee, talking to Chris or someone.'

'How do you get on with him? Sharing a room. Does he tell you anything about himself?'

'No, nothing really. Actually I did ask him what he did for a living. Seemed a natural enough question to me. But he just muttered something about social services and made it pretty obvious that he wasn't going to tell me any more. And this evening, just before we went down to dinner, I asked him if he was married and he just said "No". Nothing else. Nothing about whether he'd ever been married or been engaged or anything like that. Just "No".'

Gordon took a drink of his whisky and water. Then he said, 'What about you, George? I take it you're married.'

'Oh yes. Yes, nearly thirty years. Twenty-eight to be exact. Got two boys, Ian and Charles. Ian – he's the elder boy, twenty-six – he's at Art College. Chelsea. Started studying law but packed it in after a couple of years. Painting was always his thing, even as a youngster. The other, Charles, he's in the RAF flying fighters. Different as chalk and cheese, those two. Good chums though, always have been.' George drank. 'And you? You a family man?'

'I suppose I am, yes. We've got three, a boy and two girls, a bit older than yours of course. Anthony – I can never remember their ages – God, he must be thirty-five, thirty-six, something like that. He's doing rather well, an architect. Pauline, she's thirty-two, I *think*. She's married with two kids and June's twenty-seven. I remember her age because she was born 1972, the same year I published my *Selected Poems*. June's not married. Researcher for Yorkshire Television and I gather in line for some kind of promotion. She seems happy enough, as far as one can tell.' There was a pause while they both took a drink and then stared rather bemusedly at the table top as if it held in miniature the fragmented history of their married lives.

Gordon seemed suddenly to wake from his reverie. 'Come on, let's finish the bottle.'

When their glasses had been recharged George said, 'Would you say you were happily married?'

After a brief hesitation Gordon replied, 'I might. If I used clichés like "happily married".'

'You *might*. You don't sound very sure.'

'I don't suppose I do. But that doesn't mean I'm not sure about the quality of my marriage. It means I don't think of my life in those police-court terms. What do you mean by "happily married"? It usually means *still* married. Or it means you don't often knock each other about or get into daily shouting-matches. Another thing. It reminds me of those terrible ads on TV with those rosy-cheeked, silver-haired old couples simpering at each other because the Scottish Orphans' Society or some-such is going to give them a pension or a lovely funeral.'

'All right. I'm not a literary man like you. I don't examine every word before I use it. I use cliché. Most ordinary people do. But you know what I meant.' George sounded a little testy.

'Did I? Are you sure *you* knew what you meant? Did you mean would I be more contented if I was on my own? The answer's certainly not. Or did you mean would I be happier with another woman? This time *probably* not. No . . . wait a minute. I'm sorry George. I'm being pedantic and silly. Of course I know what you meant and the answer's yes, I'm happily married.'

George swallowed some of his drink. 'Well, I know *I* am. Phil – that's Philippa, my wife – Phil's always been a great stand-by. Wonderful really. Always there in the hard times as well as the good times. I suppose the glamour and romance wears off after a bit but it's those other things that count isn't it? Trust. Respect for each other. As for love, the romantic stuff, passionate love, that's for youth, isn't it? Or maybe you poets see things in a different light. Didn't I read somewhere that old chap Robert Graves – even when he was in his eighties – didn't he have to have young women, what he called his Muses, to keep him up to scratch?'

'I believe he did. I don't think – ' Gordon broke off whatever he was about to say. 'Oh hell' he exclaimed. 'I forgot to phone Susan. My wife.'

'A bit late now.'

'Too late. I'll have to ring tomorrow.'

'Don't worry. She'll understand.'

'I expect so. Still, I should have phoned. Drink up. About time we hit the sack.'

They finished their drinks and George said goodnight and left for his own room. Gordon went out into the corridor and visited one of the lavatories where he relieved himself of at least some of the residual beer from the session in the pub. No doubt he would have to get up in the night for another pee but he would now, with luck, be able to sleep for three or four hours.

Back in his room he undressed and climbed into bed. He extinguished the light and turned on to his right side. Just before sleep submerged him he lifted his head from the pillow and sniffed. For a second he was not sure, so he sniffed again. He could feel the wrinkling of his frown in the darkness as, for the third time, he took a deeper and longer inhalation through his nostrils. There was no doubt this time. What he could smell was celery. It was not strong but it was unquestionably the smell of celery.

Where could it be coming from, he wondered, but he was too weary to stay awake and speculate. Perhaps he would mention it next day to Chris or Serena.

# TUESDAY

TUESDAY BROUGHT a sudden change in the weather, a wash of cloudless pale blue sky and bright sunlight that carried no discernible warmth. When the morning sessions were over and lunch eaten, some of the students set off on walks, either to the village or to the crest of the hill, from where they might carry on down to the gorse-covered sweep of moorland below. Gordon, though, wandered into the library to look for something fairly undemanding to read, since he had finished his Elmore Leonard when resting on his bed after lunch.

The shelves were well-stocked, mainly with poetry collections some of which, he saw from the inscriptions on the flyleaves, had been donated by their authors when serving as visiting tutors on previous courses. Besides collections by individual poets there were some anthologies, including various *Oxford Books* of this and that, *Palgrave's Golden Treasury* and dozens of compilations of regional, thematic or politically slanted verse, mainly by contemporary writers, few of whom Gordon had heard of, let alone read.

The poetry of the past was less well represented: a single volume of Shakespeare's *Complete Works* in cruelly microscopic type, Carey's translation of the *Inferno* and *Purgatorio, The Collected Poems* of Longfellow, Felicia Hemans and Robert Bridges, and not much else. Then Gordon saw that a whole section was devoted to prose, chiefly literary criticism, though there were a few biographies, memoirs and miscellania among which he saw with delight a copy of D. J. Enright's *Interplay,* a quirky, clever and highly entertaining commonplace book which he had dipped into in a friend's house and long wanted to spend more time with.

He took this book from the shelf and was about to leave the library when the door opened and Maureen Symes, followed by her friend, Eileen Davidson, came in.

Maureen, who appeared to be a little older than Eileen was thin and rather nervous-looking. She wore a small, shining helmet of perfectly straight silver hair and her blue eyes looked both wary yet wondering. Her friend was plump and dark, a darkness probably dependent on artificial aid, and her eyes looked capable of merriment.

'Serena told us she'd seen you come in here,' Maureen said. 'I hope we're not intruding.'

'No, of course not. I was just leaving. Came to look for something to read.'

'Oh,' Maureen sounded as if she thought she had been snubbed.

'Go on,' said Eileen. 'Ask him. Don't be silly. He won't mind.' She looked at Gordon, smiling. 'She's shy. But she wants you to look at one of her poems.'

'A pleasure,' Gordon said. 'You got it with you?'

Maureen's small, pale face had turned pink. 'Yes,' she said faintly, and produced a sheet of paper from the folder she was carrying.

'Let's all sit down.' Gordon gestured towards the table and they pulled out chairs and sat down together with him between the two ladies.

He took the sheet of paper from Maureen. On it was written in small and very neat handwriting this poem:

### City Weather

The rain is falling, silver on dark pavements.
It gurgles in the gutters and the drains;
People in a hurry open brollies;
No sign of former dryness now remains.

Now what a change we see: The streets and park
Are beautiful with summer frocks like petals;
From tennis courts we hear the rackets whack;
Excited voices; then the silence settles.

Next, the misty morns when headlamps glow
Like pale chrysanthemums and we can smell
Autumnal scents of garden bonfires while
Feet rustle in the leaves that last night fell.

That was Autumn's voice; it fades and dies.
The days grow shorter and the wind is cold,

And when night falls we see the buses ride
Across the bridge like galleons of old.


When he had read it a couple of times Gordon said, 'Well done. It's very good, on the whole. One or two little weaknesses, maybe, but it runs along nicely. Had you anything in particular to ask me about it?'

Maureen spoke hesitantly. 'Well, not really. I just wondered if it was . . . '

Eileen cut in: 'She showed it to Gaby and didn't get a very encouraging reaction. What was it Gaby said? Something about being stuck in the nineteenth century, wasn't it Maureen?'

'She said we're about to move into the twenty-first century and I hadn't even got out of the nineteenth.'

'Is that all she said?' Gordon asked.

Maureen nodded. 'I thought she was a bit – well, a bit discouraging. I mean she didn't say exactly what was wrong with it. Sort of laughed at it. At me really.'

Gordon looked at the poem again and considered for a few moments. Then he said, 'I think I know what she's getting at about its being a bit on the old-fashioned side. But, as I said, it's good in its own way. I just don't think Gaby would get anything from it, even if it was faultless. I mean, judging from her own poetry, it's not the kind of thing she'd care for. For one thing it's written in metre and it rhymes. Another thing, your meaning's quite plain. No riddles.'

Eileen said, 'What are the weaknesses you mentioned a minute ago, when you first read it? Could you explain what you meant?'

Gordon looked yet again at the poem for a few moments. 'All right. Let's take the third line. "People in a hurry". That's a bit flat and prosy, isn't it? It doesn't make us see and hear and feel the scene. And then "brollies". I don't think you could talk about "brollies" in anything but comic or light verse. Why not "umbrellas"?'

'That's what I wanted,' Maureen said, 'but it wouldn't fit the metre.'

Gordon smiled. 'Yes, I could see that's why you'd used it. But that's one of the difficult things about strict rhyme and metre. You mustn't allow them to force you to say things you don't want to say. You could, for instance, have written something like . . . ah . . . er . . . what about this? "Umbrellas, sleek and black, are opened up" or

"Umbrellas, sleek and black as skins of seals" and then run the image into the next line, which is pretty weak as it stands.

'Then, in the next stanza you've put "morns" instead of "mornings". Again you've done it to fit the metre, but you can't use words like "morn" in the twentieth century. That's probably what Gaby was getting at. Ideally, we should never write anything – that is, the individual words and the order they're put together in, what we call "syntax" – never write anything in a poem that doesn't sound like natural speech. Look at the last line in the stanza, "leaves that last night fell". You'd never say "I've got to sweep up the leaves that last night fell", would you? So you mustn't write it. Same with "galleons of old" at the end of the poem.'

Maureen nodded. 'Yes, I think I see what you mean.'

Seeing how downcast she looked, Gordon said quickly, 'I still think there's a good little poem there. But why not – just as a kind of exercise – rewrite it, forgetting all about rhyme and metre. Say, in syllabics. You know about syllabics? I bet they've been talked about at your writing circle.'

'Like haikus?'

'That's right. But not necessarily as short and restricting as haikus. You know how they go – only three lines, five syllables, seven and then five again. But you can make up your own pattern of syllables and stanza-length. Thing is to concentrate on the images. You've got some good ones there. They could be worked up. Compress your first lines into something like "Rain sprays its silver on dark pavements. It gurgles in gutters. Black umbrellas swell above the hurrying heels that dance and chatter". Something after that style. Just a series of little word-pictures, but pictures that you can hear and smell as well as see.' He paused. 'Do you see what I mean?'

Maureen nodded again. 'Yes, I think so.' Then she added, 'Thank you.'

Eileen, who had been listening with as much attention as her friend, said, 'Would it be all right if we came to your morning session tomorrow, Gordon? Gaby wouldn't mind. I told her we'd ask you if we could. We thought she might be a bit cross but she wasn't at all.'

'Yes, of course, you'd be welcome. Actually it'd work out rather

well. Carol and Freda – you know them, the two teachers – they're
going to join Gaby's group tomorrow. Howard Simpson, as you'll
have seen, has deserted me. So it'll even things up. How did he
get on, by the way? Howard, I mean, in Gaby's lot?'

The two women exchanged looks that combined stifled amusement with nervous hesitancy.

'Well . . . ' Eileen said, and the word was stretched out cautiously,
'I don't want to be unkind but I must say that he didn't seem to have
the faintest idea of what we were all there for. I know Gaby's rather
hard to follow sometimes but this morning she set us something that
was straightforward enough. We had to imagine we were another
thing, not human, a creature, a natural object, an animal, a flower, a
tree. Something like that. You might not see the point of it but it was
clear enough what she meant us to do. We were supposed to describe
the world as it would appear to us if we were one of those non-
human things.'

She looked again at her friend and they both suppressed giggles.

'What did he do?' Gordon said.

It was Maureen who took up the story. 'Well, we all of us read
out what we'd written at the end of the morning.' Both women
began again, more unrestrainedly, to laugh. Then Maureen made a
firm effort to control her mirth. 'Well, Howard . . .' There was
another brief eruption of laughter before she could continue: '. . . he
solemnly read out a long – it certainly *seemed* very long – a long and
boring kind of *article* about the difference between humans and
dogs. All about the different diets they ate and the things they did for
amusement. He talked a lot about different breeds and a bit about
working dogs like shepherds' dogs and gun-dogs. Something about
communication, the ways that dogs and humans could communicate
in limited ways though they didn't have a common language. The
way dogs and humans – oh, I don't know, he seemed to go on and
on with this sort of fourth-form essay on dogs and people. I began
to wonder if he wasn't teasing Gaby. Trying to pull her leg, make her
look silly. But no. He was completely serious. Even seemed rather
pleased with himself when he'd finished reading the thing, as if he
knew he'd done something that was probably better than most of us
could hope to manage.'

'How did Gaby take it?'

Eileen answered this: 'She just stared at him with a kind of disbelieving look. Didn't smile or anything. Then she said, "Remarkable. Truly remarkable." Then she asked the next person to read out what they'd done.'

Gordon shook his head. 'I really can't think why he's come here. I'm quite sure he's never read a poem in his life, unless he was forced to at school. It's as if he's made a terrible mistake. Thought he was coming for some other kind of activity, though I can't think what. Perhaps he misread "Poetry" as "Pottery" but, even so, I can't see him as a potter any more than as a poet. Oh well, let's hope he enjoys himself, in his own strange way.'

Eileen and Maureen agreed and then thanked him for taking such trouble over Maureen's poem, adding that they were both looking forward to his reading in the evening. Then they left him, still sitting at the table, smiling faintly as he thought of Howard's essay contrasting human and canine behaviour, and he thanked providence that it was now Gaby's problem to deal with Mr Simpson. The two ladies who had just left would be much easier to work with. In fact, he reflected, his group was now an agreeable and intelligent one whose members could be depended on to listen to what he had to say and to work conscientiously.

That morning things had gone particularly well. He had talked about diction for a while, the importance of sustaining a conversational tone without sagging into prosiness and cliché. He had then introduced the subject of the importance of memory to the poet and commented on the ways in which many of the best known poems in the canon were in some way dependent on the poet's memory, quite often simply on memories of the author's childhood. Wordsworth was an obvious example but there were plenty of others.

What he had asked the students to do was to try to recall their very earliest memory that had stayed with them through the years and re-create in language the remembered experience. The results had been interesting and sometimes moving. George had written about being exposed as a boastful liar when he was a schoolboy. When he read his account of this aloud everyone was held and touched by it though Gordon thought, privately, that it would make a better short story than a poem.

Joan Palmer had written with rare subtlety and accuracy of her feelings of pity and revulsion caused by her childhood piano-teacher, who had carried with her a vague but distinctly unpleasant smell that the young girl had found increasingly nauseating. Margaret Baker had surprised with a neat and perceptive piece about losing a much-loved doll. No one had failed to produce something of interest and John Stamper's description of stealing money from his mother's purse was bleakly impressive.

Gordon grinned faintly as he wondered what astonishing irrelevancy Howard Simpson would have come up with had he not decided to transfer to Gaby's group, a defection for which he felt a renewal of gratitude.

'What on earth can the man have come to this place for?' he asked himself again. 'What in the world could he have expected to get from his time here?'

He shook his head in bemused puzzlement and, taking Enright's *Interplay*, he left the library.


Howard Simpson was sitting in his Mercedes outside Crackenthorpe Hall where he had parked in a position that gave him a clear view of the main front entrance. He had driven into Ancliffe, after the morning session with Gaby, to look for an eating place that might provide an edible lunch. His search had been cursory and unsuccessful and he had ended up with a ham sandwich and a large whisky-and-soda in The Railway Hotel. On his way back to the car-park, where he had left the Merc, he had picked up a copy of the *Daily Telegraph*, which he now held open in front of his face, though his eyes were not on the print. He was, like a private investigator in a crime movie, watching for his quarry.

As Gaby's group had been disbanding after their morning's work he had heard one of the two old farts, Bernard and whatever-his-name-was, say that they were going for a gentle walk up the hill after lunch and would anyone like to join them. When no one seemed keen, the old boy had repeated the invitation directly to two or three individuals, including Viv, and Howard had distinctly heard her say that she would be walking into Maldenwick to pick up a couple of things from the village shop. This was why he had hurried his lunch in Ancliffe and made sure he was back in plenty of time to see Viv leave the Hall.

During what he thought of as the morning's 'lesson' he had from time to time glanced towards Viv in the hope of seeing some kind of response. He had thought a lot about the unfriendliness she had shown on Sunday night and, gradually, he had become convinced that the animosity she displayed was, in fact, a strenuous attempt to conceal, as much from herself as from him, the attraction that she really felt. It was this slowly formed belief that had prompted him to switch from Gordon's group to Gaby's.

He had to admit that she had not once returned his glance during that morning, and he might have begun to have doubts about his attractiveness to her, until he read his composition aloud. When he had finished reading he had looked up and seen her gazing at him quite openly and there was absolutely no doubt that she was smiling. The smile was radiant and warm and he knew it was for him.

He decided to box clever, not move in at once, not even return her smile. He left the room without a glance in her direction. Not playing hard to get exactly, but not showing too much eagerness either. Keep her guessing. That was the name of the game.

He had to wait almost an hour before she appeared and during that time he saw Stamper come out and return after about half an hour, and the two school-marms, probably dykes, set off, obviously dressed for a long hike. When Viv came out he saw, from behind his newspaper, that she had changed from out of the smart short skirt that she had worn in the morning into jeans and a bright red anorak. She did not look in the direction of the parked Mercedes but strode off at a swinging pace, her dark hair bouncing and gleaming in the still bright sunshine

Howard stayed where he was. He thought he would give her time to get to the bottom of the steep lane and well on to the road before he caught her up and offered her a lift. He would be cool about it. Not too pressing. Casual, take it or leave it. He had an idea that she would take it.

He glanced at his gold watch. She would have reached the road by now. Exactly four minutes later he switched on the engine and drove smoothly out of the yard and into the lane. When he turned into the road and, after driving for perhaps half a minute, came into sight of her striding along on the right-hand side so that she would be facing on-coming traffic, had there been any, he felt a sudden quickening of the pulse and a small tremor of excitement. It was, he told himself, the natural thrill of the chase though he felt he would be more in control of events without it. 'Play it cool,' he warned himself, and pulled up on his own side of the road a few yards ahead of her.

His window slid down and, as she drew near, he called out, 'Hullo Viv! Can I give you a lift?'

She did not turn her head even the tiniest fraction to look in his direction but said, 'No thanks,' and kept walking.

He knew that what he should have done then was to drive on without any further attempt at communication but somehow he could not do it. He felt, not only his face and neck, but his whole body, burning with humiliation and rage. Disbelief, too. He thought of her smiling at him after he had finished his reading. That smile had been surely friendly, admiring as well. Her indifference, her display of sheer rudeness, was a female trick, an affectation, a refusal to surrender too easily. 'All right, my girl,' he said grimly and waited until she had walked on for about thirty yards before he drove very slowly forwards and again stopped the car a short distance in front of her.

As she came close he leaned his head out of the open window. 'Viv!' he called, raising his voice almost to a shout. 'You might at least show some manners. Come on. Stop playing hard to get. Hop in and let me run you into the village. I know you've got a bit of shopping to do.'

She walked straight past, without a word or a glance. It was as if he and his car did not exist.

This time Howard really shouted: 'Bitch!'

The single word brought her to a sharp halt like a soldier responding to a drill-sergeant's command. For a second she stood perfectly still; then she swung round, crossed the road to where he was parked and looked down at him, her lips compressed and her eyes bright with fury. That she was standing and looking down on him gave her an advantage that she clearly relished.

She said, speaking slowly and distinctly, as though to a child, or someone with an imperfect grasp of the language, 'I know you are a very stupid man. You can't help that, I suppose. But surely you can't be quite so stupid as to believe you could be anything but repulsive, absurd and hugely irritating to any woman with a glimmer of judgement. So why don't you just piss off in your big shiny motor car and leave me alone?'

Howard's eyes bulged and his mouth fell open as he struggled to find words to express his outrage and incredulity. As Viv was turning away, all he could manage was, 'You know what I'd like to do to you, you bitch!'

She paused for only a moment and said, over her shoulder, 'Yes, I do know. And the thought fills me with horror and disgust.' Then she walked briskly to the other side of the road and strode off towards Maldenwick.

Howard thrust his head farther out of the car window. 'No!' he roared. 'No! I don't mean that! I wouldn't touch you with a bloody barge-pole! I meant I'd like to give you a bloody good hiding! That's what I meant! I didn't mean . . . God I'd like to kill you, you bitch!'

But Viv was out of earshot or totally unaffected by this outburst and she walked on, vigorous, young, desirable and utterly unattainable.

Howard felt tears on his face and tasted the salt of them in his throat as he turned the car, wheezing with the effort as if he were manoeuvring a heavy goods vehicle, and drove back to Crackenthorpe Hall.

George Barnes, Maureen Symes and Joan Palmer were on kitchen-duty for the day. Margaret Baker had looked in to see if advice or extra help was needed but had left after being reassured that the evening meal of macaroni cheese, salad and apple-crumble was being competently prepared. George was apologetic about his lack of culinary experience and aptitude but showed a cheerful willingness to perform any task the women set before him.

Serena, too, had checked that all was going well in the kitchen before going up to the flat to try to do a little work of her own. She had been reading and rereading Melissa Hull's *The T Bone Psalms* over the past two days and she was forced to admit that she had little idea of what the poems were supposed to be about.

At lunch-time, when Gaby was eating an egg mayonnaise sandwich in the kitchen, Serena had cautiously voiced her bewilderment and Gaby had told her that she shouldn't agonise over trying to grasp the prose, paraphrasable meaning of Melissa's work but simply allow the images and rhythms to float around in her consciousness where they would find their own coherence which would be the coherence, not of logic, but of feeling. At the time Serena had felt, if not enlightened, at least hopeful of the possibility of future illumination but now, looking yet again at *The T Bone Psalms*, she still felt, not merely baffled but almost abused, mocked and belittled.

She sat at the table in the living-room and opened her exercise-book that she wrote the final drafts of her poems in. At the side of it she placed *The T Bone Psalms*. First, she read the last poem she had completed, just over a fortnight ago.

### First Frost

Frost has been busy
here along the lane,
baking the mud hard,
decorating winter's nervous weeds.

Small spiralled rosettes
of shepherd's purse glitter,
each curve furred with white.

Dandelions' blunt barbs
are sharpened by ice;
dead grasses cross their broken swords.

Torn fragments of old news are trimmed
with diamonds. A crumpled paper bag
is crystallised, small iceberg.
a milk-bottle top is a fallen halo.

Then she turned to Melissa Hull's book, opened it at random and read this:

### Birthday Message

Not exactly what I expected
but that is what they are for,
to be wrapped up in expostulations
and deposited in the compost
to discover their own nature.

Thank you and all who fail.
The tangerines have sung their piece.
I will talk to my pigeons
about love and mathematics
and open my legs to the thunder.

There was something maddeningly secretive and knowing about the poem's opacity. Her own lines looked, by comparison, rather childish, yet she felt almost sure that they were at least honest in their clarity and that *The Birthday Message* was the opposite in its pretentious obscurity. And yet celebrated professionals, like Gaby, said Melissa Hull was a fine poet and she was one who had won prizes and had lavish praise bestowed on her, presumably, by judges of discernment.

Serena sighed and was about to close *The T Bone Psalms* when Chris came into the room.

'Hi,' he said. 'You busy?'

'No. Not really.'

He looked at her more closely, perhaps hearing the greyness in her voice. 'What's up? Work not going well?'

He stood behind her and looked down at the open pages on the table.

She said, 'I don't know. The more I see and hear of poets and poetry the less I know about them. I was quite happy with my things before I came here. I knew they weren't marvellous, but they were all right. I mean they looked all right and sounded all right. Other people thought so, too, the few who saw them. But – I don't know – they're nothing like the things Gaby writes, or Melissa Hull. It may sound silly, but I'm afraid to show them to Gaby.'

Chris picked up the exercise book and looked at her poem for a few seconds. Then he said, 'I know I don't know anything about it, but I'd say yours is better than anything those two could ever write. What I've seen of that Hull woman and the things I heard Gaby read, none of it makes any sense. At least I can understand yours. I think it's a really good little poem.'

'Oh God,' Serena said, 'that's just the trouble. I write nice little poems, like "thought for the day" or something. Simple-minded.'

'I didn't mean it like that. When I said "little" I meant little like a small picture. It's a short poem. Doesn't take long to read. That's all I meant. Because it's short doesn't mean it can't say a lot. If I were you I'd forget those *Pork Chop Hymns* or whatever they're called. And old Gaby's stuff. You're better than either of them.'

'It's nice of you to say so but, like you said yourself, you don't know anything about it. So let's talk about something else.'

'All right.' Chris sounded a little piqued. 'If there's anything we can talk about without squabbling.'

Serena stood up. 'Come into the kitchen. I'll make us a cup of tea. I'm sorry I snapped at you. I've been feeling a bit low . . . Where've you been anyway?'

'I had to go into town again. I'd forgotten I'd promised to get some whisky for the Colonel and Gordon. A couple of old soaks, they are.' Chris was a pint-of-bitter man and he disapproved of the hard stuff. 'Oh yes, and I saw Stamper as I was driving into the yard. He was coming out of the Sludgens's cottage. And guess what he said when I asked him what he'd been doing there.'

'You asked him *what!* It's no business of yours what John Stamper, or anybody else, does in his spare time.'

'Well, no, I mean I didn't put it to him like that. Only in passing. You know, I asked him how he was getting on with the course, if he was enjoying it and so on. Then I just slipped it in, said sort of casually, I didn't know he was friendly with old Sludgens. And that's when he told me what he was up to. He said he'd asked them if they minded him going in and having a look at their telly. And when I said "You interested in anything special?" he said he just wanted to keep up with the news.' Chris nodded knowingly. 'And we don't need to be told what that meant!'

Serena, who was filling the electric kettle, turned from the tap and faced him. 'Chris. Please don't mention John Stamper and your stupid suspicions again. Not to me. The man said he wanted to see the News and that's what he wanted to see. Some people have grown-up interests like politics and the state of the world. But you wouldn't understand that. You've decided, for no reason whatsoever, that he's a murderer. A fugitive from justice. All very exciting but absolute rubbish. So please, just try and grow up a bit, Chris.'

'I never said he was a murderer! All I said was it looks a bit odd – '

Serena banged the kettle down on the draining-board. 'Make your own bloody tea!' she said. 'I'm going down to find some adult company for a change.' And she went out of the flat so swiftly that Chris thought he could still feel the cold wind of her flight long after she had slammed the door.

The sun was setting and the evening twilight was sharpened to a wintry chill as Carol Lumsden and Freda Jones walked down the rough path towards the Hall. They were both wearing trousers tucked into thick woollen stockings and stout leather boots, anoraks and woolly hats, the uniform of serious walkers. They had covered a good six or seven miles in a circular route over the moors and were feeling pleasantly warm and fatigued and were enjoying that sense of comradeship and well-rewarded virtue that such strenuous exercise often induces.

Earlier they had talked a little about mutual acquaintances and the local and national politics of education, but they had soon abandoned these topics for the more immediately interesting subject of the Crackenthorpe Hall poetry course and its members and instructors. They were particularly concerned about their decision, made after much discussion on the previous night, to switch for at least one session from Gordon's group to Gaby's.

Freda, who was the more timid of the two, had been worried about whether Gordon's feelings would be hurt, but Carol had answered that she had talked at length with their tutor about their wish to see how the other group worked and he hadn't made the slightest objection or shown the tiniest flicker of resentment at her request. In fact he had said that working with Gaby might give them some fresh and more up-to-date ideas about creative writing that could prove useful in the classroom.

'He's a nice man,' Freda said, 'I wouldn't like to upset him.'

'Yes, but don't worry about that. He didn't mind in the least.'

They walked on for a few more yards then Carol said, 'I forgot to tell you. While you were in the bathroom before lunch I went down to the library to look around for something to read for the Personal Choice evening tomorrow and I found an anthology of Sixties Poetry. Quite a nice hardback and it'd got photos of the authors, including Gordon. And, do you know, he was very good-looking when he was young.'

Freda was quiet for two or three paces before she said, 'He still is. For his age.'

Carol smiled. 'You think so?' Then she added, 'Yes. I know what you mean. He's got nice eyes, a nice smile. A bit on the jowly side but not bad. In the picture though he was really quite handsome, romantic-looking. I'll show it you later.'

'Have you chosen a poem yet?'

'Yes, I think so. Actually the poems in this anthology – I mean the ones by Gordon – they were pretty good, I thought. I even considered reading one of them in the Personal Choice. But then I saw that it would look as if I was sucking up or something and everybody would be embarrassed, especially him and me. So I've settled for an old favourite, *Porphyria's Lover*.'

'I thought I'd read a Dylan Thomas. Either *Do Not Go Gentle* or *Fern Hill*.'

'Good idea. Funny how he seems to have gone out of fashion.'

'My reading'll bring him back,' Freda said and they both laughed.

They were going through the gates of the Hall by now and, suddenly, they both had to jump quickly to one side to avoid being run down by the car that came, far too fast, out of the yard and swung with a fierce rasping of tyres down the lane towards the main road.

The two women stared after it. 'That was what's-his-name, Howard, wasn't it?' Freda's voice was squeaky with startled indignation. 'He could have knocked us both down! He could have killed us!'

Carol, too, sounded shaken. 'Yes, that was Howard all right. Why on earth was he driving like that! He looked as if he was trying to get away from someone or something. And where can he be off to at this time of day?'

'I don't know. But I'm going to have a word or two with him when I see him.'

They went into the building and up the stairs to their room.

Just before they reached it Carol said, 'You go ahead. I won't be a sec. I must have a pee,' and she hurried back down the corridor.

Freda reached their door and opened it. Then she stood there, not going forward into the room, immobilised by shock. A man was bending over the chest of drawers. She realised almost at once that she had seen him on the previous day pushing a wheelbarrow in the yard. Chris had told her that it was Sludgens, the odd-job man and gardener. But that this very unprepossessing-looking fellow in his filthy dungarees should be in their room and, more specifically, rummaging in the drawer in which she and Carol kept their underwear, was something both alarming and inexplicable.

She took a deep breath and said, 'You! What are you doing in here?' and her voice sounded strangely high-pitched in her own ears.

Without haste he straightened up, closed the drawer and turned to face her. It was not easy to tell whether the baring of the yellow and decaying fangs was meant to be a smile or a snarl. Then strange sounds came from that alarming mouth: 'Saul reet loof. Bin vixen bloog.' He pointed down to an electric fitting low down on the wall at the side of the chest of drawers and produced from a pocket in his dungarees a large screwdriver which he brandished in front of his nose.

Freda did not move forward into the room as she said, 'What were you doing in the drawer? You've no reason to look in there. None at all. I shall tell Mr . . . ' She realised that she had completely forgotten Chris's surname. '. . . I'll report you!'

The awful leer did not leave Sludgens's face as he nodded, as if in full and considered agreement with her decision to report him, and moved towards where she stood in the open doorway. Freda hastily skipped back into the corridor and, as he passed, she sniffed a pungent but unidentifiable odour which floated behind him like an invisible wake as he left, walking with a peculiar, slightly bow-legged, swaggering gait to the head of the stairs down which he went out of sight. He had only just disappeared from view when Carol came out of the toilet and, seeing her friend still outside the room, hurried towards her calling, 'What's the matter? You look as if you've had a fright!'

'I have,' Freda said. 'There was a man in the room.'

'What! Who was it?'

Together they went inside and shut the door.

'It was Sludgens or whatever his name is. The odd-job man. He was looking for something in our chest of drawers.'

'Are you sure?'

'What do you mean, am I sure? I didn't dream it. It wasn't an hallucination.'

'No. I mean are you sure he was going through the drawers?'

'Yes, of course I am. He had the top drawer wide open. He only shut it when he saw me.'

'Has he taken anything?'

'I don't know. I haven't looked.'

They crossed to the chest and Carol pulled open the top drawer. 'Yes. He's been in here all right. Look! Things are all over the place!' She was picking up small garments and folding them. Then she wailed, 'My best knickers! The real silk ones! They're not here! He can't have . . . Surely . . . ? . . . Could he?'

Freda nodded. Her eyes were wide with startled and gradually dawning understanding. 'Yes, he could,' she said, 'and we've got to tell Chris. Or Serena.'

'Serena,' Carol said. 'Let's go and find her.'


It was nearly five minutes past eight and the recital-room simmered with subdued conversation while Gordon's arrival was awaited. Tony Frame's light laugh was heard and then the deeper, more serious tones of John Stamper who was sitting next to him.

Joan Palmer said quietly to Viv, her neighbour, 'Have you had the chance to talk to Gaby yet? About your friend what's-his-name.'

'Dave. No, not yet.'

'You don't still suspect her, do you?'

'Yes . . . I don't know. Yes, I think so.'

They both looked at Gaby, who was seated two rows in front of them, exchanging occasional remarks with Kirsty Black on her right and Carol Lumsden on her other side. Joan noticed that Kirsty kept glancing over her shoulder to where Tony sat behind her with John Stamper and George Barnes, and she felt a mild twinge of pity for the girl.

Viv said, 'I'm going to see Gaby tomorrow. She's been banging on about one-to-ones so I've made a date for after lunch. Private. In her room. She'll get a one-to-one all right.'

'I shouldn't say or do anything rash!'

'No, you probably wouldn't. But I probably will.'

Joan moved her shoulders in a small shrug. 'You might end up looking silly.'

'That's a risk I don't mind taking.'

Of the people in the room only Chris and Serena were not seated. They were standing at the reader's table and she was speaking to him in low but emphatic tones. 'Well, you've got to talk to him about it and get the things back if you can. He's a lot more trouble than he's worth. And what can the old swine want with ladies' knickers anyway?'

'I don't know. Maybe he's a cross-dresser. I'll talk to him tomorrow, I promise . . . oh, here comes Gordon at last. I'll bet he's been at the whisky bottle.'

Gordon came towards them, carrying a couple of books under his arm and apologising for keeping them waiting. Chris moved away to his seat at the back of the room and Serena beckoned to Gordon to take his place at the table.

When he was settled she clapped her hands to attract the attention of the gathering and called, 'Quiet now please! . . . Is everyone here? . . . No one else to come?'

Tony's voice piped out, 'Howard's not here! Howard has flown the coop!'

'Howard? Not here? Where is he? When did you last see him, Tony?'

'Not since before lunch.'

'Has his car gone, do you know?'

Freda called, 'He nearly knocked me over! Me and Carol! About half past four as we were coming through the gate, back from our walk.'

'He's gone all right,' Tony said. 'Taken all his clothes and things. I was doing a bit of work this afternoon – in here as a matter of fact – and when I went up to our room he'd gone. Not a trace of the man.' Then he added theatrically, 'The scoundrel has forsaken us!'

Viv whispered to Joan, 'He's buggered off with a flea in his ear. He tried to proposition me again today and I told him what he could do. Good riddance too, the horrible creep.'

Serena said, 'All right. I expect we'll manage without Mr Simpson. So I'll get on with the business. As you all know, this is to be Gordon

reading his own work. As with Gaby's reading last night, you don't
want to hear a lot of chat from me. So I'll just say that Gordon
Napier has been one of our leading senior poets for a number of
years now and his *Selected Poems* was a Poetry Book Society Choice
in . . . er . . . when was it, Gordon?'

'Nineteen seventy-two.'

There was a light pittering from the audience of wonderment or
amusement, or both.

Serena went on quickly: 'His last collection, *The Trades of Man*,
was widely praised.' She consulted the piece of paper she was
holding. 'Vernon Scannell in *The Listener* describes it as showing a
welcome return to the threatened values of craftsmanship, eloquence
and wit.' Again a faint rustle from the gathering of *who*? and *what*?
and *where*? 'I'm sure we're all going to enjoy Gordon's reading and
I know he'll be happy to answer any questions you'd like to ask him,
either here or more informally in the pub.'

Serena retired to her seat at the side of the room and Gordon
stood up to a brief flutter of applause and cleared his throat, tasting
a hint of *Famous Grouse*. Then he said, 'I'll first say a word or two
about my rather old-fashioned views on poetry. Then I'll read some
– I promise not too many – of my own things, starting with a bit
of naïve juvenilia, and ending up with something from my naïve
senescence.'

He heard George's unmistakable gruff chuckle and grinned back
gratefully. 'First then,' he said, 'a comment on the kind of poetry I
like to read which is also, I suppose, the kind I try to write. When I
think about the poems that stay in the mind and heart, or whatever
you want to call it, almost without exception these poems are
written in a way that make use of the traditional devices of metre,
rhyme, stanza-forms and so on. These devices have been slowly
developed and elaborated over the centuries and it seems to me
madness for any poet of today to chuck them away and say, "Let's
forget what the old-timers did and start all over again."

'Of course, these forms are almost infinitely susceptible of
adaption and they change with the changes in society, language and
the tempo of our daily lives, but I'm pretty sure you can't – as a poet
– go forward unless you've studied and practised and absorbed the
treasury of means that the great ones of the past have left us.

'That fine French poet of this century, Paul Valéry, said that if your imagination is *stimulated* by the difficulties of the art, you're a poet. If it's *dulled* by those difficulties, you're not. That makes good sense to me.

'Oh yes, one last thing that seems worth mentioning. Quite a lot of the writing that I see today, that claims to be poetry, strikes me as being not only formless and artistically sterile but absurdly self-absorbed, and arrogant in its assumptions that the reader will wish to know about the writer's boring obsessions, preoccupations and so on. It's worth remembering what another very fine poet of our time said, this time an English – well, English-born – poet. He said, "Formal verse frees one from the fetters of one's ego." That was W. H. Auden and I think he knew what he was on about.

'Anyway, that's enough of theory – with a small t. Now I've got to stick my chin out and read a few of my own things which probably won't convince anyone of the truth of what I've just been saying. Still, here goes. I'll start with a couple of short pieces written when I was in my salad days and green in judgement. The first is called *A Portrait from Memory* and, come to think of it, it's probably full of the self-pity that it explicitly denies.'

Gordon was shuffling through the pages of one of his books. Then he began to read:

'Clearly I see him now, the boy who wore my name,
Standing on awkward limbs outside the game,
Hopeful but apprehensive, usually alone,
Assuming a nonchalance he has never known;
Afraid to speak because his words might spin
Back like boomerangs and split the grin
That aches on his wry mouth, as out of place
As whiskers on a ballerina's face.

I see him later, under summer limes,
Puddled with wonder and muzzy with rhymes,
Waiting for her who never arrived,
See him threaten heaven, heaven-deprived;
Swollen grotesquely by the public gaze,
Grunting and blundering through the sensual maze.

I cannot help but feel some tenderness
For that daft innocence and clumsiness
As he is pulled towards the ravenous city –
But do not misinterpret this mild pity:
It is for him. I do not pity me.
He died, his name my only legacy.'

There were one or two sighs and murmurs from his listeners, the noises that are always heard at poetry readings, polite acknowledgements rather than expressions of true feeling.

Gordon said, 'The next one, written a bit later and, I hope, a bit better, is at least less mawkish. It's called *The Death Beast*.'

He began again to read.

Viv was watching the back of Gaby's dark head. She saw it move, perhaps in time to the rhythm of Gordon's verse. She felt a flicker of excitement at the thought of their impending meeting on the following day. It was a feeling that she did not wholly understand. Somehow she sensed that she was going to find out more than simply the truth about Dave's betrayal of her.

Gordon was coming to the end of his second poem:

'. . . waited for the Beast to seek him out,
And when at length it prowled close to his side
And sniffed at him with wet myopic snout,
Indignation swelled in him. He tried
To rise and kick the mangy brute away,
Could not believe that this was really it,
That this contemptible, rejected stray
Engendered passion, rhetoric and wit.
He shrank from stinking pelage, scabrous skin,
But protestations of the mind and nerve
Were vain to help him when its teeth sank in.
We meet the Death Beast that our lives deserve.'

Joan said to Viv, 'I thought that was rather good, didn't you?'

Viv murmured non-committally, then said, 'Gaby didn't go to sleep. Not so far anyway.'

'Why should she?'

'Well, Gordon did when she was reading, didn't he?'

'Oh yes. I'd forgotten that.'

Gordon was reading again. Serena was listening with more care than she usually listened at the Hall readings. The things he had said before beginning his poems had sounded wise and, somehow, authoritative, even comforting in a way. Perhaps she would show her poems to him, or at least talk to him about them. She felt instinctively that he would be more sympathetic than Gaby. Perhaps she would get the chance to have a chat with him in the pub that evening.

Gordon came to the end of another poem. George Barnes, sitting with John Stamper and Tony Frame, said, 'That's very clever stuff, you know. He's a deep 'un is Gordon. I thought that was first rate.'

'Empson-and-water,' Tony said and, though George did not catch the reference, he knew it was meant to be dismissive.

Gordon was glancing unobtrusively at his watch. One more poem should be enough. Something light to send them off laughing. Well, maybe smiling.

He said, 'I know how difficult it is to take in poems that you've never seen before. And thank you for listening so patiently and sympathetically. I'll just read one more slight piece – a bit of light verse on a heavy theme. It's something that some of us have had experience of and others will have to face in the future. It's called *In Middle Age*:

> I have been forced to join the Force,
> Put on the uniform;
> I am an officer of the law,
> Defender of the norm.
> Reluctantly I've joined the blue
> Constables of my age;
> The hours are long, we're never free,
> Contemptible the wage.
> We wear our uniforms in bed
> And don't get too much sleep.
> Of course, we're all misunderstood:
> When we try to keep

The young from acts of vice and folly
Or the desperate old
From murderous joys or melancholy
Time after time we're told,
"You're a puritan, Gestapo man,
A grundy or stuffed shirt",
But on those rare occasions when,
Off duty, we revert
To practices of youth, we find
No pleas of ours avail:
No one smiles, "He's middle aged";
They clap us into jail.
And I suppose they're in the right;
Some one's got to be
A copper, but I'll celebrate
When at last I'm free,
And I rip off my uniform,
With boots and baton rolled,
Fling the bundle on a blaze,
Then like a twelve-month-old
I'll flaunt outrageous appetites,
Howl if they're not fed,
Be lawless and impossible,
And nightly wet the bed.'

There had been a few sounds of mild amusement from the audience as Gordon had been reading and, as he sat down, the applause
was, he thought, more than perfunctory. He felt a quick warmth of
affection for them and gratitude for their tolerance and generosity.

Serena was on her feet. 'Thank you Gordon. That was really great
. . . and listen everyone . . . if anybody wants to ask a question, now's
your chance. And then we'll be off to The Crook. Anyone . . . ? Ah
yes, Tony!'

Tony said, 'You mentioned theory with a small t, Gordon. Could
you tell us your views on theory with a large T?'

Gordon shook his head. 'Death of the Author? Deconstruction?
Intertextuality? All gobbledygook to me, I'm afraid. It'd be nice if
you could explain it all to me. I'm not being funny. I really mean it.'

'Down the pub,' Chris said, and there was an assenting murmur and scraping and scuffling of feet and chairs as the audience dispersed.


The Crackenthorpe Hall party was again disposed around two joined tables in The Shepherd's Crook and the conversation was lively. Everyone who had been at Gordon's reading was there except for Arthur and Bernard who, as lifelong abstainers, viewed public houses with slightly nervous mistrust. Eileen and Maureen, though, were present, making their first visit to the pub and, while they both expressed the firm resolution to drink no more than a single sweet sherry each, they appeared to be enjoying themselves, chatting animatedly with Margaret Baker and George Barnes.

Gordon was sitting between Chris and Serena and as soon as they had settled down with their drinks Serena said, 'Gordon, I've been wanting to ask you something. Have you read anything by Melissa Hull?'

He nodded. 'Yes, I have. In the line of duty you might say. It must be two or three years ago, I got something to review for *Volcano*. Do you remember it? It used to be a rather good little magazine but it folded after about half a dozen issues.'

'And what did you think of it? Melissa Hull's book I mean.'

'Ah, yes . . . well . . .' he paused and took a drink of his pint of bitter. 'I'm afraid I didn't care for it at all.' Then he added, 'Are you an admirer?'

'No, not really. No. I've just been reading her last one, *The T Bone Psalms*. I couldn't get much out of it to tell the truth. Gaby said it was all right. Marvellous actually, so she said.'

Chris, who had been listening to the exchange, said briskly, 'It's rubbish. At least I think it is. I couldn't understand a word of it and I don't believe anybody else could either.'

Gordon spoke with more caution: 'I must say Melissa Hull didn't seem to me much good. But she's writing a kind of verse that's fairly common these days. I'm not sure what it's aiming at. It could be a kind of surrealism without the mischief and wit of the French people of the Twenties and Thirties. But the book I was sent – can't remember the title I'm afraid – as far as I could gather it was supposed to be the daydreams and thoughts of someone – a woman

– who's had some kind of breakdown and been stuck in a loony bin. I suppose you couldn't object to the fact that the poems didn't make sense because the author might reasonably say they're not supposed to, since they're the ravings of a nutter. On the other hand it seemed to me to be perfectly legitimate to complain that – as pieces of writing, as poems – they were completely unedifying and head-crushingly boring.'

Serena thought about this for a bit and then said, 'So you think Gaby's wrong to like her stuff then?'

Gordon looked around and saw that his fellow tutor was at the other end of the table with Tony, Kirsty and John Stamper, well out of earshot in the gabble of chatter and laughter.

He said, 'I don't think Gaby and I would agree with each other on anything to do with poetry. That's not to say, of course, that I don't think her opinions are of any value. It's just that we look at the business in quite different ways. She belongs, obviously, to another generation and naturally enough she's open to influences and ideas that I'm probably not even aware of. If she says Melissa Hull's worth reading I'm sure she could give reasons why she believes this to be true. But I doubt if I'd ever be able to understand those reasons let alone be persuaded by them.'

'Would you look at one or two of my poems some time? Please!'

For a moment Gordon was startled. Then he said, 'Yes, of course. I'd be glad to.'

'I'd like your opinion. There aren't many. About half a dozen. And they're all short, you'll be glad to hear.'

Serena dug into her shoulder-bag and brought out a thin sheaf of the poems that she had typed out late that afternoon when she had decided to seek Gordon's opinion and advice. He thanked her and tucked them between the pages of his *Selected Poems* which was in his coat pocket.

Then he said, 'Now it's my turn to ask you something, Serena. What about the Crackenthorpe ghost? Do you know what kind of ghost it is? Man or woman? Has anyone actually seen it?'

'Ah, the ghost. *I've* not seen it, not so far anyway, but Ivy Sludgens reckons she's seen it a couple of times. So does her husband, but I wouldn't take too much notice of that. Ivy said it was a woman in what she called olden-days clothes. As far as I could make out she meant mid-Victorian crinoline or bustle or something like that. But someone else, a course member, just after Chris and I came here, saw another kind of ghost. He said it was a man, probably a monk in some sort of habit and cowl. He saw it one night when he got up to go to the toilet. He told us he called out and then it just vanished. But he'd been down here and had a few pints that night, so . . . who knows? In any case I don't see why a monk or his ghost should be prowling around Crackenthorpe Hall. I mean there's no connection with the Church as far as I know.'

Gordon drank more of his beer and then said, 'I don't suppose you could account . . . oh, no, never mind.'

'Suppose what? What were you going to say?'

'Well, this might sound rather silly. But I don't suppose anyone's noticed peculiar smells that can't be accounted for?'

'Smells? What kind of smells?'

'Mysterious smells.' Gordon grinned awkwardly. 'I know this sounds very peculiar but I seem to have been haunted by a smell of celery.'

Serena stared at him. 'Celery.' It was a flat statement with no note of interrogation or surprise.

He said quickly, 'I don't know whether you've heard of people sniffing odd, sort of occult, smells. I vaguely remember Strindberg in one of his diaries going on about the smell of celery. For some reason I think he associated it with evil. Well, the first night I was here – Sunday – that's only the night before last, isn't it? Seems longer somehow. Anyway, I woke up in the early hours and I knew someone was in my room. I could hear him or her or it, or whatever it was, breathing. All right, I could have imagined it or mistaken another noise – the wind or something – for breathing. But the door opened and closed. I heard it quite distinctly and I didn't imagine that. By the time I'd got the light on and got out of bed and into the corridor whatever it was or whoever it was had disappeared. But – and this is what I'm getting at – when I got back into my room there was a strong smell of celery.'

Chris said, 'Maybe it was something you'd eaten. I mean taste and smell are very close aren't they? I suppose you could've burped up the taste in your sleep, then woken up and been – you know – a bit confused perhaps?'

'No. I smelled it again last night, just before I went to sleep.'

Serena's eyes were wide. 'And did you hear breathing again?'

Gordon shook his head. 'No breathing. Just celery.'

Chris finished his pint. 'I'll have a look round your room tomorrow if you like,' he said. 'See if I can find any reason for it. Something under the floorboards maybe. Dead mice or something.'

Serena looked at the ceiling as if in mute appeal for patience. 'Dead mice,' she said, 'don't smell like celery.'

'No, I don't think they do,' Gordon agreed. 'Let's have another drink. What would you like, Serena? The same? . . . Chris?'

He reached the bar only a few seconds before Joan Palmer who was coming up to get drinks for Viv and herself. While he was waiting for Cyril to attend to his order Joan said, 'I did enjoy your reading, Gordon. Very much.' Both her smile and her low voice were pleasantly warming. 'I especially liked the more serious ones. I don't mean I didn't care for the lighter and jokey ones. I did. But the love poems and the ones about childhood and that terrible sad one – *A Sense of Loss*, was it called? – they're the ones I felt I really wanted to hear again and read them on the page. Can I get that book you were reading from? Is it in the shops?'

'I doubt it. The *Selected*'s been out of print for ages and I'm not sure about *The Trades of Man*. There might be one or two lying about somewhere but they'd be hard to find. If you've got a decent public library you might be able to get hold of them.'

'Won't your publishers reprint them if they're sold out?'

Gordon laughed without much merriment. 'No, I'm afraid not. In fact they're not my publishers any longer. They ditched me some time ago. I haven't got a publisher at all.'

Joan's smile disappeared. She looked quite shocked. 'But that's terrible! Surely there must be another who'd be only too . . . I mean your poems are so much better than . . . ' The unfinished comparison was left dangling.

Gordon was touched by her clearly genuine concern. He said, 'Oh, I expect I'll find somebody to do it if and when I get another book together.'

He was going to say something else but Cyril, the landlord, pushed two pints of bitter and Serena's glass of cider in front of him on the bar counter and told him what he owed for them. Gordon counted his loose change and found that he had the right sum. He handed the money over and, as he took the drinks, he said, 'I'm glad you weren't bored by my reading, Joan. It was very kind of you to say you liked some of the poems.'

'No,' she said with feeling. 'Not kind. I really did enjoy them very much and I want to read more.'

Cyril again interrupted with a heavily facetious 'What can I do you for young lady?' and Gordon moved with his drinks back to his place at the table with Chris and Serena.

When he was seated there he glanced over to see Joan returning to Viv and he felt a small stirring of affectionate gratitude and perhaps a tiny spark of something very like excitement as they exchanged quick, almost conspiratorial smiles.

# WEDNESDAY

GORDON CLIMBED the stairs, paused briefly at the top to recover his breath, then walked along the corridor to his room. There, he crossed to the window and looked out at the wooded valley that was again rinsed with the pale, thin light of the wintry sun.

His group had applied themselves with the same enthusiasm they had shown on the previous day and, again, some interesting and occasionally striking work had been produced. Tony Frame, who had joined him from Gaby's class, had been perhaps a little unnervingly bright and chirpy to begin with, but when they had all got down to writing either a Petrarchan or Shakespearian sonnet on some aspect of the approaching festival, or possibly, ordeal of Christmas, he had worked as assiduously as any of them, and had produced an impressively sophisticated, if rather puzzling, piece of writing.

Gordon smiled faintly as he reflected that this heterogeneous assembly of people, through the single common bond of an interest in and desire to create poetry, had already become a community. The world beyond Crackenthorpe Hall, the world of railway timetables and building societies, politics and sport, was now as remote as the Himalayas. Unexpectedly intense, though almost certainly ephemeral, friendships were established in a small fraction of the time that would have been required in the world outside; secret longings and sins of omission and commission were confessed to; unforeseen and thrilling possibilities of change began to take shape.

He turned away from the window and looked at the whisky bottle on the chest of drawers. 'Just a small one,' he thought, 'and then I'll go down and have a bit of lunch.'

He was pouring his drink when there was a tap on the door.

He called, 'Just a moment!' and put the glass and bottle down, dismissing with impatient self-censure the impulse to hide them.

He opened the door and was surprised to see Serena.

She said, 'Sorry to bother you, Gordon, but have you got a minute or two?'

'Of course. Come in.' He held the door open for her to enter, then closed it as she stood in the centre of the room, looking uncharacteristically and inexplicably nervous. 'Come and sit down. Only the hard chairs I'm afraid. Or the bed.'

Serena said, 'I don't want to take up a lot of your time. I just wondered if you'd had a chance to look at my poems.'

'Yes,' Gordon pointed to the table. 'There they are, look. I read them last night and again this morning, when I expect I was seeing them a little bit more clearly.'

'And . . . ?' She looked at him with sidelong, comically apprehensive interrogation.

'I thought they're pretty good. One or two comments I've pencilled at the side of them, as you'll see, I particularly liked the nature ones, specially the one about the laburnum. It's vivid and accurate. Very good. Made me feel quite envious.' She was looking at him solemnly, almost, he thought, mistrustfully. He said, 'I know my views aren't very fashionable at present but I'm sure, in the long run, you'd do well to avoid the Melissa Hull kind of thing and remember Milton's recipe for poetry. He said it should be simple, sensuous and passionate. He didn't mean simple-minded, of course. I think he meant direct, accurate. Not faking.'

Serena went to the table and picked up her poems and he watched her as she read what he had written in the margins.

Then she looked up at him. 'You think I should go on?'

'Writing poems? Of course you should!' He stopped himself from adding, 'It's a harmless occupation,' rightly sensing that Serena was in no mood to respond happily to any kind of flippancy.

She stood, holding the typescripts, nodding slowly to herself as she again seemed to be studying them. Gordon glanced with longing at his whisky. He waited.

At last she looked up again and said, 'Thank you for reading them. And for your help.' Then she added, 'Are you coming down for lunch?'

'I'll be there in a couple of minutes.'

'All right. And thank you again. Oh . . .' she hesitated as she reached for the door-handle. '. . . I almost forgot. What about that funny smell you mentioned? What was it? Garlic? No . . .'

'Celery.'

'Oh yes, of course. Celery. Has it bothered you again?'

'No. I haven't smelt it since Monday night.'

'Well, if you do, let me know and I'll get Chris to poke around.'

When she had gone he picked up his glass, added a little water from the tap, and swallowed the contents. There was something rather sad about the girl, he thought. Her little poems weren't bad, though he had seen far better from the students on this course. It wasn't because of her lack of striking talent that he felt mild pity for her. Perhaps it was because, despite her youth and reasonably pretty face and figure, she seemed so lacking in *joie de vivre*. Maybe she wasn't happy with Chris. Certainly he had never seen her display any signs of great affection for him.

He rinsed out his tumbler and put it back in its place on the shelf above the washbasin. Then he left the room and went down to the kitchen which was, as usual at lunchtime, busy with people preparing or eating their light midday meal.

Joan Palmer was making ham sandwiches and would no doubt be taking them up to share with her room-mate, Viv.

When she saw him she said, 'Can I make you one of these?'

Gordon, though touched and pleased by her offer, said, 'Oh, don't bother. I can do it myself.'

'No trouble.' She smiled and he suddenly wished that he had smartened himself up before coming down from his room.

George Barnes waved from farther down the kitchen where he was standing at the long work-surface, eating bread and cheese. After a few moments he moved towards Gordon, arriving just as Joan was handing him the ham sandwich she had prepared. 'No mustard,' she said. 'I thought you'd rather help yourself. There's the jar, over there.'

Gordon thanked her and, after smearing mustard on the ham, he took a bite of the sandwich.

George said, 'You're a lucky chap. I had to fix my own grub.'

Joan began to say something but broke off as Chris, in a state of some excitement, came into the kitchen and, addressing not only Serena but everyone there, said, 'Guess what! Gaby's won a big prize! She's off to Manchester. The BBC want her for tonight's arts programme – what's it called? – *Viewpoints* or something like that. She's got to record an interview.'

'What prize?' Serena said. 'What are you talking about?'

'I told you. She's won a prize. It's a big important one. International or American. It's called the Wharton Prize. Ten thousand dollars. And it'll mean her book's going to sell thousands here and in the States. Or so she says.'

'How's she getting to Manchester?'

'They're sending a car for her. Must be a big deal. The BBC phoned up about twenty minutes ago. They'd just got the news from the States that she'd won the Wharton Prize for the best book of poetry of the year and they want to feature it as the main item on the programme.'

'How did they know she was here?' Serena asked.

They rang her publishers and they told them where she was and what she was doing here. She says she'll be back for the Personal Choice this evening, if not for the meal. The BBC said they'd bring her back as soon as they've done the interview.' Chris went to the fridge and opened it but evidently failed to find what he was looking for. He said, 'Anyone seen the Brussels pâté?'

'I think it's over there,' George called. Margaret was making sandwiches with it.'

Gordon was aware that Serena was looking at him with an ambiguous, questioning expression. He grinned at her. 'Are you thinking you'd be wiser to ignore my advice about poetry and join up with the Melissa Hull School of Gibberish? If you are, you're probably right. That is, if you want to win prizes and get on radio and TV. But that's not the same thing as writing good poems.'

'No . . . ' she said, stretching the word as if measuring its sincerity. 'I suppose you're right.' Then she said quickly, as if trying to reassure herself, 'Yes, of course you are. Of course you're right.'

Chris approached, taking a bite from a hunk of bread liberally spread with pâté. 'Who's right?' he asked. 'Right about what?'

'Nothing that would interest you,' Serena said and turned away.

Chris shrugged and smiled a wan apology at Gordon. 'I think she's been overdoing things. She's not very strong and gets tired.'

Gordon nodded sympathetically. 'It must be a strain running these courses.' Then, partly to change the subject, he said, 'You mentioned that Gaby would be back for the Personal Choice session. I'd been meaning to ask. Do you think Gaby and I should choose something as well as the students?'

'Yes. It's what usually happens. In fact the best way to run the evening is for everybody to sit round the big table in the library and you and Gaby start with your choices and maybe say a few words about why you've chosen them. Then you go round either clockwise, or the other way, so everybody gets a go. That sound all right?'

'Yes, sounds fine. I look forward to it.'

Joan said, 'I must take these sandwiches up to Viv. She'll be starving. Have you had enough, Gordon? Or shall I make you another?'

'I've had plenty thanks. It was very kind of you to make me one and it was delicious.'

As she left with the plate of sandwiches George remarked. 'She's quite a good-looking woman, that Joan. Don't you think so, Gordon?'

Gordon, still looking towards the door through which she had just left, nodded. 'Yes,' he said, 'very.'


Viv said, 'You've been a long time doing those. I'm starving.'

Joan put the plate of sandwiches down on the table under the window.

'High drama downstairs,' she said. 'It seems Gaby's won some big international award and she's got to go to Manchester to record an interview for the BBC. An arts programme called *Viewpoint*.'

'She's what! Manchester? She can't! She's seeing me at two o'clock. Has she really gone?'

'I think so. I'm not sure. Chris said they were sending a car for her.'

'The bitch! She's afraid to face me! I knew she'd find some excuse.'

Joan stared. 'Viv! What are you talking about? Didn't you hear what I said? She's won a prize. Thousands of dollars. It's an international award, big news in the arts world. She's not running off to Manchester to avoid seeing you at two o'clock. It's not an excuse, so don't be silly.'

Viv frowned, sulky and obstinate, but only for a second or two.

Then she smiled, though rather reluctantly. 'All right. But she should've told me. It's bloody rude of her to go off without saying a word.'

'I expect she forgot in the excitement. Be fair, Viv. Who wouldn't? Chris said she'd be back this evening for the Personal Choice thing. So sit down and eat your lunch.'

They both sat at the small table and each took a sandwich and bit into it.

'Thinking of Personal Choice, what are you going to read?' Joan said, munching.

'Not sure. I thought I'd read that Sylvia Plath, *Daddy*. That, or the one you showed me the other day about the lady's maid who wears the posh woman's pearls to warm them for when she'll put them on in the evening. What was it . . . ?'

'It's called *Warming her Pearls* by Carol Ann Duffy. You'll find it in the library in that *Penguin Modern Poets* I was looking at. Unless somebody's taken it away.'

'I'll go and have a look later on. What about you? What are you going to read?'

'I'm not absolutely sure but I think I'll read an Elizabeth Jennings poem called *One Flesh*. It's about her mother and father when they're old, in bed. She can't imagine them being young and passionate and the fact of her own conception seems unbelievable. It's very touching. I'll either read that or a lovely one by Philip Larkin about a pit explosion. Difficult to decide, but I'll most likely go for the Jennings. It's probably easier to take in on a single hearing. The Larkin one's a bit more complicated. I think you'd need to see it on the page.'

When they had finished their sandwiches they decided to go down to the kitchen and make themselves some coffee and then to go into the library to copy out the poems they intended presenting that evening. In the hall they passed Tony and Kirsty who suspended their low-voiced conversation to offer greetings and wait until they were alone again before continuing.

Kirsty said, 'You should've told me you were going to join Gordon's lot. I'd have come with you. I wondered what had happened to you when you weren't there this morning. I was worried.'

'Gaby knew where I was. I told her I was going to give Gordon's bunch a try.'

'But why didn't you tell *me*?'

'I don't know. I didn't think . . . I'm sorry. Yes, perhaps I should've done.'

'Well, come for a walk now. Or take me on your motorbike. That'd be lovely. Let's go for a ride!'

Tony shook his head. 'I'm sorry, Kirsty. Some other time maybe. But I really must find something for Personal Choice tonight. I thought I'd made up my mind but, thinking it over, I realised it wasn't quite the thing. So I've got to see what I can find in the library.'

'What was the one you didn't think would do?'

'Actually it was a translation by Craig Raine of a poem by Rimbaud. Or maybe "version" is a better word than translation.'

'A poem by who?'

'Rimbaud, a French poet.'

'That's funny. My uncle had a dog called that. Though I'm sure Uncle Clive never read any poetry of any kind, let alone French poetry.'

'How strange.' Tony smiled rather mysteriously.

'Why didn't you think it would do? What's it about?'

'I thought it might not be suitable for elderly ladies. Or young ones, probably.'

'Why not? Tell me what it's about.'

'Naughty things. You know what those French poets are like.'

'I don't. I don't know any French poetry. Tell me.'

'I'll show it you some time.' He had started towards the library, with Kirsty following. 'But what are *you* going to give us tonight?'

'I'm reading *Poem Girl*. D'you know it? It's by Brian MacDuff.'

'I don't think I do.'

'I'll go and get it if you like. I wrote it out yesterday. Lucky to find it in Jake Terrabit's *Love Ya, Baby*. It's a brilliant anthology of love poems.'

They were in the library by now.

Tony said, 'No, don't do that. I'd much rather wait and hear you read it tonight.'

George Barnes and John Stamper were sitting at the long table and each had a small pile of books at the side of the one he was reading.

John looked up, smiled faintly and nodded a greeting before returning to his reading.

George said, 'Hullo. Made your Personal Choice yet, you two?'

'I have,' Kirsty told him, 'but Tony hasn't.' Then, turning to Tony: 'I'll see if I can find *Love Ya, Baby* again. You're bound to find something good there. And there was another anthology of love poetry if I can't find Terrabit's. I forget the editor but it's called *Singing in the Wilderness*. Funny title, isn't it?'

'I suppose it is,' Tony said. Then he continued: 'It's sweet of you to help me look for something, Kirsty, but I think it's better if I do it on my own. Tell you what. You go and have a little walk or something and then come back and make some tea. I expect I'll be ready for a cuppa by then . . . All right? See you later.'

Kirsty looked, at first, as though she might insist on staying in the library but then she seemed to change her mind. 'Okay, see you later,' she said and went out of the library and up to the room she shared with Margaret Baker who was, for once, not in the kitchen organising or helping to prepare dinner but sitting at the window table writing on a pad of lined A4.

'I thought you were going out for a walk,' Margaret said.

'I changed my mind.'

Margaret put down her pen. 'What's the matter dear? You don't look very happy.'

Kirsty sat on her bed. 'I don't know. I'm all right really. It's just that people, things – everything – always let you down, turn out disappointing somehow.'

'That's a gloomy way of looking at the world, specially for someone young and pretty like you. Life ought to be a feast. Excitement, adventure, fun!'

'Well, it doesn't seem like that to me. I mean, look at this course. I came on it for one reason only and that was to meet Brian MacDuff. And what happens? He doesn't show up. And who've they got in his place? Some old codger nobody's ever heard of.'

'Oh, that's not true!' Margaret protested. 'Gordon's a well-known poet. He's published lots of books and he writes things in the *Guardian* sometimes. Book reviews. I've seen them. I recognised his name. And he's not *that* old!'

'Yes, I know. I shouldn't have said that. It's not his fault Brian's not here. But it was a big disappointment. And then there's Tony. At first he was nice and friendly. I thought he really liked me. And then he switches from Gaby's group without telling me he was going to, and now it seems almost like he's trying to avoid me.'

'Tony? Oh, I'm sure he's not avoiding you. What happened exactly?'

'Well, only a few minutes ago I asked him if he'd like to go for a walk or a ride on his motorbike and he said he had to go to the library and find a poem for Personal Choice. I mean he'd already picked one but he said it wasn't what he wanted and he had to choose another.'

'That doesn't sound unreasonable, Kirsty. After all, he's come here like the rest of us for the poetry. The social side's all very nice, and nobody enjoys it more than me, but the poetry's the thing we're all here for and he's right to put it first. Don't you see that, dear?'

Kirsty nodded, but she did not look convinced or greatly cheered.

'Take it from me,' Margaret said. 'If you just relax and enjoy the course, show a bit of sparkle, try not to get so intense, you'll find Tony'll be glad enough for your company. Now I've got to go downstairs and see what they're up to in the kitchen. Eileen and Arthur are the cooks. That chap Howard Simpson was supposed to be on duty but – well, you know about him. I shouldn't think anyone'll miss him anyway. So just you cheer up, Kirsty. Laugh and the world laughs with you. Weep and you weep alone.'

Margaret put her writing materials away and headed for the door where she hesitated before opening it.

'You all right, dear?' she said with a slight frown of concern. 'Why don't you come down with me and have a cup of tea?'

Kirsty attempted a smile. 'Yes. I'm all right. You go ahead. I'll be down shortly.'

Margaret looked at her steadily then, apparently satisfied, she nodded once and went out of the room.


They were all gathered in the library and seated round the long table. Gaby was there, having arrived back from her trip to Manchester shortly after the evening meal had begun. She was now at the head of the library table with Gordon, who was to begin the evening's entertainment, on her right. The rest of the students had positioned themselves on either side, with Chris and Serena at the other end. Some had brought paperback or hardback volumes from which they would read their chosen poems while others carried notebooks or single sheets of paper. The room simmered with low conversation and small eruptions of laughter and Gordon thought he could sense a quite eager anticipation in the air.

Serena banged on the table and called, 'Now then, please! If everybody's ready we'll make a start. It's just after ten past eight. I reckon we'll be finished by about half past nine unless somebody's chosen *Paradise Lost*. Now remember. I'd like each person just to say a word or two – well, maybe I mean a sentence or two – about why they've chosen whatever it is they're going to read. When they've read their piece, some of you might like to make a comment on their choice. Not too rude, I hope.

'Okay. We're going to start with our tutors at the top of the table. Gordon begins, then Gaby, then we go clockwise round the table – including me and Chris – and ending with Margaret. So shall we make a start? . . . Gordon?'

Gordon opened the copy of *The Oxford Book of Victorian Verse* which he had found that morning in the library.

He said, 'I thought I'd go back into the not too distant past for my choice. I was going to read Browning's *A Toccata of Galuppi's* but decided it was probably a bit too long and maybe too well known. So I've chosen a little poem that you may not have come across before. It's a sonnet with an irregular rhyme-pattern in the last six lines, and it's by one of Tennyson's two elder brothers, Charles. Because of some inheritance from a rich uncle he changed his name to Turner, so he's known as Charles Tennyson Turner. It's a simple poem about a little girl looking at a globe. You might think it's a bit sentimental but I feel any charge of that kind's swept away by the marvellous last line. Here it is then: *Letty's Globe*:

> When Letty had scarce pass'd her third glad year,
> And her young artless words began to flow,
> One day we gave the child a coloured sphere
> Of the wide earth, that she might mark and know,
> By tint and outline, all its sea and land.

She patted all the world; old empires peep'd
Between her baby fingers; her soft hand
Was welcome at all frontiers. How she leap'd
And laughed and prattled in her world-wide bliss;
But when we turned her sweet unlearned eye
On our own isle, she rais'd a joyous cry –
"Oh! yes, I see it, Letty's home is there!"
And while she hid all England with a kiss,
Bright over Europe fell her golden hair.'

There were some appreciative sighs and a general murmur which
sounded unanimously approving.

'What book is that from?' Margaret asked. 'It's lovely.'

'It's the old *Oxford Book of Victorian Verse*, edited by Arthur
Quiller-Couch. I don't know whether you can get hold of it now
because they've brought out another, edited, I think, by Christopher
Ricks.'

The short silence that followed this was broken by Gaby: 'Oh, it's
my turn is it? Right . . . well, like Gordon I'm going to read
a short poem but, unlike Gordon, I've chosen one by a twentieth-
century poet. It's by John Simkin who died a year or two ago while
still in his creative prime. I hope you'll all agree it provides a nice
contrast to Gordon's choice with its sheer energy and passionate
manhandling of language to force it to embody the poet's vision. It's
called *Cold Star Dance*.'

Gaby opened what was either a paperback book or a magazine
and read, in her rather harsh and monotonous poetry voice:

'Again the white time comes, the coldness,
so they, skald and scholar of skyscrawl,
jongleur of black icecream and nightingales,
minstrel of sly emoluments,
note this, my ancestral company,
spinning its fandangos of brilliancies
while constellations sway and jig
to airs of blind compulsion.
They tune their pulse and passion to the cry
of reeling fulgencies and kneel
in thwarted hunger as you pray

> for your small moiety, your due,
> that Yaweh might withhold the thunderbolt,
> beguiled by hymns you paint on silence
> and welcome you to sit with episodes
> of heroism, tall as paradise,
> consuming dark felicity
> and drinking deep of bitter joy.'

Gaby sat with her head lowered while some of her listeners released little noises of awed wonder in the manner of poetry audiences who feel that some response is called for but are not quite sure how it should be vocalised.

Then George Barnes said, 'It sounded rather impressive, I suppose, but I haven't the faintest idea what it was about. I wonder if you could explain it to us, Gaby. Or to those of us who couldn't understand it. I hope I'm not the only one.'

Gaby looked up and smiled, a patient, perhaps long-suffering smile. 'I don't think poems can be explained. To explain is usually to explain away. The poem you've just heard, *Cold Star Dance*, is an enactment of its theme. It is the creative spirit verbalised. The only way to put it into other words would be to write another poem.'

George looked at her with bafflement. 'Oh, I see,' he said, without conviction.

Gaby turned to Carol Lumsden on her left. 'What have you got for us, Carol?'

'Me? Oh, ah, yes. Well, I've chosen something from the nineteenth century too. Like Gordon, I mean. It's called *Porphyria's Lover* and it's by Robert Browning. I chose it because it's very dramatic and though it was written well over a hundred years ago it's about something that's only too common today, a sex murder by a psychopath.'

Carol read the poem well and without any misguided attempt at dramatisation and it was received with sounds of approval.

John Stamper said to George, his neighbour, 'That was great. What was it called again?'

'*Porphyria's Lover*. Browning.'

'I'll have to have a look at his stuff. The only ones I know are *The Pied Piper* and *Home Thoughts from Abroad*.'

Freda Jones began to introduce her choice, Dylan Thomas's *Do Not Go Gentle Into That Good Night,* and her reading of it was followed by Arthur Kirk presenting A. E. Housman's *Into My Heart An Air That Kills* and his friend Bernard's defiantly spirited performance of Masefield's *Sea Fever.* Then it was George Barnes's turn.

He said, 'I had a bit of trouble making up my mind which one to read. I thought a lot about Kipling's *Danny Deever* – a bit too long – and *Recessional,* but in the end I picked a very short one by someone I admit I'd never heard of until I came across this poem in an anthology called *The Albatross Book of English Verse.* The poet is Anne, Countess of Winchelsea, and she lived in the seventeenth and early eighteenth centuries. I've got her dates here – 1661 to 1720. I think you'll see why I, as a military man, like this little poem so much. Here it is then:

> Trail all your pikes, dispirit every drum,
> March in slow procession from afar,
> Ye silent, ye dejected men of war!
> Be still the hautboys, and the flute be dumb!
> Display no more, in vain, the lofty banner.
> For see! where on the bier before ye lies
> The pale, the fall'n, th' untimely sacrifice
> To your mistaken shrine, to your false idol Honour.'

'That was damn good,' John Stamper, who was sitting next to George, said. 'You read it well too.'

'Nice of you to say so . . . I think you're on now.'

John opened the book that was on the table before him but he did not at once read from it. He said, 'Like most of us, I suppose, I had some trouble settling for the poem I was going to read. Not knowing as much about it as most of you, I felt I was unsure about my own judgement. I have to say that Tony was a big help here. First, he put me on to Thomas Hardy. He said if I liked Frost I'd probably like Hardy's poems. And I did, most of the ones I read. Then Tony said what about trying Edward Thomas. He was a great friend of Robert Frost, in fact it was Frost got him started on writing poetry. But you most likely know all that. Anyway, I liked

Thomas a lot but in the end I chose something completely different from either of them. I was browsing through a book in the library and I came across this one by a man called William Ernest Henley. I looked him up in *The Companion to English Literature* and found out he was born in the middle of the nineteenth century and died when he was in his early fifties . . . What else? Oh yes, he'd been ill as a boy and he'd had one foot amputated. Seems he believed poetry should be realistic and he was a friend of Robert Louis Stevenson and he was supposed to be the model for Long John Silver.

'Sorry I've been going on for so long but I was excited by the poet and what I found out about him. Well, here's my choice. It's called by its first line, *Madam Life's a piece in bloom* and it shows a tough, honest view of what life's all about:

> Madam Life's a piece in bloom,
>     Death goes dogging everywhere:
> She's the tenant of the room,
>     He's the ruffian on the stair.
>
> You shall see her as a friend,
>     You shall bilk him once or twice;
> But he'll trap you in the end,
>     And he'll stick you for her price.
>
> With his kneebones at your chest,
>     And his knuckles in your throat,
> You would reason – plead – protest!
>     Clutching at her petticoat;
>
> But she's heard it all before,
>     Well she knows you've had your fun,
> Gingerly she gains the door
>     And your little job is done.'

When John had finished, one or two perhaps slightly startled intakes of breath were heard, followed by a restrained but lively buzz of talk. Then Tony, from higher up on the other side of the table, called, 'Very good, John! A great choice!' and there were murmurs of endorsement.

Serena, whose turn to read came next, said, 'It was a very interesting poem John. One question though. What was that word "bilk"? Can you tell us what it means?'

'Yes,' John answered. 'I had a fair guess at it from the way it was used in the poem. "You'll bilk him once or twice, but he'll trap you in the end." I guessed it meant cheat or avoid paying for what you've been given but to make sure I looked it up and that's exactly what it did mean.' His secretive, slow smile might have been complacent but somehow it wasn't.

'Right. Thank you.' Serena said. 'I ought to have guessed.

'Now it's my turn and I'm going to read something from our own time, Philip Larkin's *The Trees*. I think this is an absolutely brilliant poem. It's very short and simple – well, simple on the surface – but there's a terrific lot of feeling and meaning packed into it. What to look out for – or listen out for – is the imagery, the "unresting castles thresh" and the gorgeous last line where the word "afresh" is used three times, one after the other, and you can actually hear the noise the leaves make in the wind. Oh, and one more thing. At teatime I told Gordon what I'd chosen, and we were talking about the poem and some of Larkin's other things, and he told me that the verses in *The Trees* are exactly the same in rhythm and rhyme as Tennyson's *In Memoriam*. That right Gordon?'

Gordon, at the other end of the table, nodded and Serena read her choice of poem which seemed to give pleasure to everyone. Then it was Chris's turn to read his choice.

He said, 'As I'm sure you all know by now I'm not an authority on poetry, in fact what little I do know about it – and it's very little – I've picked up on these courses. All the same this doesn't mean I don't like it or haven't got my own likes and dislikes.

'I'd like to read a poem by one of the poets who came to Crackenthorpe Hall not so long ago as guest reader. I thought he was terrific. I expect you've all heard of him – Kit Wright, the tallest poet in the country, probably the world, and for my money one of the best.

'The poem I'm going to read is *Personal Advertisement*.'

'No!' Serena squeaked. 'Not that one! You can't read that one!'

'Why not? It's great. It's about the funniest thing I've ever read.'

'But he's written so many lovely ones. Why not read *Elizabeth* or one of the poems for Anna, or *Red Boots On*. You told me you like that one.'

'I do, but I like *Personal Advertisement* better.'

'If you read it I'm not staying here to listen.'

'Why not? What's wrong with it?'

'You know what's wrong with it. It's crude. It's indecent.'

The course members were beginning to whisper and mutter. There was a quickly restrained laugh from someone, probably Tony.

'All right,' Chris said. 'I won't read it. But I strongly recommend it to everyone. I'll make sure the book's in the library. It's called *Bump-starting the Hearse* – a great title if ever there was one – and it's on page 33.'

'What are you going to read then?' Serena asked him.

'Nothing. If you won't let me read that, I pass.'

Serena's eyes sparked with anger and her lips were tightly compressed. Then she said, 'That's very childish and stupid. But if that's what you've decided we'll go on to the next reader. Tony. What have you got for us?'

Tony said, 'I'm very sorry we're not allowed to hear Chris's choice. But you're the boss, Serena. My own choice is a bit more up to date than Serena's *Trees*. It's got its roots in the tradition of English or European poetry but it has a playfulness and cleverness that will, I think, steer us into the new millennium. The poet is American. You may have heard of him, Jim Rowanberry. The title is *The New Wallpaper*. So here it is:

> The deus ex machina should be employed
> only for events external to the drama,
> according to Professor Slocombe,
> though Aristotle said it first.

> "That's as maybe," Ivor remarked,
> "but the hydrangeas still need watering
> and we all know about Zelda
> whose position grows impregnable by stealth."

> The Philharmonic this time played the full version.
> The Fall of Pondicherry left dark bruises
> visible only from the swollen tip of the lighthouse.

She was found eventually in the attic,
suspended from the Oregon branch
and wearing only fisherman's waders.'

Tony looked up from his book with eyebrows raised and an enigmatic smile. His audience exchanged uncertain glances and made little noises difficult to interpret.

Then Joan Palmer said, 'Can you tell us why it's called *The New Wallpaper*? I can't say I understand any of it, but I'm sure there wasn't any mention of wallpaper.'

'You're quite right. No reference of any kind to interior decoration.'

'So why call it *The New Wallpaper*?'

'Teasing,' Tony said. 'The poem tells us things are neither what they seem to be nor what they claim to be. It signals things that don't materialise. It has the inconsequentiality of life. And, of course, life's absurdity.'

George Barnes muttered, 'Poppycock!' as Joan, with a slow smile of indulgent dubiety, said, 'I see. Thank you.'

'Maureen,' Serena said briskly, 'let's have your choice,' and Maureen surprised everyone by reading a funny and rather risqué poem by Fleur Adcock called *Smokers for Celibacy* which caused much real laughter, and her friend, Eileen, read a short but immensely effective piece, *Armistice*, by Patricia Beer.

After Joan had read Elizabeth Jennings's *One Flesh* it was Kirsty's turn to present her choice.

She said, 'I decided it would be nice to read something by the poet who should have been one of our tutors here at Crackenthorpe Hall. I mean, of course, Brian MacDuff. That's not the only reason I chose him though. I happen to think he's one of the best poets around today. This poem's called *Poem Girl*:

My favourite poem is what you are
and what to me you'll always be.
I could read you over and over,
Always finding things new to me.

I love the way you walk along the street,
tall stilettos on your metrical feet.
I could never get tired of you.

I love the way your beautiful eyes
are almost exactly like each other,
but not quite. I call them eye-rhymes.

Most of all I love your varied rhythms,
the rise and fall of breast when breathing fast;
I love the alliteration of your lips
and, neither least nor last,

the lovely languorous line of your hips,
and when all this has been said,
I love to learn you line by line
on the white pages of our bed.'

A couple of sympathetic *ahs* came from the audience but George grunted to John Stamper, 'No need for the girl to say MacDuff should've been here. Tactless, with old Gordon sitting a couple of feet away.'

John said in a loud half-whisper, 'If that's the best he could do, a good job for us he couldn't come here.'

Serena called, 'What are we having for the final poem of the evening, Margaret?'

Margaret Baker said, 'Something by one of my favourite poets, Emily Dickinson. It's one of her best-known and I expect most of you know it well but I'm sure no one will mind hearing it again. This is it, then – *The Snake* by Emily Dickinson.

She read the poem with unaffected clarity, which seemed to impress everyone, and the evening's performance came to an end and the assembly began to break up and disperse.

Margaret said softly to Kirsty, 'Remember what I told you, dear. Don't try and push things with Tony. Be a bit distant, as if you don't care one way or the other. Remember you're the prettiest girl here by a long chalk. Wait for him to make the running.'

'Suppose he doesn't?'

'I think he will.'

Chris called out, 'Anyone for the bus to the pub! We'll be leaving in five minutes!'

Serena, Gordon noticed, had already left the library and he suspected that she would not be joining the pub party. As for the rest of the company there was an atmosphere of mild excitement

generated, perhaps, by the feeling that the Personal Choice evening
had been very successful and no one had failed to make a satisfactory
contribution to that success. He thought, with a little surprise, that
he had rather enjoyed the session himself.

As he glanced round the room he saw Joan Palmer, who was
talking with Viv and Margaret, look towards him and smile, and
again he thought he read something sympathetic, a hint of recognised consimilarity in that smile. Then George was at his elbow
saying, 'I take it you're going to the pub, Gordon,' and the two of
them went off to collect their coats against the chill of the night.


'He didn't even notice I was there,' Kirsty said. 'He was laughing and
joking with old Gordon Napier and Stamper and that old Colonel
chap. The only woman he looked at was Gaby.'

She and Margaret had just returned from the evening in The
Shepherd's Crook and the older woman was feeling pleasantly tired
and was looking forward to getting into bed. Kirsty, though, showed
no signs of tiredness and looked as if she would be ready to stay up
chattering for hours.

Margaret said, 'You're quite wrong dear. Tony did keep looking at
you. I saw him two or three times. At least.'

'Well, *I* didn't.'

'No, of course not. He made sure of that. He only looked at you
when he knew your attention was somewhere else. That's the kind of
young man he is.'

'What d'you mean? What kind of young man?'

'Well . . . you know. He likes to be the centre of attention. A bit
of a show-off. The kind of person who thinks other people should
wait on his pleasure. Rather spoilt, I'd say.'

'How d'you know? You've hardly spoken to him. I don't think
he's like that at all. Well, not much. I mean he's clever and good-
looking and of course he knows he is. But he can be very nice. He
was nice at first but now he's gone off me. I think he fancies Gaby.'

'Oh, I don't think so. She must be ten years older than him, at
least. Fifteen probably.'

'Lots of older women and young men fancy each other. It's a well-
known fact.'

Margaret yawned and then began to undress. 'That's something that goes on more in stories and films than real life. Come on Kirsty. Get to bed and have a good sleep and things'll look different in the morning.'

'I'm not tired. I couldn't sleep.'

'Yes you could. If you went to bed you'd soon find you could sleep. I can hardly keep awake.'

Kirsty had not sat down since they had come back from the pub and she was still moving restlessly about the room. She said, 'You go to bed. I won't stop you sleeping, I promise.' Then she added, as if speaking to herself, 'I could go out. Yes, I will. I'll go out.'

'Go out? Where? Where on earth do you think you can go at this time of night?'

'Oh, I don't know. I could go down and make a drink of something. Or I could . . ' She left the sentence unfinished.

'You could what?'

'I could go and see Tony.'

Margaret froze in the act of taking off her skirt.

'You could *what*? Don't be silly. Of course you couldn't. Not at this time of night. It's getting on for twelve. He'd probably be in bed.'

'What's wrong with that?'

'Kirsty!'

'Well, what *is* wrong with that? He's by himself. That man Simpson – the one who's cleared off – he was his room-mate. Tony's got a room to himself now.'

'But you can't go knocking on people's doors – on a young man's door – at this time of night. It's not . . . well, I mean you just can't.'

'It's not a young man's door. It's Tony's door.'

'But what will he think? It's so . . . well, obvious. Or that's how it'd look. I mean you wouldn't want him to think you're . . . you know, just kind of saying . . . ' Margaret faltered and she stopped speaking.

Kirsty said, 'Playing hard to get didn't work, did it? So I'm going down there to see him. If he doesn't want me, at least I'll know the score. If he does – bingo! I'll see you in the morning.'

Margaret sat down on her bed. 'I do hope you know what you're doing,' she said. 'You could get hurt, dear.'

Kirsty looked determined and excited by her own audacity. 'Yes.

I know what I'm doing. Wish me luck.' And she went out of the room.


Chris found the living-room of the flat in darkness but then he saw the thin strip of light under the bedroom door. He switched on the lamp in the living-room and looked into the bedroom. Serena was not there but he knew from the faint sounds from the bathroom that she was taking a shower, as she usually did before going to bed. He thought about calling out but changed his mind and went into the kitchen where he boiled a kettle and fixed himself a mug of instant coffee.

He was taking his first sip when Serena appeared in the doorway wearing a blue towelling robe. She looked pink and rather pretty, he thought.

'Would you like a cup?' he asked.

'No. It's much too late.'

He moved with his coffee back into the living-room and sat down at the table with it. Serena followed but remained standing.

He said, 'Everyone in the pub seemed in high spirits tonight. The general feeling seemed to be that everything had gone well with the Personal Choices. I thought so, too, didn't you?'

'If so, it was no thanks to you.'

He put his mug down. 'Now wait a minute. I didn't do anything to spoil it. More the other way round. But listen, Serena, I don't want to squabble over it. The evening went well and that's what matters.'

'Not for me it didn't. Not when you did your best to spoil everything. It was all right till then, but you had to try and ruin things with that disgusting poem of Kit Wright's.'

'Disgusting! You sound like Mary Whitehouse. It's a witty, clever bit of writing and when Kit read it here he had everyone in stitches. You know he did. You were there. And, come to think of it, I seem to remember you were laughing as much as anyone.'

'Perhaps I was. But it was a different occasion, a different kind of course. They were all young students from the same college. They were here for a lark as much as anything. But surely even you can see that you can't read things like that to a mixed lot of old ladies and gents and school teachers.'

'I think they'd have loved it.'

'Well, I think they'd have been horrified.'

Chris took a drink of his coffee. 'In any case, why go on about it? I didn't read the thing so what are you worried about?'

'You made a scene. You embarrassed me in front of everyone. It was so childish. You were like a naughty kid. "If you don't let me do my party piece I'm not going to play!" That's what you sounded like. You could have read one of Kit's other poems. You know you like lots of them. But no. You had to sulk and make it look as if I was being unreasonable and it was all my fault.'

Chris seemed to reflect for a few moments before he said, 'Look, sit down, love. Let me make you some coffee. I think we'd better have a talk. This isn't just about tonight's reading and whether I should've chosen that poem or not. It's about you and me and the way we've not been getting on lately. You're not happy here. Certainly not with me. Not any more. Isn't that true? Isn't that what's really worrying you?'

Serena did not accept the invitation to sit. She said, 'You may be right that we're not happy together any more but your performance this evening's a good example of *why* we're not. I mean your insensitivity, your selfishness, childishness. You must have known that reading that particular poem wasn't suitable, you must have known I'd be embarrassed. But even when I told you, you still wanted to go on with it. You wanted to make me look silly or a spoilsport or something in front of everybody. It was typical somehow. I mean you just go sailing on, doing all the things you feel like doing but not bothering about *my* needs, what *I* want. And another thing. You're so bloody feeble. What about that Sludgens business? You said you'd talk to him today. And have you? . . . Of course not. I knew you wouldn't. And what am I supposed to say to what's-her-name, the teacher, Carol? What am I going to tell her when she asks me about that bloody horrible old man nicking her knickers?'

Chris grinned involuntarily. 'I like that. Sludgens the knickers nicker. It's a bit of a tongue-twist – '

'Oh, fuck off!' Serena snapped and swung round and went back into the bedroom, slamming the door behind her.

Chris remained at the table, staring bleakly at his cup of cooling coffee. He considered going after Serena and trying to coax her into a more amicable mood but quickly decided that this would be a hopeless enterprise. What he really needed, he thought, was something a bit stronger than *Nescafé* to drink. Perhaps he could try tapping on Gordon's door to see if the old boy was still up and willing to share some of his *Famous Grouse*. Failing that he could go down to the office and open one of the bottles of wine that he kept there for sale to course members. One thing was for sure: he wasn't going to join Serena for what would certainly be a continuation of their row.

He got up and went out of the flat and began to descend the two flights of stairs to where the male members of the course had their rooms. He was half-way down the second flight when he was startled and puzzled to hear, coming from the dimness below him, strange and disturbing sounds of sighs and moans and perhaps sobs and, for a second before dismissing it, he felt a tremor of superstitious fear.

He tiptoed down and, when he had almost reached the foot of the stairs, he saw a huddled female figure crouching there, head sunk low and arms crossed over her breast in a pathetic attempt at self-embracement. He stopped on the step above the one she was sitting on and said, almost in a whisper, 'Excuse me . . . who . . . is it . . . are you . . . Oh! It's Kirsty, isn't it?' Then louder: 'Kirsty! What is it? What's wrong?'

There was no intelligible reply, only a renewal of the sighs and moans, the same piteous note repeated over and over. He bent and touched her shoulder and he could feel that she was trembling.

'Kirsty,' he urged, 'please tell me what's happened. What's wrong? What are you doing here?'

Still no answer, only the same monotonous keening.

Chris descended the last two steps and sat down next to her and very gently placed his right arm about her shoulders. With his left hand he cautiously felt for one of hers, found it and squeezed it softly.

He said, speaking close to her ear, in the low, coaxing voice he would have used to soothe a fractious or frightened child, 'Tell me what's the matter, love. Tell me. Tell me what's happened. Why are you so upset? What's wrong? Come on, Kirsty, tell me what's up. I won't let on to anyone else if you don't want me to. It'll be our secret. Just tell me what's upset you, love. Go on, you can tell me.'

The moaning noises now seemed to come a little less frequently and were punctuated by different sounds, small gulps and sniffs, but still she seemed unwilling to say anything coherent.

Chris said, 'Tell you what. Let's go and make a drink. Tea or coffee. Anything you fancy. What about a glass of wine? How would that be? Kirsty?' He gave her shoulder a slight squeeze. She shook her head. 'Okay, just as you like, love. Just as you like. But we can't sit here all night. It's cold. The heating's off and doesn't come on again till seven in the morning. We'll be frozen.' She was quieter now but he could still feel her trembling. 'Who's your room-mate? I've forgotten who you share with. You haven't had a row with her, have you? Have you, Kirsty?'

She shook her head and muttered something he did not catch.

'What's that? What did you say? I didn't hear what you said. What was it?'

When she didn't answer, he said, 'Listen, I've got an idea. There's a couple of empty rooms on this floor. There's one down there, next but one to Arthur and Bernard's. What about going in there? At least we'll be a bit more comfortable and I can get us a drink or something and maybe you'll be able to tell me what the trouble is. What about that, Kirsty? Or would you rather I took you back to your room? Would that be best? Shall I take you back?'

She shook her head again.

He said, 'Come on then. Nice and easy.' Still holding one of her hands and keeping his arm about her shoulders he very slowly and carefully began to rise, drawing her gently with him, taking great care not to make any sudden movement that might alarm her.

The sounds she was making now were reduced to regularly spaced sniffs and little whimpers which reminded Chris of a sick puppy he had once nursed as a boy. With low murmurs of encouragement he led her slowly along the corridor until they reached the door of the room he had spoken of. He opened it and took her inside, switching on the light as they entered. As the room was flicked into bright detail she pressed her face into his chest, at the same time mumbling something unintelligible. He led her to one of the two beds and together they sat on the edge of it.

'What was it you said then, Kirsty, a moment ago? I didn't quite hear.'

She withdrew her face an inch or two away from where it was

pressed close to him and, keeping her head well down, she said in a tear-blurred, tiny voice, 'I must look a fright.'

'I'm sure you don't,' Chris said in almost a whisper. 'Though you gave me a fright, sitting there on the stairs in the shadows. I thought you were the Crackenthorpe ghost!'

A minute convulsion of her body and just audible grunt could have been a pathetic attempt at real or simulated laughter.

Encouraged by this, he went on, 'Hey! Let me see your face. Come on, love. Let's have a look at you. I'm sure you look as pretty as ever.'

Very cautiously he released the hand he was holding and placed two fingers gently beneath her chin and applied the tiniest of pressures there. She resisted for a few seconds and then lifted her face with its smeared make-up and tear-stains and tremulously attempted a smile. She looked, he thought, like a young child waking from a nightmare.

He said, 'I knew you would! You look lovely! So tell me what's wrong. What happened to upset you?'

When she stayed silent he went on, 'Look. I'll go and get a drink of something. Then we can talk. What would you like?'

She shook her head.

'Isn't there anything you'd like? Are you warm enough? You could put that duvet round you if you're cold.'

She said in a faint, but quite clear voice, 'I'm all right now.'

He waited for a moment or two before he spoke. 'Well then. You going to tell me what the trouble was? Why all the tears?'

She seemed to be considering whether or not to tell him. Then she began to speak very quickly and in little more than a hoarse whisper: 'It was Tony and that man Stamper. It was horrible! I couldn't believe my eyes but it was true. I couldn't believe it. It was the most horrible thing I've ever seen . . .'

'What was? Tell me Kirsty. What was it you saw?'

'They were in bed together! In Tony's room!'

'What! How d'you know? I mean how – what were you doing there if . . . I don't get it.'

'I went down to see Tony. I thought . . . I don't know . . . I sort of thought we were friends. I didn't feel tired so I thought I'd go and see if he was awake and he felt like – well, at first, when we first talked together, he seemed nice and friendly and I thought maybe he . . . you know . . . sort of fancied me a bit. And then he started acting like he wasn't so keen after all but Margaret said he was playing it cool like and I got confused and wasn't sure what was happening. Anyway, I thought I'd go and see him. And that's what I did. I went down to his room. I knew – well, I *thought* I knew he'd be alone 'cause that Simpson bloke he was sharing with had gone home. So I knocked on the door and nobody answered. I thought maybe he was asleep or something. But then I saw there was a light showing under the door so – well, I opened it. And there they were. Him and Stamper. In bed – or on the bed really. I mean the sheets and stuff were all over the place. They were on top. And they had no clothes on! They were both naked and they were – I couldn't believe it – they were . . . you know . . . it was unbelievable. It was horrible!'

'Jesus Christ, Stamper! I can't believe it! Are you sure it was him?'

'Of *course* I'm sure. I'm not blind!'

'No. Sorry. Of course you're sure. Silly of me. I didn't mean it. I mean it's a bit hard to take in. It must have been a terrible shock for you. Terrible.'

She said, 'I'd no idea he was like that. I just couldn't believe my eyes.'

'I dunno. I've always thought he's a bit of a weirdo. I've been keeping an eye on him. I'm not at all sure that he – and this is between me and you, Kirsty – I wouldn't be surprised if he's not a psychopath. Even a killer!'

'Tony? Oh no, I don't think he'd do anything violent. He's not –'

'No, not Tony. Stamper.'

'Oh, *him*. I don't know anything about him. Except . . . well, you know. I can't bear to think about it. And how am I to face Tony again? I won't know what to do or say. I'll feel such a fool, such a stupid idiot!'

'You don't know how *you'll* face *him*? I'd have thought it was the other way round. I can't see how he'll have the nerve to face *you*.'

Kirsty shook her head slowly. 'I don't think Tony'll worry about me,' she said. 'He'll be just the same, as if nothing's happened, if I know anything about him. I don't think he'll give a monkey's what I feel like. He knows I fancied him and he just made a fool of me. I feel so . . . so . . .'

Chris could see she was close to tears again. He tightened his arm around her. 'Don't you worry your head about Master Tony. If he wasn't gay he'd have been doing the chasing. Any normal bloke would feel dead lucky to meet a girl as pretty as you.'

She looked up at him again. 'You really think so Chris? Am I really pretty? You're not just saying that because . . . you know . . . all what's happened? Not saying it to cheer me up?'

'Of course you're pretty. You're lovely!' And he bent his head down to her upturned face and kissed her lightly on the forehead. As he did so he felt a stirring of sexual desire which surprised and slightly shocked him because, until that moment, he truly believed that his concern for her was disinterested, almost fatherly.

What happened next surprised him even more.

Kirsty, her face still raised to his, said, 'Why don't you kiss me properly?'

Chris hesitated, but only for a moment. When he put his mouth to hers he felt her lips part and then open wide and her tongue began to flicker against his own lips and then penetrate them, busy, searching. He embraced her with both arms and they rolled backwards and sideways on to the bed. He released one hand to take off his spectacles, which he dropped on the carpet, and then they began again to kiss and fondle each other, Kirsty astonishing him with her boldness and what could only be a much-practised deftness.

'Christ! You're lovely, Kirsty,' he gasped.

'Take off your things,' she commanded. 'Quick! Come on!' And she wriggled free of him so that they could both, in a frenzy of haste, get rid of their clothes and return to their love-making on the narrow bed.

'One for the road,' George said, 'and then we'll hit the sack.'

He poured whisky into both glasses and got up from the table and added water from the washbasin tap.

As he sat down again he said, 'I've no idea what happened to John. He wasn't in the room when I went to get my tooth-mug or whisky-mug or whatever you'd call it. Can't think where he got to after the pub crowd came back.'

'He's a bit of a mystery-man,' Gordon said, after he had taken a sip of his scotch and water. 'I don't suppose you know much more

about him than you did the day you came here, even though you're
sharing a room.'

'You're quite right. I don't. He never says anything very much.
Always perfectly friendly but he's always a bit – I'm not sure what
the word is – sort of on guard, if you know what I mean.'

'Seems to be enjoying the course, in his own quiet way.'

'Yes, I'm sure you're right. He's done a lot of reading and plenty
of writing, too, though he never shows me any of it. That was a
funny old poem he chose tonight, wasn't it? I can't remember the
author's name. Had you ever come across it before?'

Gordon nodded. 'Oh yes, I know it well. Henley's the poet, W. E.
Henley. He wrote one you probably came across in your school-days
called *Invictus*. Remember these lines?

> Out of the night that covers me,
>     Black as the pit from pole to pole
> I thank whatever gods may be
>     For my unconquerable soul.

'The last lines are the ones everyone knows:

> I am the master of my fate:
> I am the captain of my soul.

'It might be a bit on the grandiloquent side but it's pretty stirring
stuff. The thing about Henley was he had such a wide range. He
wrote a sequence of hospital poems around the time he was having
his foot off and these are tough and realistic and very well observed.
Then there's his use of the vernacular – oh God, I'm beginning to
lecture again! Sorry.'

'Not at all! Jolly interesting. Always like to listen to a man
talking when he knows his stuff. Wish I could quote things like that,
just off the top of my head. Wonderful gift.' George swallowed some
of his drink. 'I say, old Maureen gave us a bit of a shock, didn't she?
That poem about cigarettes and sex. Bit near the knuckle, wasn't it?
I mean for someone like Maureen. Or does that sound chauvinist
piggy?'

Gordon said, 'I was surprised. It's a good poem though.'

'Oh yes, I thought it was very clever. Again I've forgotten who
wrote it.'

'A poet called Fleur Adcock. A very good poet too.'

'I expect you knew that one as well.'

Gordon said, almost apologetically, that yes, he did know it.

'Not much you don't know about poetry, is there?'

'Yes, quite a lot. In any case it's all relative. Compared with some people I've read next to nothing.'

George ignored this and said, 'What about your wife, Susan? Is she keen on poetry? I suppose she must be or she wouldn't be able to – '

Gordon interrupted: 'Oh my God! I didn't ring her!'

'When? Today? Were you supposed to?'

'Ever. I mean I haven't rung since I've been here. What day is it tomorrow? Thursday, isn't it? Oh shit! I really meant to ring before supper but I got talking to Chris about . . . ' his voice trailed off into disconsolate silence.

'Ring in the morning, first thing. Tell her you couldn't get to the phone or it was out of order or something. She'll forgive you, I'm sure. Though I'm not so sure she would if she'd seen you in the pub this evening with that Joan Palmer girl.'

'What? What are you talking about? What's Joan Palmer got to do with it?'

'Well, you did seem to be getting very matey, looking into each other's eyes and so forth. She's a nice-looking woman. I felt a bit jealous to tell the truth.'

'Oh rubbish! We were talking about Philip Larkin. She's got the right ideas about poetry. By that I suppose I mean she thinks pretty well as I do.'

'I thought she was giving you definitely tender looks. You wouldn't object if she had been would you? I mean if she gave you the old come-hither.'

'Christ! I haven't heard that expression for a few decades.' Gordon grinned, mildly embarrassed and perhaps, he had to admit to himself, a little excited by what George was suggesting. 'She's young enough to be my daughter!'

'Maybe she is. But you weren't looking at her in what you might call a fatherly way in the pub.'

'Bollocks,' Gordon said, 'And drink up.'

George lifted his glass but, before he drank from it, he said, 'You must agree she's a good looker, Gordon. So tell me. Would you be tempted? If the chance was there?'

'No . . . I don't know . . . It's not going to happen anyway. Now drink up and bugger off. I want to get to bed.'

George finished his drink and stood up. He took his empty glass and moved towards the door. Gordon went ahead of him to usher him out of the room but stopped suddenly as he reached for the door-handle.

He said, 'Wait a second, George.' He sniffed the air twice before he spoke again: 'Can you smell anything?'

George looked surprised; then he, too, sniffed a couple of times and nodded. 'Yes, now you mention it. I think I can.'

'What is it? What can you smell?'

George sniffed again. 'It's . . . I don't know. Sort of earthy, perhaps a bit herby.'

'Celery? D'you think it's celery?'

More sniffing by both of them.

'No . . . something else . . . I know . . . I think . . . mushrooms!'

'Are you sure it's not celery?'

'Yes, quite sure. It's mushrooms.'

Gordon said, 'Had you noticed it before? While we were sitting there having a drink?'

'No, I don't think so. I'm sure I didn't. That's a bit odd isn't it? What about you? Did you suddenly notice it?'

'Yes, just as we got up to move away from the table. I've smelt it before. In fact I smelt it the first night I was here.'

'It's not really unpleasant is it?'

'I suppose not. No.'

'If it worries you I'd get young Chris to have a look around and try and find out where it's coming from.'

'I might do that.'

They exchanged good-nights, and George left, and Gordon got ready for bed. When he was between the sheets his last thought, before he sank into sleep, was of Joan Palmer who was, as George had observed, a nice-looking woman, though whether the tender looks that George claimed to have seen signified a more than casual interest seemed unlikely. Unlikely but perhaps not impossible.

# THURSDAY

THE FINE WEATHER continued, though few of the students took advantage of it to go for long walks in the afternoon because most of them were too busy working at their poems or exercises. Even on the breaks for coffee, tea or meals, much of the talk, Gordon noticed, was more or less directly concerned with the practice or nature of the art of poetry.

There were changes in the formation of the study groups but numerically they stayed remarkably even. On Thursday morning Gordon found, rather to his surprise, that John Stamper had decided to accompany Tony who had elected, with the teachers, Freda and Carol, to move to Gaby's fold, but Bernard and Arthur had joined Eileen and Maureen in Gordon's group. More surprising than John's switch to Gaby was the appearance of Kirsty among Gordon's students, a Kirsty, moreover, who seemed somehow changed, quieter, less self-assertive than the pugnacious little person he had first encountered. Joan Palmer, he was pleased to see, showed no interest in shifting to the less orthodox and possibly more exciting tutelage of Gaby.

His morning session was spent in discussing and studying examples of the villanelle form, and then the students began to settle down to attempting the composition of an original one. After they had been working for half an hour or so, Gordon moved about the library to see what progress each was making. This gave him cause, or excuse, to sit quite close to Joan's side while he made suggestions for a change in the final word of the first line which would not adversely affect sound or sense but provide a larger store of possible rhymes. He was mildly disturbed by her proximity and obscurely moved by the summery fragrance that sweetened the air about her. What he felt was not simple sexual interest but something closer to romantic nostalgia, and his memory was teased by spectral images and sensations, perhaps from puberty or even earlier, when he had, by design or luck, found himself sitting close to some imperfectly recalled object of desire, a girl of his own age, maybe, or possibly a loved teacher at his primary school.

He said, 'Of course, you might manage with the word you've got but I think you'll find it difficult. Plenty of near-rhymes of course, but in a strict traditional form like the villanelle I don't think anything but pure rhyme will do.'

'I'm sure you're right,' Joan said, 'I'll change it.' A brief pause while they both considered other possibilities. Then she said, 'What about "descends" instead of "goes down"? That'd be better, wouldn't it?'

Gordon nodded. 'I'd have suggested it myself if you hadn't come up with it. You'll find lots of rhymes for "descends".'

As he rose she looked up at him and smiled. 'Thank you. I'll see what I can do with it now.'

He moved away and forced himself to resist the temptation to look back at her, but the image of her head bent over her work was distinct in his mind, and a few words of a Yeats poem drifted, unbidden, into his consciousness:

> Overcome – O bitter sweetness
> Inhabitant of the soft cheek of a girl –

before he dismissed them with self-mocking brusqueness and went over to where George Barnes was sitting.

'How you getting on, George?'

George's grin was a little embarrassed. 'Sorry,' he said. 'Hope you don't mind but I'm not trying to do the – what-you-call-it – villa something. . . '

'Villanelle.'

'I copied down the one you talked about. Here it is, look – the one by what's-his-name – Auden. *If I Could Tell You*. I think it's a bit too tricky for me, though I'll probably have a crack at it when I get home. So what I've been doing is trying to get that sonnet about Christmas finished.'

'Fine. How's it going?'

'Not too bad, I hope. I won't show it you now, if you don't mind.

I'd rather wait till it's finished. Or as finished as I can make it. That all right?'

'Of course.'

Gordon was about to move away when George said, 'What's this chap like who's coming to read this evening? Zip or Zap or some such name. Do you know his work?'

'Zak Fairbrass. Yes, I've read some of it, not a lot. He's all right. A bit agricultural for my taste but quite a lot of people think he's good. Powerful's the word they use.'

George nodded and went back to his sonnet and Gordon continued his surveillance of his students' efforts until it was time to break for lunch.

He was on his way through the hall towards the stairs when Chris came out of the office and called his name. Gordon stopped.

Chris said, 'I'm very sorry Gordon but I forgot to tell you yesterday. Your wife phoned in the morning, around eleven. All that business with Gaby's prize and the BBC and a few other things just put it out of my mind.'

'What did she say?'

'Nothing much. I don't think it was important. She just said tell him I called. I think she only wanted to know if you were getting on all right. Not catching cold or anything. Sorry I forgot to tell you.'

'I'll ring her now,' Gordon said.

'Come in here and use our phone.'

Gordon went into the office and tapped out his own number on the telephone. He heard the distant double rasp of the call and waited for Susan to answer. No answer came. He looked at his watch. Twenty minutes to one. She was probably out shopping, or maybe she'd gone over to Pauline's in Ealing for lunch. He waited a few more seconds before he put the receiver down.

'No reply. She must be out.'

'Try again later. Don't bother with the pay-phone. You're welcome to use this one.'

Gordon thanked him and started to leave the office when Chris said, 'Oh, by the way, what about that funny smell in your room? You noticed it again?'

'Well, yes. Only faintly, but it's there. George Barnes noticed it, too, but he thought it was something else, not celery. He said more like mushrooms.'

'I'll have a sniff around when I get a moment,' Chris said. 'I'm wondering if it might be dry rot or something. And again, I'm really sorry about forgetting your call.'

'Don't worry. I don't suppose it was anything important.'

Just before Gordon reached the door it opened and he stepped aside to allow Serena to enter the office. She looked, he thought, pale and vaguely peevish, though she attempted a small and joyless smile of greeting.

'See you later,' Chris called and Gordon went out but, as he walked away, he heard their voices raised in what could only have been exchanges of an acrimonious kind.

'What I need,' he told himself, 'is a restorative snifter.'


'What did your lot do this morning?' Viv said, and then took a bite of bread and liver pâté.

Joan sipped some of her orange juice. 'Oh, we – or most of us – tried to write or struggle with something called a villanelle. Not very easy, though I found it rather fun in a way.'

They were seated opposite to each other at the small table in their room.

'What was that word again? A what?'

'Villanelle.'

'Anything to do with villains or villainy?'

'I don't think so. Though, come to think of it, Gordon told us it comes from an Italian word, "villano" meaning "peasant" and that might be connected with "villein", and they were sort of peasants, I think. Our modern villains used to be thought of as kind of low-born, roughnecks, though I don't know so much about nowadays. I dunno really. That's just guesswork.'

'But what's it all got to do with poetry?'

'Well, the villanelle, way back in Italy, was just a kind of country song, a peasant song I suppose. Nothing like the complicated things we were trying to write. But what happened was this. The French sort of took it over in, I think, the late sixteenth century and a chap called – wait a minute, I've got his name here . . . ' She left her seat and picked up the cardboard folder that was lying on her bed and opened it.

Back at the table she said, 'Ah yes, here we are. Jean Passerat. apparently the old Italian villanelles didn't have to be in any special form, nor did the French ones at first. But this Jean Passerat chose to write his villanelles in this very intricate way, and they became so popular that everybody started imitating them and it sort of set the pattern.'

Viv sipped at her orange juice, then ate more bread and pâté. 'And what's the pattern like then?'

'Well, it's – oh, too difficult to explain. But I've got one here. This is a modern English villanelle, a different metre from the old French ones, but the same pattern of rhymes and repetitions. Look – you see how the first and last lines of that first little verse are repeated alternately – oh, work it out for yourself!'

Viv looked for a minute or two at the sheet of paper on which Joan, like most of the others in the group, had copied out Auden's *If I Could Tell You*. 'My God,' she said, 'that's too much like hard work, even thinking about it, let alone making one up.'

Joan laughed. 'Oh, I don't know. I don't think they're quite as difficult to do as they look. I'm going to try and finish mine anyway. I don't suppose it'll be much good but at least I'll get it more or less right. What about you? What did Gaby's lot do today?'

'Some sort of game. Everybody had to write ten lines of – well, let's call it poetry. It could be about anything you like and of course it didn't have to have rhymes or anything like that. Then we cut them all up, so all the lines were in separate strips of just one line – with me?'

'I think so.'

'Right. Then Gaby put them all in the wastepaper basket and shook them so they were all mixed up, then everybody took out ten of these strips of paper – you might find you'd got one or two of the lines you'd written yourself, but not necessarily – and, using these and adding four lines of your own you were supposed to make up a poem. You weren't allowed to alter any of the words in the lines you'd picked out of the basket so it wasn't very easy.'

'Did you manage to do it?'

'Yeah. After a fashion.'

'What was it like? Have you got it with you?'

'It was rubbish. To tell the truth, I didn't really try very much. I was thinking more about what I was going to do when I go and see Gaby . . . ' She looked at her watch. 'In about ten minutes.'

Joan was about to eat some of her lunch, but she stopped with the food half-way to her mouth. 'Don't do anything silly,' she said. 'I'm quite sure you've got things wrong about Gaby and what's-his-name.'

'I don't think so. Too many coincidences. I'm sure she got her paws on him.'

Joan took a bite and chewed a little, then she said, 'Do think before you say anything about – I'm sorry, I've forgotten his name.'

'Dave.'

'Oh yes, Dave. I can't help feeling he was just impressed by Gaby as a poet and a teacher. I can quite see any man – anyone – being sort of bowled over by her. I mean she's got a very strong personality. I should think she's the sort of person who attracts hero-worship or something of that kind. I can imagine people – certain kinds of people – sort of falling under her spell, even becoming disciples. But, somehow, I can't see her responding in – you know – the way you seem to think she has with Dave. In fact she doesn't seem to have much time for men. Shows a kind of impatience, maybe even contempt.'

Viv smiled, but not reassuringly. 'Aren't you forgetting the poems? Dave's poems? The ones I found hidden in that book? They were *sex* obsessed. They weren't in praise of Gaby's powers as a teacher or a poet. They were about her body and her powers as a good fuck.'

Joan's eyebrows rose and her eyes widened. Then she slowly shook her head and said, 'Don't blame me if Gaby makes you look a fool. My guess is that she could be rather good at that.'

'All I want from Gaby is for her to admit the truth. Then Dave had better watch out. And so had she.'

Viv picked up her glass but returned it untasted to the table. 'Wish I'd got something stronger than that to drink,' she said.

'I'm glad you haven't. You're crazy enough when you're sober.'

Viv stood up. 'Don't worry Joan. I can look after myself. I'm going to have a pee and then I'm off to see Gaby. I'll be back later. Will you be going out?'

'No. I'll stay here and do a bit of work. I want to see what happens with you and Gaby.'

'All right. See you later.'

'Yes. And please, Viv, be careful what you say. And do.'

Viv's grin was wild and reckless. 'I don't suppose I'll say a great deal. But I'll probably strangle her.'

She stopped for a moment at the door and looked back at Joan with an excited, glittering smile. 'You get on with your villainy or whatever it's called and I'll get on with mine. Bye now. See you soon.'

She went out and along the corridor to the bathroom. Before she came out, she stared a little grimly into the mirror, gave her reflection one decisive nod, and made her way quickly to Gaby's room and rapped on the door. She waited and found that she was breathing more quickly than usual and was aware of a tremulous sensation of something between anticipation and apprehension.

There was no sound from behind the door. Anger began to rise and thicken the emotional mix. She was about to knock again, more loudly with both fists, but the door opened and Gaby stood there.

'Didn't you hear me? I called "Come in".'

Viv shook her head and Gaby stepped back, gesturing for her visitor to follow her into the room which, Viv observed, was furnished in exactly the same way as the one shared with Joan, except there was only one bed.

'Come and sit over here,' Gaby said, indicating the table and two chairs beneath the window. 'I can't offer you anything to drink, I'm afraid. We'll have to settle for plain living and high thinking.'

'And plain speaking,' Viv said with a note of belligerence in her voice.

'That too, if that's what you want.' Gaby spoke carelessly, untroubled.

'It is.'

Gaby smiled faintly and they sat down at the table facing each other.

'Okay. Where would you like to begin?'

'Dorset. That poetry course at Oaklands, when you and my partner got together. Dave Mottram. remember? Last August. That's where I'd like to begin.'

Gaby did not answer immediately but gazed at Viv with her slight, ambiguous smile. 'Oh yes, you said something about this on the first evening here, didn't you? I didn't know you were still worrying about it. Whatever it is. Tell me more.'

'Dave went on that course and, like I told you, he came back a different person. Until then we'd got on fine. Had a few squabbles, like everybody does, but we were okay. We were a real item. And then he went to Dorset and when he came back he talked about nothing but you. It didn't matter what we were on about, he brought you into it. Gaby told me this or Gaby said that. Like you were the voice of God.'

'He didn't mention any other names? People on the course? Other students?'

'No. I think he told me the other tutor's name was Selway, Solway, whatever it was. But he didn't say much about him. Too busy banging on about how marvellous you were.'

'James Selway, that was my colleague at Oaklands. No, your Dave didn't work with him. He stayed with my group all week.'

'Ah! So you *do* remember him!' Viv's dark eyes flashed with anger and triumph. 'You said you couldn't put a face to the name! That's what you said on Sunday night! You said you'd met hundreds of new people since the Oaklands course and you couldn't place him. That's what you said, wasn't it?'

Gaby seemed neither disconcerted nor alarmed by Viv's outburst. 'Yes, I think I did say I couldn't remember him. And it was true, at the time. But afterwards I began to think about it. I mean you seemed so . . . er . . . *concerned*, so *passionate* about it, I racked my brains and tried to remember every student on that course and, sure enough, I *did* bring Dave to mind. I'd forgotten his second name – what was it? – Motting? . . . Mottham?'

'Mottram.'

'Mottram. I see. But we didn't use surnames much, hardly at all. I mean everybody was on first-name terms, like we are here.'

'Yes, I *bet* you were. Specially in the sack. You'd hardly say, "Hold me tight Mr Mottram" or "You've got a lovely bum Mr Mottram", would you?'

Gaby's smile broadened and in her eyes glinted what might have been sparks of mischief. 'No, I wouldn't. But, then, the possibility of my ever being, as you put it, in the sack with him, or anyone like him, simply doesn't exist.'

'Oh no? Then what about those sexy poems he wrote? All about dark secret foliage and soft and juicy fruits, white branches of the pliant flesh, stuff like that. You mean to tell me they weren't love-poems? Or lust-poems. You mean to say they were pure imagination? They didn't come from real experience? Because I don't believe you.'

'He showed you those, did he? I *am* surprised.'

'No, he didn't show me them. I found them. Hidden in some boring book about politics he thought I'd never think of opening. Of *course* he didn't show them to me.'

'They weren't very good, were they?' Gaby said thoughtfully. 'Seemed a bit adolescent, as if he'd been wanking over a girlie magazine.'

'Don't try and get away from the facts! I don't give a shit whether they were any good or not. Thing is, they were all about you and him bonking away happily while I was sitting at home with my knitting. So to speak.'

'No, not exactly.'

'What do you mean, not exactly?'

'I mean those slushy bits of writing were *not* about your Dave and *me*. I'm not saying they weren't attempts – feeble as they were – at verbalising actual experience. In fact I'm pretty sure that that's just what they were. But they were nothing to do with me, my dear. Nor, I'm afraid, anything to do with you, either.'

There was a brief silence. 'What do you mean? I don't see . . . I'm . . . '

'I mean that Dave was having it away with a girl – well, hardly a *girl* – called Dilly. And I truly can't remember *her* surname so don't ask me.'

Viv stared uncertainly at Gaby. Then she said, but her voice carried little conviction, 'I don't believe you.'

'You don't?' Gaby's eyebrows were raised and her expression was one of mildly amused but compassionate disbelief.

'But . . . why . . . why did he go on about you so much if it wasn't you? Gaby this and Gaby that. He was obsessed. It must have been you!'

'No, it wasn't me, Viv. No way was it me! And if he was droning on about me when he got back from Oaklands it was really because he was longing to talk about that Dilly woman, and of course, he couldn't, directly, so he was using my name as a kind of shield.'

Viv still did not look convinced.

Outside, a cloud must have passed over the wintry sun, for the room suddenly became more dim and shadowy. The two women sat in a longer silence, each gazing at the other. Then Gaby began to speak again in a lower, softer voice, that was almost caressing. 'Listen to me, Viv. Your Dave is not worthy of you – don't say anything please, just listen. That woman, Dilly, – she was much older than you – older than me, come to think of it – she was a predator, one of those faded divorcées who somehow manage to attract younger men. I know how they do it. I've seen it often enough. They use flattery and a kind of corrupt sensuality that men like your Dave, for some reason, find irresistible. I suspect that it's something to do with mummy, something incestuous, but that's by the way. What you should do, Viv, is get rid of him. You don't deserve to be besmirched by him. You are very beautiful. And you should be loved and cherished. But not used and betrayed by men like him. You deserve a cleaner, sweeter, purer love than he, or any man, can offer you. Don't you realise now that you are so much better, so much lovelier, lovable, true, honest, clean, so infinitely superior to him and his kind?'

Gaby's voice, so unlike the rather harsh one that she used for her workshops and readings and normal daily intercourse, began to work upon Viv's senses in an almost mesmeric way. This voice was warm and of a dark, velvety texture, and its rhythms were like the gentle rise and fall of the waves of a placid summer sea; it was insistent, but not forcefully so, and its low music and the repetitive phrasing created, along Viv's nerves and in her bloodstream, a faint vibration and throbbing, delicate but unwavering, that very slowly intensified. She found that her senses were now becoming confused so that she could smell the honeysuckle fragrance of Gaby's words and taste their elusively sweet sound. She felt that she was breathing with Gaby's spicy breath.

The words flowed out: 'We women should deny the brute male his power-mad piercing, his mindless, selfish violations. You know now, don't you my love, that I would never allow that Dave, or any other man, to violate the sacred me, the female me that is wholly woman, woman that could not submit to anything or anyone that is not woman too. I think you are beginning to see and, more important, to *feel*, to *know* in the wise blood and senses, what your true destiny should be.

'I thought when I first saw you, when you spoke to me with hostility, that your aggression was not true aggression, your show of enmity was an expression of your fear of, and attraction to what you really knew, what you really wanted. Do you see? I think you do. I think you see and feel the truth of what I'm telling you.'

Now, it seemed warmer and more shadowy in the room and Gaby's eyes, dark and glistening with a deep, almost juicy liquescence, were conveying a message, strange, appalling perhaps, in its unexpectedness and in its power to thrill and to bewilder. Viv became aware that Gaby had stopped speaking, though the cadences of the voice seemed still to linger in the air. The spell had been completed and the physical words were no longer needed. Viv was also conscious of a slight tremor, a sustained frisson, like the tiny trembling of a breeze-troubled spider's web, in all of her limbs, as Gaby very slowly rose from her seat and stood over her and held out both hands.

'Come, my darling,' she whispered. 'Let's go and sit on the bed. We'll be more comfortable there. Come on. You have nothing to be afraid of . . . come my love . . . come . . . '


Joan sat at the table with her half-finished villanelle in front of her. After a few botched attempts during the morning session she had just managed to complete the lines of which she had made a fair copy in her notebook:

> These summer evenings as the dusk descends
> I hear a silent music in the air;
> I see the spectral faces of old friends.
>
> Those I have hurt and never made amends,
> Inflicting pain I never can repair
> These summer evenings as the dusk descends.
>
> I cannot say why this dumb music blends
> So softly with those shadowed places where
> I see the spectral faces of old friends

With unshed tears I turn away . . .

She took her ball-point pen and scored out the last line. Then she read over the three tercets she had, at least for the time being, finished, speaking them in a half-whisper to herself. They didn't sound too bad, she thought. She wasn't absolutely sure what her words meant but she felt that she might have managed to convey something of a mood of melancholy regret for the irredeemable past. All right.

Presently she was able to substitute for the line she had crossed out a new one which had, if nothing else, the virtue of ending with the necessary rhyming-word for *descends*.

This moment when the bruised heart comprehends

and, after many false starts, she succeeded in completing the stanza:

A little of the burden all must bear
These summer evenings as the dusk descends.

Again she read through the whole of what she had composed and permitted herself to feel a tentative sense of satisfaction. One more tercet to write, then the final quatrain, and it would be, for better or worse, finished.

What would Gordon think of it? she wondered, and she realised that his opinion mattered to her quite a lot. She found herself thinking what a nice man he was. She knew that he would never say anything deliberately unkind about a student's work, no matter how poor the effort might be, but she felt that she would be able to tell whether or not his approval was sincere.

There was something endearing about his quiet devotion to his art and his modesty about his own achievement, something a little sad, too, about the impression he gave of wry resignation to his being largely ignored by the fashionable criteria of the literary press and other media. Something else too. More than once he had smiled at her in a way that she believed was reserved for her alone, a smile that in its slightly self-deprecatory, quizzical way had become a thing to look forward to receiving. After tomorrow she would not see him again, except perhaps, briefly, on Saturday morning to say goodbye. The thought saddened her a little, then she shook her head at what seemed like her foolishness and returned to the task of finishing her villanelle.

After three failed tries she managed to write:

> I feel ~~that some kind~~ *a tender* influence extends
> Promise of forgiveness if I dare
> See the spectral faces of old friends.

She sat looking at the words on the paper, wondering if it was permissible to make that tiny omission of the personal pronoun at the beginning of the last line and decided that she would leave it for Gordon to decide.

And now for the quatrain at the end. She wrote down the obligatory final couplet first:

> These summer evening as the dusk descends
> I see the spectral faces of old friends.

Now, all she had to do was find two lines that would make some kind of sense when stuck on top of the couplet. This proved less easy than she had hoped but, after many abortive starts, she produced this:

> Love and courage share the same bright ends
> Without which we are left with our despair.

Then she read the entire poem through, at first silently and then aloud. She thought it sounded all right, better than she had hoped when she was struggling to get it finished. Then she suddenly thought of Viv.

She looked at her watch. Ten minutes to four! Had she really been working on her villanelle for almost two hours? And what on earth could Viv be up to with Gaby?

It was extraordinary how this verse-writing business could absorb your attention so completely. She had quite forgotten her fears that Viv might behave in some wild and even violent way with her tutor, but now she felt her anxiety returning more acutely. Surely Viv and Gaby had had more than enough time to say to each other whatever had to be said. Even if they had come to blows, the contest would have been decided by now.

Joan slipped her villanelle into her folder which she put away in one of the drawers. She looked at her watch again. Could Viv simply have forgotten her promise to come back to their room and tell her how the confrontation had gone on? It was possible. It was possible that she had gone out somewhere to cool off after the altercation, if that was what their meeting had turned out to be. Or maybe she'd gone down to the kitchen for a soothing cup of tea. If that was what she'd done she might at least have called in here first, Joan thought, and she felt a small spark of impatient anger.

She moved with vague indecision about the room; then she picked up a copy of a book which she had taken from the library on the previous day, *New and Collected Poems* by Robert Conquest, and sat down to read. She had known of Conquest only as the author of *The Great Terror*, the famous book about Stalin's purges in the 1930s, until Gordon had mentioned that he was an entertaining, skilful and much underrated poet of the Larkin and Enright generation. She had, so far, greatly enjoyed most of the poems she had read but now she found concentration impossible and, after only a few minutes, gave up and decided to go down to the kitchen to see if Viv was there and, whether she was or not, make herself a cup of tea.

Chris said, 'Where are the cooks? Should've started by now, shouldn't they? Who's on, anyway?'

He looked up at the list pinned up on the kitchen wall above the fridge. 'Tony, Kirsty and Viv.'

Serena took a sip of her tea. 'Margaret's taking Kirsty's place for some reason I couldn't make out. I think they've had a row, Kirsty and Tony I mean. Margaret said they'd had some sort of quarrel. No idea what it was about. Anyway Kirsty refused to work with him, so Margaret's stepping in as usual. I expect they'll be down here in a minute. I don't know what you're worried about. It's only bangers, mash and peas tonight, so that won't take long.'

Chris heaved himself backwards on to the work-surface and sat there, swinging his feet just clear of the floor. 'What time's Zak Fairbrass's train getting in, did you say?'

'Six-fifteen at Ancliffe.'

'I thought I might look in Gordon's room, see if he's been imagining those odd smells he's been going on about. Could be dry rot or something. Probably not, but just could be.'

Serena said nothing.

'What's wrong, love? You're looking a bit peeky. You feeling all right?'

'I'm all right.'

'You don't look it.'

'Thank you.' She put down her unfinished tea and started towards the door. Then she stopped and turned back to face him. 'Where did you go last night?' she said.

'Last night? Oh, *then*. Yes. Well, I went down to get a drink after you'd gone to bed. A glass of wine or something. Didn't feel like . . . well, you know. We'd had a bit of a squabble about the Personal Choice thing – me wanting to read Kit Wright's poem. I didn't feel tired and didn't want to come in and stop you sleeping. You know what I'm like when I'm restless. You wouldn't have been able to – '

Serena broke in. 'You didn't come back till God knows when. It must have been at least three or four o'clock in the morning. What the hell were you doing till then?'

'Oh no, it couldn't have been as late as that. But I *was* gone some time.' He hesitated before continuing. 'I'll tell you. Something very peculiar happened. I didn't know whether to mention it but maybe I should. So I'll tell you.'

'Well, go on and tell me.'

'Yes. Right. Well, as I said, I was going down for a drink. I felt I could do with – well, never mind. Thing is, I got half-way down the stairs and guess what – there was little Kirsty, sitting in the dark, crying her heart out!'

'What? Where? Sitting where?'

'On the stairs. You know how dim the night-light is. I couldn't see who it was at first. Just this little huddled figure. Then I saw it was Kirsty. In a terrible state she was.'

'Why? What was wrong with her?'

'I told you. She was crying, hysterical, a terrible state.'

'I know you did. But *why*? Why was she hysterical?'

'Ah, yes. Well. Here's the part you're not going to believe. She'd had a terrific shock. What happened was, she thought she'd go and see Tony. I mean, as she said herself, she really fancied him and he was on his own – got his own room – now Simpson's buggered off. She thought she'd go and see him. Thought they'd have the room to themselves, be a nice chance for a bit of nooky. So – '

'She said *that*?'

'Eh? What? Oh, well, not those words exactly but it was obvious what she meant.'

'And she was crying all the time she was telling you this?'

'Yeah, well, sort of. She was talking in between sobs like. I mean that's why I was so long coming back. It took a helluva time for her to get the story out.'

'All right. What story? What happened? According to Kirsty.'

'Well it seems she went along to Tony's room – and we're coming to the bit you won't believe. I could hardly believe it myself. She went in and found he was – have you guessed? I bet you have. He was in bed with somebody else.'

Serena's interest, despite her scepticism, was aroused. 'Who with?'

'Right. Wait for it. This was the thunderbolt. He was in bed with John Stamper!'

'What!'

'He was in bed – or if I understood her right, *on* the bed with Stamper. And Kirsty was in no doubt what they were up to.'

'I don't believe it!'

'No? Well, I don't think you'd've had any difficulty believing it if you'd seen Kirsty last night. She was in shock. She'd had what must've been the worst experience of her young life. She was weeping and moaning and shivering and didn't know what to do with herself. Take it from me, Serena, that girl'd had a terrible shock. Unbelievable.'

'John Stamper . . . it doesn't seem . . . I mean are you sure she'd not . . . '

'I'm quite sure. When she'd got her act together a bit and was making plain sense, it was obvious what she'd seen. Both of them on the bed, bollock-naked. And they weren't comparing tattoos.'

Serena did not say anything for a few seconds and, when she

spoke, her voice was coldly inquisitorial. 'And where were you and Kirsty when she was telling you all this?'

'I told you. Sitting on the stairs.'

'For two or three hours. I don't believe it!'

'We were. For most of the time, that is. Then we came downstairs, came in here as a matter of fact. Had a cup of coffee. She needed it, poor kid. She was – '

'Yes, I know, in a terrible state. And were you able to console her?'

'I did my best.'

'I *bet* you did.'

'Hey now, Serena. What you trying to say? The poor girl was distraught. Think of it. The guy she fancies rotten turns out to be the other way inclined – and making out with John Stamper of all people! Can't you see what a kick in the teeth it was for her?'

Serena nodded. 'Specially since he's a murderer.'

'What?'

'John Stamper. He's a killer and rapist, isn't he? Isn't that what you thought? You had him weighed up all right.'

'No, I never said that. Not for sure. But he's a very weird guy. Nothing would surprise me about Mr Stamper. I can't think what – ' Chris did not complete his sentence for the kitchen door opened and they both looked round to see who was coming in. It was John Stamper, followed by Tony and, only a matter of seconds later, by Margaret Baker. Tony looked his usual cheerful self and Stamper wore his habitual, watchful, rather enigmatic expression that Serena had always thought rather attractive. She found that she was trying to visualise the scene that, according to Chris's story, had so shocked Kirsty. She found the exercise both difficult and oddly disturbing, so she abandoned it as quickly as she could.

'We've come in search of the cups that cheer but do not inebriate,' Tony announced as he filled and switched on the electric kettle. Margaret was busy with mugs and teabags when the door opened again and Joan came in.

'Just in time,' Margaret said. 'You don't take sugar do you, Joan? You know where the biscuits are.'

'Anyone seen Viv?' Joan asked the tea-drinkers.

Heads were shaken and Chris said, 'She's not been in here. Not in the last half-hour, anyway.'

Joan took her mug of tea from Margaret. 'Thanks . . . I'm worried about her.'

'Wait a minute,' Margaret said. 'I think I *did* see her. Not absolutely sure, but I think I saw her car going out of the gate. She drives that little red thing, doesn't she?'

'Ford Fiesta,' Chris said.

'When was this?' Joan asked Margaret.

'About half an hour ago. I'd been down to see Mrs Sludgens to see if I could buy a few of their free-range eggs – I'm afraid I can't eat the battery-hens' ones, poor little things – and when I was coming away I'm fairly sure I saw Viv's car whizzing out of the gate.'

'Was she driving it? Did you actually see her?' Joan said.

'No, I can't say I did. I only saw the car, sort of out of the corner of my eye. I couldn't swear who was in it. I just assumed it was Viv. Why? You seem worried, dear. What's wrong?'

'I *am* worried. A bit.'

'What's the trouble?' Chris said. 'What you worried about, Joan?'

'Anyone got any trouble, Chris is your man,' Serena said. 'He's a dab hand at sorting out people's troubles.'

Joan paused before she spoke, aware that she might be about to appear, if not foolish, an irrational worrier. Then she said, 'I don't think – I mean I know it might look as if I'm making a fuss over nothing very much but I can't think why Viv's cleared off. I was supposed to see her – oh, an hour ago at least. I can't understand why she'd suddenly drive off somewhere without letting me know. If she has, if that *was* her car you saw, Margaret.'

'Wait there a sec,' Chris said. 'I'll go and see if it's gone.'

A minute later he was back. 'Yeah, it's not there. She's gone off in it somewhere.'

Tony said, 'Why shouldn't she go out in her car, Joan? What are you so concerned about? You don't think she's run away, like Mr Simpson, do you?'

Joan shook her head and frowned. 'Look, I don't know whether I should talk about any of this but I can't help feeling worried. Actually I feel a bit silly, too – it all seems so – well, so unlikely, melodramatic even, but the fact is Viv's kind of obsessed with Gaby. I don't mean a silly crush or something, not that kind of obsessed. I mean – well, do you remember – any of you – when Viv spoke on that first night on Sunday when we were all introducing ourselves? She didn't talk to everybody, she just fixed on Gaby and went on about Gaby tutoring a course at some place in Dorset where she'd met Viv's partner, someone called Dave. Maybe you've forgotten but she seemed very intense, strange and sort of accusing about it.'

Tony said, 'Yes, you're right. I remember thinking something funny was going on there.'

'Yes something was. Viv's talked to me quite a lot about what's been bothering her. Mind you, I don't think for a moment that she's right, but she's got a wild idea – in fact she's certain – that her Dave and Gaby had some kind of fling on this course. I don't believe it but *she* does, absolutely. Anyway, she's been swearing that she'll get at the truth and – here's the worrying part – she seems after some kind of revenge. Well, today, she went to Gaby's room for some sort of confrontation. I know this seems very unlikely but she was over-excited and – I don't know how to put this without sounding daft – but I do feel she's potentially violent. She's told me the only reason she's here is to get at Gaby. She even said – of course, I know she was joking, or half-joking, – she even said she'd strangle her.'

Margaret said, 'Don't you worry, Joan. I expect Viv's gone into town to get something she's run out of. She'll be back any moment now.'

'But I can't imagine her going off without seeing me first. She knew I was anxious to know how her session with Gaby had gone. She definitely promised to come back to our room after she'd seen Gaby. I've got an uneasy feeling that something's wrong.'

'What could go wrong?' Margaret said. 'Viv's a very lively girl but I don't think she'd do anything nasty to anyone.'

'I hope you're right. I wish I knew where she's gone and what happened with her and Gaby.'

'That's simple,' Chris said. 'Let's go and talk to Gaby. She'll tell us what happened. If anything did. Come on.'

'Chris the fixer,' Serena said.

Joan went with him out of the kitchen, followed by Tony and John, who were clearly determined to witness whatever drama, if any, might take place. Chris paused at the foot of the stairs, looking back at them both, as if to tell them that their presence was not welcome, but then he seemed to change his mind and proceeded up the stairs to the floor where the women had their rooms. The four of them stopped at Gaby's door. Chris knocked on it sharply. When there was no response he knocked again, a sustained and loud tattoo, but there was still no reply from within.

'Right!' he said purposefully and opened the door and stepped into the empty room.

The others followed and stood there, looking around and seeing nothing unusual except that the bed was unmade, the duvet pushed back to the foot of the mattress from which it spilled over on to the floor, close to a fallen pillow.

Chris stepped nearer to the bed, peering down at the undersheet. 'My God!' he said. 'Look at that! It looks like blood!'

John moved swiftly to join him. He gave one short nod. 'That's what it is,' he said.

Tony giggled. 'Murder most foul!' but then added quickly, with a glance at Joan, 'Sorry. Stupid of me!'

Chris, looking at no one in particular, said, 'D'you think I'd better ring the police?'

'Hang on a minute.' John's voice sounded suddenly authoritive and, to Joan, he seemed in a few moments to have grown taller. 'No need to panic.'

Tony, who was an admirer of the fiction of Martin Amis, said, 'John is a police.' He looked as if he were proud of his secret knowledge but, at the same time, not sure whether he should have revealed it.

'What?' Chris looked from one man to the other. 'What did you say?'

'I said John's a police – a policeman. He's a detective.'

Stamper had moved over to the chest of drawers, taking no notice of the exchange between Chris and Tony. The top drawer was slightly open. He pulled it farther out and extracted a blue cardboard box and held it up. 'Tampax,' he read aloud from the box, 'medium to heavy flow.' He dropped it back into the drawer which he closed. 'I don't think we need to start looking for the murder weapon.'

'Is that true?' Chris was staring at him. 'Are you really a copper?'

John nodded. 'Detective-Sergeant. I like to keep quiet about it when I'm off duty.'

'This seems like an odd place – ' Chris began but Joan interrupted:

'Where can they have gone? I don't understand it. What can they be doing?'

'*And* Viv's supposed to be on kitchen-duty,' Chris remarked, an uncharacteristic note of petulance in his voice.

Joan stared at him and he turned away with a slight shrug.

John opened the wardrobe in which Gaby's clothes were ranged, smart and orderly on their hangers. 'Well, I don't think they'll have gone far,' he said. 'I expect we'll be seeing them both before very long.'


Serena said, 'This evening we are very lucky to have Zak Fairbrass with us as our guest reader. I'm sure he needs no introduction from me but I'll just mention that his last book, *Dark Reservoir*, was the Poetry Book Society Choice and Andrew Mission said in *The Observer* . . . said . . . ' She looked down at her notes and read: ' . . . Zak Fairbrass's latest collection shows all of the astonishing linguistic power we have come to expect from this poet of the natural world whose exultant and visionary pantheism is in such refreshing contrast to the urban nihilism of so much contemporary poetry.'

Gordon, sitting between George and Joan Palmer near the back of the recital-room, exchanged smiles with Joan.

She whispered, 'What does urban nihilism mean?' and he gave a small shake of the head.

Serena went on: 'Zak's entry in *British and American Poets of Today* reads like this: "He is one of the most exciting talents to have appeared on the poetry scene during the past two decades and his explorations of the darker, more destructive forces in nature and in the human psyche are presented in language and imagery of dazzling variety and power."

'Well, I don't think that leaves anything much for me to say and in any case it's not me you want to listen to. So here he is . . . Zak Fairbrass . . . '

Serena slipped away to her chair at the side of the room and Fairbrass rose slowly from his seat at the table to face his audience. He was a big man in his late thirties with short-cropped hair of indeterminate colour and a bony, slightly equine face, with pale blue eyes. He wore in one ear a delicate and surprising earring. When he began to speak it was with a pronounced Yorkshire accent, but one curiously tinged with what sounded like a Texan drawl.

He said, 'The first poem' (he pronounced it paw-em) 'I'm going to read is one I wrote some while back after I'd been staying with some friends in Andalucia. It's called *Bull Rushes* – not bulrushes, all one word – but Bull . . . Rushes.' He seemed to glare at his audience as if challenging them to comment or contradict. Then he began to read in a sing-song yet rather rasping voice:

> 'Not the marsh or water plant,
> reed-mace, cat's-tail, or clubrush
> no thing of passive stasis this, but rush
> like blood-rush to the fortress forehead
> where the coarse hair curls and burns;
> thunder-rush of bludgeoning muscle,
> the great horns make massive music
> and the score is death.
> I, matador, male and maker, move
> not one retreating step but stay,
> honed pen poised to strike and pierce,
> plunge deep in blackness, shrill in the black blood
> where prophecies – '

His voice stopped abruptly and his mouth stayed open as he gazed to the back of the room where the door had opened to admit two latecomers, Gaby and Viv. Heads turned and all eyes were directed towards the two women. They were both smiling and looked a little flushed, as if from the cold night wind, and their smiles were mischievous, excited and conspiratorial.

Gaby called, 'Zak! I'm *so* sorry! We got held up. Couldn't be helped. Just give us a couple of seconds and we'll be with you.'

They were taking off their coats as they advanced into the room, and space was made for them in the second row from the front.

Joan, who had told Gordon a little of the afternoon's events, whispered, 'Well, they don't seem to have come to any harm,' and he nodded as Zak Fairbrass resumed his performance by starting *Bull Rushes* from the beginning again.

It was not long before Gordon found himself sinking into the torpid state of reverie that poetry-readings seemed to induce these days. In fact, he thought, there had never been a time when he could truthfully say that he enjoyed listening to poets declaiming their own work. For him, the reading of poetry had always been a private activity, even a secretive one in his school-days, when he feared he might be accused of pretentiousness or effeminacy by his sport-worshipping companions. And now, when familiar verse was spoken by its author or by an actor, the sounds he heard were never quite the same, or quite as satisfactory, as the verbal music that his silent reading created in his head. As for unfamiliar work, he simply could not comprehend it unless he followed the printed words on the page.

Then there was the additional distraction, or irritant, of the personality of the poet-reader, the idiosyncratic gestures of voice or body, the facial expressions or the real or affected displays of modesty, humility or aggressive arrogance, the carefully rehearsed impromptus, the adoption of a public face, all of this seemed good reason to keep away from poetry readings.

And yet, when he had once voiced these objections, and probably some others, to Susan she had said, 'If you feel like that about readings why do you do them yourself?' and he had answered, 'Because I get paid,' but he had known that this was not the whole truth, that there was something seductive about the temptation to perform one's work in public, to entertain, impress, or even touch the deeper emotions of an audience.

Another thing: there were people, quite a few, who genuinely preferred to listen to poetry being read by someone else rather than read it for themselves. Susan was one. In the early days of their life together he had often read poetry to her in the evenings and, as a consequence, he had been forced to revise the suspicion that those people, who would rather listen than read, understood little of what they heard, for she quite frequently surprised him by perceiving nuances and connections of meaning and association that, in some cases, had completely evaded him.

Dear Susan, he thought. Where was she now? He had telephoned again just before the evening meal but again there had been no reply. The most likely thing was that she'd decided to stay in Ealing with Pauline rather than come back to a lonely flat. He would have rung

Pauline but he had forgotten to bring his diary on this trip and he could never remember her number.

All the time he was vaguely aware that the poet's voice was pounding away, a rhythmic meaningless background to his thoughts, and, conscious of a slight feeling of guilt at his failure to attend, he made a deliberate effort to bring the words into focus.

Zak was holding the book he was reading from in his left hand, almost at arm's length, while his right hand waved and flapped in the air, perhaps in time to the rhythm of his lines, though sometimes his gestures seemed of a more dramatic and hortatory kind. Suddenly one finger pointed to the ceiling as he declaimed:

> '. . . and then
> from blood-clotted hair between taut thighs
> the butting skull thrusts. Skies wheel
> dark over curlew-canted moors;
> for a spiked, apocalyptic tick
> silence shrieks. And then the thin
> and juddering cry of nativity floats
> white annunciation through bruised air.'

Some of the audience made little murmuring noises of awe and wonder while Zak stared out over their heads with his strange pale glare. Then he began to shuffle through the pages of his book until he found what he was looking for.

'Next,' he said, 'another paw-em in the tradition of English nature poetry. I like to think that John Clare wouldn't mind this one. It's called *Pied Wagtail* and I don't think I need to say more than that. Here it is then:

> He struts in pied gear
> but he is no piper;
> this titch is athlete and acrobat.
>
> See, now, he runs and leaps
> springheel, but not to swank;
> what he is doing is dining,
>
> devouring insects as they ascend,
> gobbling them in fast gulps.
> His tail belies his name,

No doggish side-to-side wagger,
it shifts up and down, up and down,
dark admonitory finger.


In flight both aircraft and stunt-pilot
he loops the loop,
but he can also hover


motionless over stream or river,
to dip and sup on surface denizens.
loved by some, a cocky charmer,


to water-gnats and midges he
is a lethal shadow and a legend
of infinite power. He is the God terror.'

More thoughtful and appreciative murmurs and Gordon tried to sneak an unobserved glance at his watch. George, on his left, said, 'I see what you mean about agricultural. Doesn't he ever write about humans?'

'I think he'd say that he does, by metaphor and allegory.'

'Oh.'

The reading went on and Gordon drifted off, not quite into slumber but rather close to its inviting borders. He did not know how much time and poetry had passed when he was nudged by Joan who must have noticed his drowsiness.

She said softly, her lips close to his ear, 'I think he said this is going to be the last poem.'

He found her nearness both comforting and, in a muted way, stimulating. For a moment he felt the desire to touch her, not passionately but affectionately, to hold her hand, or even put an arm about her shoulders, though he quickly stamped on the impulse with impatient and self-mocking briskness. He tried hard to concentrate on what Zak was now announcing.

'And so,' the poet said, 'the paw-ems that I write aim at handling the kind of experience that takes us into other worlds while never leaving the world of men. I think a lot of you will probably know the one I'm going to finish by reading. It's something of a favourite with anthologists though I wouldn't go as far as to say it's my *Innisfree*, if you know what I mean. It's called *Wolf Man*, and here it is.' He began to intone.

Chris, who was sitting by himself near the door, was watching Kirsty. Shortly before the reading began she had come in with Margaret and had given Chris a careless smile and nod before going off to find a seat. This was the first time he had seen her since they had parted in the early hours of the morning and he had been waiting for this meeting with a mixture of mild apprehension, curiosity, and something less easy to define, an expectation of some kind of acknowledgement of their secret encounter perhaps, or a proprietorial claim on his attention. What he had not anticipated was her easy, casual greeting, as though nothing of any significance had occurred between them.

He could see her sitting with Margaret at the end of the second row and she was gazing up at Zak as he declaimed his poem and, though he could see only her profile, he could tell from her parted lips and total stillness that she was enthralled.

Zak was now punching the air with his right fist, almost like a soccer goal-scorer, but then his fingers opened and the flat of his hand was brandished in what could be seen as a sketchy Fascist salute or a signal for the audience to stay where they were as he chanted:

'. . . mists blurring the marshes,
a burly wind has bundled the clouds away.
The early stars were too venturesome,
they have been chomped by ravens,
spat out as dead cinders on the marl.
Soon the dark time, my time, will be here.
I wait in my hovel among cold bones
reading the black catechism of my religion.
I pray to the Wolf Zeus.
I have been instructed in the rites.
On Mount Lycaeus I munched sheep's bones and liver
garnished with wrists, elbows and plump nates.
If I could abstain for nine years I would be human again.
This is too much to demand.
I know where I must go.

The tombstones wait as patiently as ever,
itching under their coats of moss.
My whiskers bristle above the hard white collar.
I am at pains to conceal my tail.
The screech-owl yells its summons.
It is time to go.'

He very slowly lowered both the book and his gesturing right hand while continuing to stare with a curious look of defiance and what might be outrage in his unnervingly icy gaze. Then his head came down, and he stayed with chin on chest in an attitude of submission, and the audience heard him say, 'Thank you,' very quietly and humbly, and they began to applaud.

Chris saw that Kirsty was clapping with such enthusiasm that he thought she might well damage the palms of her hands.

Zak sat down at the table and Serena came to his side and the clapping petered out politely to allow her to be heard.

'Thank you, Zak,' she said. 'I'm sure everyone was as impressed as I was by that wonderful and powerful reading.' Then addressing the audience: 'Zak doesn't wish to take questions. As he says, you might as well question a tree or the ocean about its nature as ask a poet about his poems. But he'd be glad to have a chat informally with anyone at the pub.'

There was some more applause and then the assembly began to disperse. Chris saw Kirsty hasten to be the first to reach the poet and begin to talk to him with great animation. Zak looked down at her upraised, eager face and the slight rearrangement of the shape of his mouth was probably evidence of a smile. Then, together, they moved towards the door, followed quickly by Serena.

Kirsty did not give Chris even a glance as they went out, leaving him to examine his feelings, which were confused and confusing: relief was there, but only very faintly; jealousy was present, surprisingly strong and unequivocal and, somewhere, intermingled, a sad, irrational sense of loss.

# FRIDAY

THE CLEAR BRIGHT WEATHER of the previous three days was transformed. A strong north-easter swept across the valley and threw hail and sleet like frozen grapeshot against the windows of Crackenthorpe Hall. The louring skies were dark and lights were switched on for the morning workshop sessions, but there was no accompanying gloom among Gordon's students who seemed as keen to work as ever.

There had been, he thought, a muted excitement among them, a touch of end-of-term high spirits, but this had resulted in few lapses in concentration. He had set them to work on what they all agreed was an interesting exercise. This involved his choosing a short poem from the established canon that would not be easily recognised in the form in which he would present it to his class. What he had done was to make a rough prose paraphrase of the poem on the previous afternoon and Serena had made copies of it which he handed out to his students. This piece of writing, he told them, must be regarded as a prose draft of an unwritten poem and, using it as such, they were to write their own versions of that poem, choosing any form they wished.

The poem he had chosen was Keats's sonnet, beginning, 'Bright Star, would I were steadfast as thou art – ' and the students produced some strange and sometimes entertaining compositions which, at the end of the morning, they took it in turns to read aloud before Gordon declaimed the original to exclamations of recognition and wonderment.

Now Gordon was on his way back to his room to treat himself to a small whisky and water before lunch. He climbed the stairs, paused on the landing to recover his breath, then walked on to his door and was reaching for the handle when he stopped, his hand almost touching it, listening. He was almost sure he had heard a sound from inside the room. A second or two later he heard another noise, which could have been caused by a chair or table being moved, and quite convinced that someone was there he opened the door and stepped into the room.

Chris was in the act of straightening up from a crouching or perhaps kneeling position close to the wash-basin and in one hand he held a chisel and in the other a hammer.

'Hullo Gordon,' he said. 'I hope you don't mind me coming into your room while you're out but I'd got a few minutes to spare and it seemed like a good chance to check for dry rot. That smell you talked about. Could be dry rot. I believe the people who ran things here before Serena and me had a bit of trouble with it. That was downstairs in the library though, not up here. Anyway, I've had a couple of floorboards up and I can't see anything. Can't smell anything either. I'm told dry rot's got a pretty strong smell.'

'Sorry you've been put to any trouble.'

'No trouble. Have you smelled it since – when was it? Couple of days ago?'

'I don't think so. I mean no, no I haven't.'

'Oh well, we can't be too careful. Last night tonight. I expect you know we always have a bit of a party. Serena fixes a punchbowl – pretty good it is too – and if people want anything else – sherry or something – they can let me know and I can get it for them when I go in to do the shopping. Anybody just wanting red or white wine they can get it from me in the office.'

'We don't go to the pub then tonight?'

'No. Not on the last night. What happens is we have the students reading their own things after we've eaten. That's like Personal Choice night, in the library. When they've read their poems we wheel in the punchbowl and stuff. Margaret Baker's going to make some little snacks and we have a few drinks, sort of wind up the course, and everybody's happy. We hope.'

'Sounds quite fun,' Gordon said.

Chris grunted. 'Yeah. It usually is, though you'd be surprised. Sometimes odd things happen. People get over-emotional. Something to do with being cooped up together and not seeing anything of the outside world for a week. And all that what-you-call-it . . .

introspection . . . scratching away at emotional spots. I've seen tears and I've seen punch-ups at last-night parties.'

'Really? I hope we don't get either of those tonight.'

'You never know.'

Chris moved towards the door, then stopped. 'Gordon . . . ' he hesitated awkwardly. 'I was wondering if . . . '

'What?'

'Well, I was wondering if you think – or rather what you think of Serena's work, her poetry. What you've seen of it. I mean do you think it's any good?'

'Ah, er, yes . . . well . . . it's . . . er . . . '

Chris said quickly, 'Don't feel you've got to be tactful. I mean I wouldn't dream of telling Serena what you've said and I'm sure you wouldn't tell her I've asked you about it. I don't want to put you in a spot but it's important – very important – for me to know whether she's any good or not. This is strictly between ourselves, Gordon. It's not for her I'm asking. It's for me. I mean *I* want to know if she's any good, if there's any chance of her making it. I know I could help her, if only I was sure. You see, I've no idea really about poetry. Don't understand most of the stuff we've got in the library. I've just got this feeling it's not really her thing. When I first met her – about eighteen months ago that was – she was writing stories then. Didn't get them published or anything but they seemed pretty good to me. At least I knew what they were about. Her poems – well, even when I *can* understand them they don't seem up to much, they don't seem to be saying anything the slightest bit interesting. Not like her stories. They kept you wanting to go on reading.'

Gordon said cautiously, 'She's very young.'

'Twenty-six.'

'Well, that's young, isn't it?'

'Keats was dead by then, wasn't he?'

Gordon blinked, and then he grinned. 'Yes, true. But Keats was exceptional. Edward Thomas didn't write any poetry till he was in his late thirties. He was exceptional, too.'

'All right. She's young. But you've not really answered my question. Tell me honestly, Gordon. Do you think she's a poet? Do you honestly think she's got real talent?'

'I don't know. Probably not – look, you're sure you won't repeat a word of this to Serena?'

'Absolutely. I swear it. Not a word.'

'Very well. From the little I've seen of her work I'd say she's not especially gifted. Her poems look to me very much like the kind of thing that any literate young person could write. On the other hand I've seen worse stuff in the poetry magazines and even between the covers of books.'

'You mean like Melissa Hull?'

'Well, yes, I think I do. The kind of thing that deliberately sets out to frustrate understanding. There's a lot of it about. It's what I call The School of Gibberish. I suppose, in a way, it's quite a smart idea. I mean, if you write that sort of thing, critics can't take you to task for the weakness or banality of the content because it's impossible to say what the stuff's about. You can't say it's wrong-headed or banal because it's completely unintelligible. And you can't criticise it on the grounds of structural or formal weaknesses because it hasn't got any shape beyond a typographical one. But that's not what you want to hear about. At least Serena doesn't write that kind of rubbish.'

Gordon glanced at his bottle of *Famous Grouse* on top of the chest of drawers. 'Can I offer you a drink? I haven't a spare glass I'm afraid but you could get one from the kitchen.'

Chris shook his head. 'No thanks, but you go ahead. I'd better be going anyway. And thanks for your words about Serena's poetry. It's what I thought, and I think she half knows it herself.'

'Be careful what you say. People are very touchy about their poems. More than almost anything I can think of. It's like criticising their children.'

'I'll be careful.' Chris was at the door now, but he paused again. 'Oh, I almost forgot. I meant to ask you. What did you think of Zak Fairbrass's stuff?'

'Powerful . . . well, that's what all the reviewers say.'

'Yeah, but what do *you* think?'

'I think it's ham-fisted, a bit silly and in its own way sentimental. It's a mix of horror movie and muscle-bound Beatrix Potter. But a lot of very respectable people in the literary world think highly of it and would strongly disagree with me.'

Chris nodded thoughtfully. 'Seemed a funny sort of bloke. Kirsty seemed to go for him in a big way. When I took him to the station this morning she insisted on coming along to see him off.'

'Did she now? I'd have thought he's a bit long in the tooth for her.'

'I don't think she'd agree with you.'

'No . . . well. I suppose not . . . ' Gordon's eyes again flickered towards the whisky bottle.

Chris said, 'Right. I'm off. Be seeing you.'

'Yes. See you later.'

The door closed behind Chris, and Gordon at once poured himself a drink. The wind howled outside the window and flung another handful of hailstones at the smeared pane. Gordon swallowed the whisky and water, rinsed out the tumbler and went down to the kitchen for lunch.


Joan returned from Gordon's morning workshop to find Viv sitting at the table with a mug of coffee.

She said, 'I see you've managed to get up at last.'

Viv smiled a slow, lazy and secretive smile but made no reply.

On the previous night, after Zak Fairbrass's reading, she and Gaby had not travelled in the minibus to the pub but had driven there in Viv's Ford Fiesta and, when in the bar, they had sat apart from the main group in a corner of their own, conversing only with each other.

Joan had no idea of what time Viv had come back to their room, for she had been fast asleep, but she knew that it must have been well into the early hours of the morning because she had not gone to bed until after midnight and even then she had not immediately fallen asleep. When the time came for today's workshops to begin Viv had not stirred from her deep slumber.

'What happened yesterday?' Joan demanded. 'You were supposed to come back here and tell me how you'd got on with Gaby.'

Viv's smile was unchanged. 'Sorry. Things didn't work out quite the way I thought they would.'

'Evidently not. No fisticuffs? No hair-pulling? No strangling?'

'Nothing like that.' Viv's smile widened a little. 'Come and sit down and I'll tell you what happened. Some of it.'

'I want my lunch.'

'We'll go down for lunch later. Come and sit down.'

Joan, looking a little resentful, took the seat at the table opposite to Viv. 'Go on then. Tell me.'

'All right. What do you want to know?'

'Everything. What happened. Why you didn't come back. You *promised*!'

'Yes, I know I did. I'm sorry Joan. Really I am. But the way things turned out it wasn't possible.'

'Why not?'

'Because I had to go with Gaby. We had to get away somewhere quiet, to be on our own for a bit. Actually we'd both been through a – well, I can only say shattering experience. We had to calm down, in private, just the two of us.'

'But why? What happened? What about your chap, Dave? What did she have to say about that? About him? What you thought had happened.'

'Not a lot. Except she told me he'd spent most of his time on that course at Oaklands screwing some old bag he'd met there.'

'You mean it wasn't her? It wasn't Gaby? There was some other woman?'

'Yes. You were quite right, Joan. In a way. You said all along he hadn't been with Gaby. You thought he was just impressed by her mind or personality or something. It wasn't that either. When he came back and started banging on about Gaby, what he was doing was using her name as a kind of screen to hide the person he really was obsessed with. The one he wrote those stupid, dirty poems for. The one he was screwing all that week.'

'You quite sure that's true? I mean you were absolutely certain that Dave and Gaby had been at it, weren't you? Now you admit you were wrong about that. Mightn't you be wrong about the other things, too?'

'No.'

'Why not? Why are you so sure?'

'Because I *know*. Gaby told me.'

'But how did *she* know? Presumably she wasn't there when it was going on. She wasn't an eyewitness.'

'She knew. Everybody knew. It was obvious.'

'You only have Gaby's word for that.'

'Yes.' There was something maddening about the smug certainty of Viv's smile.

'In any case, I still don't see why you didn't come back here and tell me what had happened. We were worried, you disappearing like that.'

'*We* were worried? Who's *we*? Who did you talk to about us?'

'Only Chris and Serena . . . I think . . . oh yes, I'd forgotten. Tony and John Stamper were there too. I didn't tell anybody anything much. Only said I was worried because you hadn't come back from seeing Gaby. What did happen, anyway? You haven't really told me.'

'Nothing. I mean nothing that's any concern of anyone but Gaby and me. We talked. She told me a lot of things. She understands all sorts of things I'd never even thought about. I don't know. I think she might have changed the whole direction of my life. I'm sorry Joan but, to tell the truth, I forgot all about you, all about coming back here. All that mattered was that Gaby and I had to get away from the place for a while. Had to be on our own, away from everybody, everything.' Viv's smile had at last faded and she was staring at Joan with intense seriousness.

'Where did you go?'

'We went to a pub. Not the local, The Crook. Another one, just the other side of Ancliffe. It was nice and quiet. We had so much to talk about. We must have been there for hours.'

Although vestigial annoyance lingered, Joan's curiosity was aroused.

'What on earth did you find to talk about all that time?'

'Everything. All kinds of things. I can't really tell you because it would sound different if I tried. It would sound commonplace, ordinary, even silly if I tried to tell you. I mean Gaby's got a kind of magic – I know you'll think I've gone off my head talking like this. But the things she said and the way she said them made me see the whole of life, the whole world – everything – men, women, love and all that – in a new and marvellous and kind of scary way. It was fantastic.'

Joan was looking at her closely now. She said, 'You and Gaby talked. Is that all you did? You just talked? How long were you in Gaby's room before you went off to the pub?'

Slowly the inward-looking, secretive smile returned to Viv's eyes and mouth. Then she said, 'Long enough.'

The two women looked in silence at each other for a moment or two. Then Joan said, 'Long enough for what?'

Viv's smile was unwavering and it now contained a tiny hint of mockery. 'For what had to happen,' she said, 'and that is nobody's business but mine and Gaby's. So let's go down and have something to eat, shall we?'

The students' reading of their own work began shortly after eight o'clock in the library where Chris had persuaded Sludgens to light a log fire, its bitter-sweet scent and cheerful blaze adding to the atmosphere of mild excitement and festivity. At the evening meal of boeuf bourguignon and rice (with cauliflower cheese for the vegetarians), followed by black cherry gateaux, more wine than usual had been bought and consumed so, as they all waited for the evening's entertainment to get under way, there was a sharp edge of nervous anticipation in the air, and the laughter and conversation were louder and more boisterous than on previous occasions.

As on the Personal Choice event, Serena, sitting with Chris at one end of the long table, was in charge of the proceedings and she had to call out three times and bang quite loudly on the table-top before all the noise subsided and she was able to begin her introductory remarks. 'You don't need me to tell you,' she began, 'that this is the last event of the course and in many ways it is the one we look forward to most. As you've been told, but I think it's worth mentioning once more, each person will read only one poem or, in the case of it being a *very* short one, maybe one other. In any case, no one can read for more than five minutes. This means, allowing for any introductory remarks and so forth, the whole thing shouldn't take more than an hour and a half. When the readings are over we'll bring in my super punchbowl and we'll have a little party.

'Right. Now for the real business. We'll start here, on my right, with Bernard. Then we'll go round the table anti-clockwise – Maureen, Eileen, Arthur and so on. If each of the readers will say just a few words about their poem – that is, if they feel like it – so much the better. The main thing though, of course, is the poetry. So, to start with, let's hear Bernard.'

Bernard stood up and opened a large, spiral-bound notebook. He cleared his throat and smiled nervously. Then he began, 'I know you'll think – well, some of you will think – my poem is a bit old-fashioned. But it's the only way I seem able to write verse. I suppose we all try to write the kind of poems we like to read and, in the end, that's what I've done. I haven't given it a title, but you could just take the first few words and call it by those – *When I was young* . . . All right . . . here it is:

When I was young I never guessed
What lay in wait for me:
Lack of breath and hair, girls' eyes
That look but do not see.

Or, if they see, the thing they see
Is something useless, sad;
Not a brisk and handsome chap,
A lively golden lad.

The hand that swung the cricket bat
And hurled the spinning ball
Is withered now and scarce can grasp
Anything at all.

The eyes that gleamed with health and fun
Are dulled with pain and cares;
The limbs that sped o'er hill and dale
Can hardly climb the stairs.

A wise, compassionate old man
Should have counselled me,
Told me to avoid strong drink
And live abstemiously.

So I would now be heartier
And not a wretched sight,
A lonely man with nought to come
But dark and endless night.

But if I warned some lively lad
To change his ways or he
Would end his days in misery
He'd only laugh at me.

> For church bells to the young are sweet;
> They speak of joy and birth;
> The young are deaf to bells that call
> The old to lie in earth.'

Bernard sat down and murmured something to Maureen on his right who was joining in the enthusiastic applause.

Tony, near the bottom of the other side of the table, called 'Great stuff Bernard! You *are* a bit of a Shropshire lad, aren't you?'

Bernard grinned and nodded. 'So you spotted the influence, Tony! I wondered if anybody would.'

George muttered to Gordon, 'Nobody could miss it, could they? Still, it wasn't bad, was it?'

Now Maureen had risen and was turning the pages of a rather battered notebook. She spoke with more confidence than Bernard had shown because she was accustomed to reading aloud at the meetings of her Writers' Circle.

She said, 'I'm going to read a very short poem, or you could call it a little sequence, about the different seasons in the city. It probably doesn't sound like it, but I've spent a lot of time and hard work trying to get it right. Originally it was written in regular metre and rhyme but Gordon suggested I did it in syllabics. So that's what I did. It's called *City Weathers*:

> Rain spits and sizzles silver
> on dark pavements, gurgles in gutters.
> Heels click; jumble of slick umbrellas.
>
> Summer frocks, airborne petals
> drift through the park. From green courts we hear
> thwack and twang; then voices bouncing high.
>
> Headlamps in the morning mist
> bloom, pale chrysanthemums, the scent of
> old memories. Leaves scuffle on stone.
>
> Autumn's contralto lingers,
> fades and dies. Darkness. The last bus leaves,
> gold galleon, sinking in the night.'

Maureen's audience was clearly impressed and she sat down, smiling pinkly and pleased.

Joan, on Gordon's right, said, 'I thought that was rather good, didn't you?'

He nodded. 'Yes. I hope she doesn't switch altogether from metre and rhyme though. The first version was all right, too, in its way.'

Chris was speaking in a low voice to Serena: 'That was nice and short. We should get through pretty smartly if there's more like that.'

Serena frowned. 'It was a good poem. And *not* because it was short.'

Eileen was now introducing her offering, an account of a childhood memory of a Sunday School outing which ended in her miserable humiliation when, on the return journey from the seaside, she was sick over her best dress. The poem was composed in regularly rhyming pentameters, and the narrative was competently handled, though there was nothing particularly memorable about the language or imagery.

Next, Arthur read another anecdotal piece in rather rugged rhymed couplets about the first moon-landing in 1969, when he was returning from an evening concert to his home in the Leicestershire village where he then lived, and he saw old Ernie, one of the regular patrons of the local inn, staring up at the sky. The poem ended with Ernie calling out in great excitement for Arthur to join him:

> 'Ernie called me over. "Look up there!"
> He cried, his finger pointing up to where,
> Unveiled of cloud, the moon shone pale and bright.
> "Did you see it?" he enquired. "My sight
> Ain't what it used to be but I could swear
> I spotted movement on the moon up there!"'

A few chuckles accompanied the clapping and then it was George's turn to read. He whispered to Gordon, before he stood, 'I feel more windy than I did in action,' and then he rose. 'I'm going to read a sonnet,' he said. 'You can blame Gordon because he set us working on sonnets. Christmas was the subject he said we should write about. So what I'm trying to say in this one is that Mary thought everyone would think she was off her head if she told them an angel had come along and told her she was going to have a baby. They'd think she was mad. But when the shepherds – these ordinary men, came to the manger and said they'd seen an angel – a crowd of angels actually – this came as a great relief to her. She knew she wasn't crazy. Well, that's the general drift. I call it *Mary and the Shepherds*:

> The lamplight flickered in the cattle-shed
> As she was mauled by claws and teeth of pain;
> Her piteous cries for mercy all in vain
> As her racked body writhed on that rough bed.
> The air was cruelly cold, or so they said
> Afterwards, when she was once again
> Herself, and not the creature who had lain
> For hours that night in agony and dread.
>
> She was a mother now. At last she slept
> Until the shepherds came and begged to view
> Her newborn child. With joy she laughed and wept.
> That they had seen an angel made her glad
> Beyond all words, because these men, she knew,
> Were plain folk like herself, and were not mad.'

George sat down to exclamations of admiration from Margaret, and general applause which carried an undercurrent of surprise that the old soldier should produce such an unmartial poem.

He looked a little embarrassed but decidedly gratified by the reception his performance received. 'I do believe they liked it,' he said to Gordon.

'So they should. It was pretty good. I bet you worked hard at it.'

'I did. Spent hours on the damn thing.'

Joan murmured, 'Oh dear. It's me now.'

Gordon touched her arm lightly. 'You'll be fine,' he said.

She extracted her villanelle from her folder and stood up. The noise of conversation dwindled and died away into an expectant silence.

She said, 'I've done a villanelle. Those who've worked with Gordon will know about the form. It's very tricky but not quite as difficult as it looks. Perhaps I shouldn't say that. I mean maybe mine's no good at all, but at least I think I've got the pattern right. I haven't given it a title, mainly because I'm not sure what it's about. So I'll just call it *Villanelle*. It goes like this:

> These summer evenings as the dark descends
> I hear a silent music in the air;
> I see the spectral faces of old friends.
>
> Those I hurt and never made amends,
> Mistakes I know I never can repair
> These summer evenings as the dusk descends.
>
> I cannot say why this dumb music blends
> So softly with those shadowed places where
> I see the spectral faces of old friends.
>
> This moment when the bruised heart comprehends
> A little of the burden all must bear
> These summer evenings as the dusk descends.
>
> I feel a tender influence extends
> Promise of forgiveness if I dare
> See the spectral faces of old friends.
>
> Love and courage share the same bright ends
> Without which we are left with our despair;
> These summer evening as the dusk descends
> I see the spectral faces of old friends.'

Again the listeners' response contained surprise as well as admiration, and Gordon, seeing her faintly flushed and grateful expression was touched by a feeling of protective tenderness that was, he knew, not quite paternal.

He whispered, 'That was terrific, Joan. And beautifully read. Lovely.'

Then John Stamper stood up. He was holding a reporter's notebook which he riffled through until he found the page he wanted. 'Ah yes, here we are,' he said. 'This is the one. I did quite a lot of drafts but this is the final one. It's a sonnet, like George's. I don't mean it's as good as his but it's about the same subject from a different angle. Christmas. Mine's set in modern times though. One for today:

> Expensive fragrances enrich the air,
> Strong Havana, delicate *Chanel*,
> As limousines, outside the great hotel,
> Disgorge the wealthy, powerful and fair
> Who seem oblivious of those who stare
> And shiver on the pavement and expel
> Their misty sighs of longing as they smell
> The other, savoury scents, from inside there.
>
> This is Christmas Eve. Tomorrow sees
> The birthday of the Saviour of our kind,
> Though some, it seems, are saved so they can freeze,
> Hungry and unhoused, as they have slept
> So many times before while others dined
> In this, the city over which Christ wept.'

Through the sound of clapping and a few appreciative sighs Gordon heard George mutter, 'A darned sight better than mine, damn his eyes.'

Joan must have overheard for she said, speaking across Gordon on her left, 'No. I liked yours better. Truly. It's a lovely poem!'

George beamed. 'Nice of you to say so. Still, John's was pretty good, wasn't it?'

'I still prefer yours.'

Tony was now on his feet. 'Upstaged again,' he said. 'Anything after John's superb sonnet will seem trivial. Especially my poor things. However, I'll try to compensate for their deficiencies with my golden-voiced delivery.

'I think you said we're allowed five minutes, Serena. So I'm going to read two tiny pieces and then a little surprise, a sort of *found* poem. Don't look alarmed, dear, I promise I won't run over time.

'Here's my first little snippet. It's called *Wearing Out the Answer-phone*:

> Bananas are my favourite tune.
> I sing them when I take off my dress
> to immerse myself in the Gardener's Companion.

> My neighbour knocks on the wall
> with yellow knuckles.
> I can see them shining.
>
> If you have something to tell me
> whisper it softly.
>
> I know about the confetti in my hair.'

The reaction of the audience was the quietest so far. There was a perfunctory patter of applause and a couple of uncertain titters.

Then Gaby called out, 'I liked that very much Tony. It reminds me of Melissa Hull.'

Tony nodded. 'Yes. Good. It was meant to,' he said. 'And now for the next little one. It's called *Millennial Elegy*:

> After the Eastern Bloc collapsed
> he developed a passion for patience
> (lower case) and became a fellow-traveller
> with ragamuffins led by one Nahum
> who had failed to graduate.
>
> It was later, in the supermarket,
> near to the check-out, he was browbeaten
> by bully-boys to change his tunic
> who were not to know their deed
> would sink the white long-boat in the loch.
>
> All of this would be recorded
> and filed away in stone archives
> with the photographs of passers-by
> clad in diaphanous ninon,
> all too late for the last sitting.'

If anything the response to this was less enthusiastic than ever but Tony did not seem in the least abashed by this.

'And now,' he said, 'begging your indulgence. Here, on this scrap of paper, are a few stanzas from an unpublished poem called *Mummy*. I understand, from a source I've promised not to reveal, the manuscript was found in an attic in a Devonshire farmhouse. You might like to hazard a guess at the name of the author.' He began to read, affecting a Deep South drawl:

'You stand at the window, mummy,
In the picture I have of you
With your permanent wave and your cupid's bow lips
And frock with waistline hugging your hips
And your eyes of such deep-sea blue.

No wonder the whole world loved you
And the beaux lined up to woo.
You looked like a movie star,
I'd have paid for a seat to watch you eat
The hearts they served up for you.

But what was it made you choose
The man with the Aryan nose
And big black coat and a hook of steel
Instead of a hand, and an iron mouth
That chomped and swallowed you.

But I could make him spew.
He just had to look at me,
And that's what he did, he up-threw,
And you were as good as new,
Once I'd mopped all the goo off of you.

Mummy, you're looking good now,
All I want is you.
We've got rid of the shit in the bottomless pit
And now it's just me and you.
Mummy, mummy, you darling, it's true.'

Tony smiled round the table, eyebrows raised in a kind of benign interrogation, then he returned the sheet of paper to his yellow folder and sat down. At first there was no applause at all, then the lightest flutter of clapping followed quickly by whispering and muttering which steadily increased in volume.

Joan said to Gordon, 'It wasn't really by Sylvia Plath, was it?'

'No. It was a Tony joke. A parody. Not bad either.'

George said, 'What did you say? What was it?'

'A parody of a poem by Sylvia Plath called *Daddy*. You've heard of Plath?'

'Yes. Heard of her. Don't think I've ever read anything by her though.'

Serena interrupted the talk: 'That was very clever Tony. But we'd better get on. You're next Viv. What have you got for us?'

Viv, sitting next to Gaby, smiled and shook her head. 'Sorry. I haven't got anything. Nothing suitable, anyway.'

Serena began to protest but Gaby's voice briskly rose over hers: 'Viv hasn't anything she wants to make public. She's done a lot of good work but doesn't feel any of it's quite ready for public performance. Even among friends. And that must be respected of course.'

Serena looked as if she might try to persuade Viv to change her mind but Chris said quickly, 'It's Freda then. Hope you've got something worth putting on show.'

'I don't know about that,' Freda Jones said, 'but I'll give it a try. It's a short poem called *Autumn*. Not a very original title I'm afraid. The point I'm trying to make, without actually stating it, is just as the season of autumn has its consoling beauties quite different from spring and summer, so does the autumn of life – in other words middle age – have compensations to offer. I hope. Here we go then . . . *Autumn*.'

Freda read the poem, which was written in five rhyming quatrains and contained some quite sharply drawn visual images, though the metre was, Gordon thought, too plodding to be wholly satisfactory. She sat down to friendly applause and, after a few moments, her friend, Carol Lumsden, rose to read.

Carol said, 'When I was very young, no more than about sixteen or so, I used to have, as a bedside book, a little anthology of what was then called Modern Poetry. The book was one of my dad's and it must have been at least twenty years old when I was reading it, and that was longer ago than I care to specify. Anyway, there was a particular poem in this anthology that annoyed me then and has annoyed me ever since. It's quite well known – I expect you've all come across it – and it's by a woman called Frances Cornford who was a friend of Rupert Brooke. It's the one that begins "O why do

you walk through the fields in gloves missing so much and so much?
O fat white lady whom nobody loves . . . " and so on.

'Well, for years and years I've wanted to have a go at Cornford for
her insensitivity and snobbishness, and that's what I've tried to do in
this piece of verse. I've given it the title of *To a Georgian Lady Poet*.
So here it is:

> O poetry lady who travelled first class,
> Watching the meadows and trees as they pass,
> Why did you sneer in your silly pink hat
> At the woman in gloves? Because she was fat?
> Or because she wore gloves? I can't quite see why
> Either could possibly justify
> Your scorn and judgmental superior pose;
> You'd no right at all to look down your thin nose.
> And how come you possessed the ineffable gall
> To claim she was loved by no one at all?
> I very much doubt that her life was without
> The spices of loving, although she was stout.
> There might have been medical reasons for
> That avoirdupois and the gloves that she wore;
> So there's no real excuse for your sniffy disdain,
> Or the rubbish you wrote as you rode on that train.'

This went down very well with everyone, though Gordon
suspected that there might be a few who were not familiar with the
poem's target. He wondered if Carol knew that Chesterton had
been angered by the poem and had aimed his own barbed shaft at
it, but he decided he wouldn't ask her because, if she didn't know
of its existence, to be told would almost certainly spoil her sense of
achievement.

'I know that fat white lady poem,' George said, 'and I agree with
Carol. I never thought it was funny, if that's what it's supposed to
be.'

Kirsty was now on her feet, clutching a notepad, looking
nervous but still a little belligerent. She said, 'I don't know whether
you remember but I came here because I thought Brian MacDuff was
going to be one of the tutors. But I'm glad I came now because, if I

hadn't, I probably wouldn't ever have got to know Zak Fairbrass's poetry. I still like Brian MacDuff's things but I see now that they're not in the same class as Zak's, Zak Fairbrass, that is. I mean it's the difference between talent and genius really. I was lucky enough to spend some time with him last night and we talked about all kinds of important things, the environment and politics and the third world and all that. Anyway, after he'd gone back this morning I thought some more about all the things we'd discussed and I spent all afternoon writing this poem called *Vengeance of the Trees*.' She held her notepad in both hands and, in her rather flat, monotonously pitched voice, began to read:

> 'There were no trumpets, or not the kind
> that humans can hear. Except for the rustle
> of leaves they advanced in silence,
> coming from mountains, valleys and hills
> and parks and big gardens of rich people,
> juniper and fir, elm and poplar,
> chestnut, oak and tree of heaven,
> maple and cedar, all the trees in the world
> were on the move, marching towards the city
> where the rich fat cats were hiding,
> or trying to hide, all to no avail
> because the trees would get their revenge
> for all the awful things inflicted on them
> In the names of profit and progress.'

The listeners, unsure of whether or not the poem had ended, failed to react for a couple of seconds; then Gaby led the quite vigorous clapping and Kirsty sat down, still contriving to look childishly pugnacious though she was clearly pleased with her own performance. Chris, Gordon noticed, was not applauding but looking at Kirsty with a sceptical and rather sour grin.

Margaret Baker, the last one to perform, then stood up and read a rather charming little poem about her cat, Sheba, who during the day seemed a mild, affectionate, entirely domesticated character, but at night became transformed, a predatory beast who terrorised the smaller neighbourhood creatures though, the next morning – as Margaret said:

'. . . at breakfast we would find
Sheba on the carpet, curled,
Purring softly, tame and mild,
In our human sunlit world.'

When everyone had stopped clapping and congratulating Margaret, Serena stood up and said, 'Chris and I are going out to the kitchen for a few minutes to see that the punchbowl's all right. As you see, there's wine and glasses over there so, if you want to start on that, you're welcome to. The punch won't be long . . . Come on, Chris . . . '

Margaret called , 'I'll come with you and get the snacks!' and she followed them out of the library while the others, chattering, started to rise from the table and gather in little groups as the end-of-course party began.


Serena's punchbowl was a great success and she received compliments from most of the people at the party. It was also very potent, though its strength was disguised by the innocent spiciness and fruitiness of its fragrance and flavour. Even Bernard and Arthur were seen clutching glasses of the stuff, and Maureen and Eileen were drinking with evident relish and the brightness of their eyes and the frequency and slight shrillness of their laughter were testimony to its potency.

Gaby, who was standing with Tony and John, was saying, 'But what's the purpose, what's the *relevance* of parody? I know it can be very clever, Tony, but isn't it basically destructive? Isn't there something mean and envious about it?'

'I don't think so,' Tony said. 'I suppose it's a lightweight genre but it can work as criticism when it's done well. Hugh Kingsmill's parodies of Housman make a point about the old doom-and-gloom-monger as well as being skilful and funny and the J. K. Stephens Wordsworth sonnet is marvellous.'

'Housman, Wordsworth . . . well, yes, maybe it's all right to take the piss out of guys like that but it's a different matter when it comes to a great poet and tragic figure like Plath.'

'You mean she's beyond criticism? Is that because she's a woman or because she killed herself? Or both?'

'Of course not. Neither. It's because she's a great poet.'

'Ah, I see. And Housman and Wordsworth aren't up there in the same league?'

'Well, no, they're not. Certainly not Housman anyway.'

Gordon, who might have enjoyed debating that, was standing a few yards away with Joan and George and, a moment later, they were joined by Chris who announced, 'I just heard something on the News. Those rapes and murders – I expect you've read about them. They've arrested somebody for them. About time too.'

John must have overheard this for he muttered an excuse to Tony and Gaby and crossed quickly to Gordon's group. 'What was that you said, Chris? Something about the murders? An arrest?'

'Yeah. On the News. They've got somebody for them. Well what they actually said was a man's being held for questioning. I don't think they gave his name.'

'Where? Where's he being held? Did they say?'

'No . . . wait a minute. Yes. Yes they did. Somewhere in Buckinghamshire. I think it was Aylesbury.'

'Thanks.'

John moved away and interrupted whatever Tony was saying. 'Sorry. I've got to go. Something's come up. Excuse me, both of you.' And he pushed his way through the crowded library to the door.

Tony stared after him and then said, 'Forgive me Gaby I've got to go and see what's going on!' and he, too, hurried out of the room and up to the bedroom, that John still nominally shared with George, to find him throwing his belongings haphazardly into his bag.

'What's happening, John? What are you doing? Why are you packing?'

John fastened his valise and went over to the wardrobe where his cap and raincoat were hanging. 'I've got to go, Tony. It's that big case I mentioned the other day, the one I was working on before I came up here. It was my case. I should never have taken this leave. Sorry Tony but I've got to go. They've picked up a suspect. Chris heard it on the News. I think I know who they've got and I need to be there for the interviews. So that's it. Must go.'

'But you can't! Not at this time of night. Wait till morning, John. Please. If you get an early start you'll be there before noon tomorrow.'

'I told you. I've got to go. Now.' He was pulling on his raincoat and then his cap.

Tony looked very young and forlorn and powerless. He said, 'Let me carry your bag down.'

John grinned faintly. 'I think I can manage it.'

He picked up his valise and went out of the room, followed by Tony, and they both descended the stairs and went out to where John's four-year-old VW Golf was parked.

The rain was still falling but the wind was not so strong now.

John threw his bag on to the rear seat of the car and turned and looked at Tony. 'You get back inside, son,' he said, 'You'll get soaked out here.' He sounded more like a policeman than ever before.

'I wish you'd wait till morning.'

John shook his head. 'No can do. Sorry.'

'Drive carefully then. And you'll write won't you? Or call me. You've got my number and address, haven't you?'

John nodded. 'I'll be in touch. Don't worry.'

They embraced for only a moment before he got into his car. He did not lower the window for a final word of farewell or reassurance.

Tony stayed there in the steadily weeping night as the car engine snarled and grunted into life and the beams from the headlamps leaped forward and the rain flickered and glittered in them as it swept down. The car moved away and Tony saw its rear-lights disappear as it turned out of the drive and into the rough road that led down to the main thoroughfare. He waited for a few seconds until the noise of the engine had died away and then he went back inside.

He could hear the hum and buzz of talk and laughter coming from the library. He hesitated, but only very briefly, before he went back to the party.

Kirsty saw him come in. His dark hair was wet and curling from the rain, and the drops on his eyelashes and face might have been tears. She was half-way through her third glass of punch and feeling warm and at ease with herself and the world. The image of Tony and John, naked on the bed, came suddenly into sharp focus, a memory that, deliberately or not, she had managed to keep, for most of the time, locked away in some mental compartment of defensive forget-fulness, but now it did not bring with it the expected feelings of shocked revulsion; instead there was something almost appealing and obscurely exciting about it.

She said to Margaret and Serena who were with her, 'Excuse me a sec. Just going to have a word with Tony.'

He saw her approaching but, before he could make an unobtrusive escape, she was close to him, looking, he thought, just a trifle pissed.

She said, 'You're wet. What you been doing, Tony?'

'Singing in the rain.'

Kirsty giggled. Then she said, 'Have some of this. It's lovely. Here, take my glass. I'll get another.'

'No. No thanks Kirsty. I've got a bottle of Chablis over there that we'd only just started when John had to go.'

'Where? Where's he gone? Why'd he have to go?'

'He's a policeman. A detective. An arrest's been made in a big case he was working on and he had to go and question the prisoner.'

'You're kidding me again.'

'No. It's true. That's why he had to go.'

'Oh . . . well, come on. Let's go over there and get your wine. A drink'll cheer you up.'

As she and Tony moved away to find the bottle of Chablis Chris joined Serena and Margaret. He gazed thoughtfully after the younger pair and said, 'She seems to have made a good recovery from her terrible experience, doesn't she?'

'What experience?' Margaret said.

Serena spoke quickly, before Chris could say anything more: 'She had some bad news but she doesn't want it talked about. Remember, Chris? She specially asked us not to talk about it to anyone.'

Margaret looked from one to the other, eyebrows slightly raised.

Chris nodded. 'Yeah. Silly of me. I forgot.'

George was saying, '. . . honestly Joan, I can't think how you did it. Don't you agree Gordon? That – what-you-call-it, villa-something – I couldn't even work out how it's put together, let alone write one myself.'

Gordon smiled at Joan. 'I agree with George. It was fine. You should be very pleased with it.'

'But your sonnet,' she protested to George, 'was at least as good. It was Petrarchan, wasn't it Gordon? Well, that's every bit as difficult to do as a villanelle.'

George beamed. 'All right. We're both geniuses. You agree with that, Gordon?'

Joan said, 'You were quite right, Gordon, about the way the form helps you if you've got the patience to stick at it and get the things finished. I mean if you finish a villanelle and get it right it's almost bound to be at least readable.'

'Yours was more than just readable.'

George said, 'What about a refill? How's your glass Joan? . . . Gordon? Drop more of the red stuff?'

Gordon handed over his empty glass. 'If you'll excuse me, I'll be back in a minute or two. Something I've just remembered.'

At the other end of the room Kirsty took another sip of punch. 'Tony,' she said, 'what did you think of Zak Fairbrass's poetry?'

'I thought it was . . . ' Tony paused while he searched for the right word. 'Elemental,' he said.

Kirsty peered at him uncertainly. 'What do you mean? I don't know what that means exactly.'

'It means, ah – pertaining to the elements, fire, earth, air and water. Fairbrass's poetry is earthy. You could say it's fiery, too, I suppose. Don't know so much about airy – though I think you could say it's quite often wet.'

'He's a great poet though, isn't he? Such power.'

Tony drank some of his wine. 'To tell you the truth, Kirsty, I didn't go a bundle on him or his poetry, if that's what it is. But perhaps I'm not the person you should be talking to about him. I've never been very keen on the notion of the poet as Tarzan, or King Kong.'

Kirsty smiled indulgently. 'You do say some silly things.'

'I know. I can't help it.'

Kirsty lowered her voice unnecessarily, indeed against the noise of the party, almost inaudibly, and looked around as if ensuring that she, or they, were not under observation. 'Tony,' she said. 'I don't want you to think I don't understand. I do want us to be friends in spite of . . . you know . . . everything. You don't think I'm homophonic, do you?'

'Think what? I didn't quite catch what you said.'

'Homophonic. You know, prejudiced about gays.'

'Ah, homophonic. Goodness me, no! Not for a minute did I think that.'

Kirsty nodded and smiled with self-satisfaction and sipped a little more punch.

Upstairs, above the library, Gordon was standing in the middle of his room holding an open book in his hands. It was his own *Selected Poems* and he had decided to give it to Joan Palmer. He knew that he had two other copies at home so the gift was not extravagantly generous. What he was now hesitating over was the matter of an inscription. Should he simply write his full name on the flyleaf or title-page or should he add a conventional 'best wishes'? Or should he sign his full name over the printed words on the title-page and then add a personal message from 'Gordon' and, if so, what kind of message?

He felt real affection for her and was tempted to express this, but his natural reticence and fear of appearing presumptuous or absurd were deterrents. Finally he came to a decision, placed the book on the table, bent over and wrote on the flyleaf *To Joan with love and best wishes from Gordon* and, tucking the book under his jacket, he went back down to the party.

George greeted his return: 'Ah, there you are! We were wondering what had happened to you. Here's your drink. I'm just about ready for another.'

Gordon took his drink. 'Why not get yourself one?'

George drained the little that was left in his glass. 'I think I will. What about you, Joan?'

'No thanks. I've got plenty here.'

When George had gone for his refill Gordon brought out the *Selected Poems* from under his jacket. 'I've got this for you,' he said. 'It's a bit worn-looking but not too bad.'

She took the book, glanced at the title on the spine and said at once, 'Oh no, I couldn't possibly. It's terribly nice of you Gordon but – '

'Why not? I've got a couple at home. I really would like you to have it. Honestly, I mean if you really want – look out. George is coming back. Please take it.'

George arrived with his fresh glass of wine. 'Most of the punch is gone,' he told them. 'What's that you've got, Joan?'

'Oh, just a book,' she said and she and Gordon exchanged brief complicitous smiles.

George looked from one to the other but did not comment. Then he said, 'It's been a funny old week hasn't it? Seems longer. A bit odd to think that none of us – well, very few of us – are ever going to meet again.'

They all three looked around at the lively assembly and each smiled, though with a touch of valedictory melancholy.

Well out of their hearing, Gaby was saying, 'What do you say to slipping out to the pub Viv? It's only just after ten. It's so noisy in here. Let's go in your nice little car, shall we?'

Viv nodded and they put their glasses on to the table and moved to the door.

Both Eileen and Maureen, who were chatting with Arthur and Bernard, noticed them and Eileen called out, 'Not going yet are you? The night is young!' Then she laughed rather wildly as Gaby answered, 'Maybe. But *I'm* not,' and she and Viv went out of the library.

Kirsty was saying to Tony, whose smile was beginning to resemble a frozen grimace and whose eyes were inclined to skitter away from his interlocutrix's eager gaze, 'I can see – course I can – it's obvious why you don't go for Zak's kind of poetry. It's so masculine, if you know what I mean. There's nothing airy-fairy about – '

'Excuse me Kirsty . . . ' there was a note of desperation in Tony's interruption, 'I think Carol's leaving and I simply must have a word with her about . . . ah . . . so excuse me for a moment or two.'

Carol was surprised when Tony joined her and Freda and Margaret for, during the course, he had seemed scarcely aware of their existence. Now he was smiling at them in a most friendly way.

'Ah, Carol,' he said, 'I must tell you how much I liked your Frances Cornford demolition job. Lovely! I thought you got it just right. Not too vitriolic. Just the right measure of contempt the thing deserves.'

Carol's usual self-possession was more than a little disturbed by Tony's unexpected praise. She blinked and her complexion, already warmed by Serena's punch, seemed to deepen a shade. She said, 'Oh. . . . well, yes. Thank you.' Then she added, as she regained a little composure, 'It wasn't a patch on your Sylvia Plath take-off though.'

Tony did not look in the least embarrassed by Carol's praise. He said, 'Actually, she wrote one or two quite pretty poems.'

Carol looked puzzled, even a little shocked. 'Pretty? Sylvia Plath?'

'No, no, Frances Cornford. Have you seen the ones in Larkin's *Oxford Book*? Only three or four, but a couple of them are rather lovely in a low-key way.' He turned to Margaret. 'I liked your pussy, too. *And* your sad little Autumnal piece, Freda. Well, it's been a lovely evening and it's beddy-byes for me. So good night and sweet dreams.'

Then with an almost benedictory raising of one hand, he turned and headed for the door without looking back at Kirsty who was standing alone, clutching her now empty glass and watching his departure with bemusement.


'I think it all went rather well,' Chris said as he brought two mugs of instant coffee into the living-room and put them on the table at which Serena was already sitting. 'Not a drop of your punch left.'

'No. An awful mess though.'

'We'll clear that away in no time tomorrow. Ivy'll come in and help. Then we've got a whole day to ourselves.' He sat down at her side and touched her left wrist gently. 'You were great tonight Serena. I was proud of you, the way you ran the readings and the party and everything.'

She said, 'I wasn't very proud of you when you nearly told Margaret about Kirsty and – you know – Tony and John Stamper.'

'I thought Kirsty would've already told her, seeing they share a room. I wouldn't have thought Kirsty's one to keep quiet about a thing like that.'

'Well, I'm sure she did keep quiet. If she'd have told Margaret, everybody in the place would have been going on about it. I don't mean Margaret's specially a gossip-monger but that kind of thing's bound to be talked about.'

'Yeah. I'm sure you're right. I should've thought of that.'

'Oh well. No harm done.'

He thought he heard something conciliatory in her voice, an absence of the edginess that had been present for the past few days.

He said, 'It's been one of the odder ones, hasn't it, this course?'

A pause. Then: 'Yes, I suppose it has.'

They sipped their coffee. 'Next week's should be easier. They're all teachers from the same London Borough, aren't they?'

Serena nodded but did not say anything.

'Tired, love?'

'A bit. Not very . . . I was thinking . . . '

'What? What were you thinking?'

'Oh, I don't know . . . about Kirsty and Tony and that night.'

'What about it?'

'You fancied her a bit, didn't you?'

'Who? Kirsty? No! Not at all. Not a bit.'

'You spent a long time that night with her. *Comforting* her.'

'No . . . well, yes. It must've seemed like that. But I didn't really have any choice. I couldn't just leave her there. She was in a truly awful state. I know she got over it quick enough once Zak Fairbrass came on the scene but – '

'There you are, you see! You *did* fancy her or you wouldn't be jealous of her fancying Zak.'

'Jealous! I'm not jealous. I couldn't care less who she fancies. I was just mentioning it, That's all. I was surprised how quick she got back to normal after the Tony and Stamper business. Or what seems to be normal for her.'

Serena moved her chair a little so that, if he turned and faced her, they could look straight into each other's eyes.

She said, 'When you were comforting her, how did you go about it? Did you cuddle her? Did you hold her tight? Did you kiss her? Did you – '

'No! I didn't! You've got it quite wrong Serena.'

'You didn't *touch* her?'

'No . . . well . . . yeah, maybe I touched her. Yes, I did. I remember I did. It was the least I could do, the state she was in. Or seemed to be. Crying and all that. Yes, I just put my arm round her shoulders but that's all. I swear it.'

'Look at me Chris.'

He stared back steadily, earnestly, honestly.

'Did you screw her?'

'No I did not.'

She held his gaze but it did not waver.

He said, 'I don't want anyone but you Serena. That's the truth. I only wish you felt the same way about me.'

Her eyes softened a little and her mouth relaxed into almost a smile. Then she said, 'They'll all be gone tomorrow.'

'You *don't* feel the same, do you?'

The smile defined itself more openly. 'Sometimes . . . perhaps.'

He found some encouragement in this. 'Listen love,' he said. 'Things haven't been easy for us since we've been here. There's been a lot of strain, a lot of responsibilities. But I reckon we're doing a pretty good job on the whole. Now, what I really want is to see you happier. I want to keep your work here down to a minimum so you can have more time for what you really want to be doing. Your writing.'

'*What* writing?' Serena spoke with what seemed like fairly bitter self-contempt.

'Your poetry.'

'My poetry's not worth shit. I've been kidding myself about that for long enough. Almost any of that lot tonight have got more talent than I've got. Those old schoolteachers and Joan Thingummy, they can all write better stuff than I could ever do.'

Chris digested this slowly. Then he said with some caution, 'I know I don't know anything about poetry. But I've been meaning to say something for a long time. If you think it's stupid or I haven't the first idea of what I'm on about, just tell me to shut up. But listen to me for a couple of minutes and think about it. Will you do that?'

Serena was looking at him with curiosity and perhaps even a little apprehension. Some time passed before she said, 'All right, I'm listening.'

Chris took a rather deep breath. Then he began: 'You remember the early days when we were in Shepherd's Bush and I was working at Timson's and you had that job with the Secretarial Agency? Yes, of course you do, I know. But wait a minute. The thing I remember most – I mean apart from us being happy and in love and all that – the thing I remember is how hard you worked after you'd got back from that bloody office. I can remember, even on nice summer evenings, you used to go into the bedroom and work away for hours at your writing. But it wasn't poetry then, was it? You were writing stories. And very good stories, I thought.'

Serena shook her head. 'Kids' stuff. I didn't know what I was trying to do.'

'No Serena. They were good. All right, I'm not a critic. But I'm not a total idiot either. I've read a lot of novels and stories. You know I have. We've read the same ones and talked about them, haven't we? Well, quite a lot of those things we read I find hard to remember now. But a couple of those stories you were writing then, I still remember. I remember them – not just what they were about but the *feel*, the atmosphere. That one about the girl running away from the little market-town in Oxfordshire or somewhere and coming to the big city, looking for adventure and romance and God knows what wonderful things and ending up begging at Charing Cross Station.'

'Oh that!'

'Yes, that. The plot wasn't important. It was something else, the feeling I got of what London is really like. The smells, the noises, the weather, the loneliness.'

Serena looked thoughtful but unconvinced. 'I suppose that one wasn't too bad. Nobody wanted to publish it though. I sent it to half a dozen mags and tried the BBC but I got nothing back but rejection-slips.'

'Yeah, well. I expect like everything else, competition's tough. But it was a good story. I've seen a lot worse in print.'

'One little story doesn't prove much.'

'It wasn't only one. There were others. I remember one about the schoolgirl who thinks she's pregnant. That was kind of funny and touching and real. It was good, Serena. It really was.'

She lifted her mug but replaced it on the table without drinking from it. Then she said, 'What are you trying to say, Chris? What's all this about?'

He hesitated before he spoke. 'Like I said, tell me to go and take a running jump if you think – or if you're sure – I'm talking total crap. What I've been thinking, seeing all these people coming here, all wanting to write poetry, some of them doing it pretty well, too, but none of them, or very few, ever getting published or anything. What I've been thinking is maybe you should go back to – I mean maybe your real talent is for prose, those stories.' He went on quickly, before she could protest: 'I'm not saying your poetry isn't any good. Don't think that. I know for a fact Gordon likes it. But looking at it from the outside – I mean looking at the whole poetry scene – it looks like it's full of bullshitters and fakes as well as the really talented people and it's not always easy to tell which is which. I reckon it's a simpler matter to tell a good story from a rotten one. Almost any reasonably intelligent person who reads a bit knows a good story from a bad one.'

Serena was frowning slightly. 'Stories,' she said, 'are just as hard to get published and everybody knows publishers hate collections of short stories. All they're interested in is novels.'

'Well . . . ?'

'What do you mean, well?'

'Why not? Why not write a novel?'

'A novel!' Serena laughed but without much sign of being amused. 'What on earth would I write a novel about? I'm twenty-six and I've only been out of the country a couple of times and one of those was on a school trip. I haven't been anywhere, don't know anything. I couldn't write a novel.'

'I think you could.'

'And what makes you think so?'

'Those stories. They were good, Serena. They kept you reading. They got you involved. They were about real people, real situations, places. You believed in them. I mean they made your reader believe in them.'

'But even if that's true they were only like miniatures. Little bits of life. Only one or two characters – one proper one as a rule. And only a few pages. A novel! You've got to have lots of characters, a plot, and a background you know all about. I don't know anything about anything or anywhere.'

'Yes you do.'

'What do I know about? School, working in an office or a shop. A fortnight in Majorca. That's about it.'

'What about this?'

'What do you mean? What about what?'

'Crackenthorpe Hall. This place. These people, or people very like them. You and me. Stamper and Tony. Gaby and Viv. Old Gordon and his whisky bottle. The Colonel. All of 'em. I don't need to tell you I couldn't write a novel or anything else to save my life. But *you* could, Serena. I'm sure you could. It's all there for you. You could do it, love. I know you could.'

For a second or two Serena looked almost aghast, as if he had said something outrageous or sacrilegious, but then a widening of the eyes and a sudden brightness in them that was almost mischievous, a slight parting of the lips, showed that she accepted the possibility that Chris's suggestion was not, after all, beyond reach.

She said, 'No. I couldn't. It's too . . . I don't know . . . I couldn't . . . could I?'

'Yes. Of course you could. You could take a week like the one we've just had. It's got a built-in beginning, middle and end. That's what novels are supposed to have, aren't they? You've got a real mix of characters. You can make up stories about them if you feel like it, or just put it down the way it really was. Call it *Poet's Licence* or something like that. Maybe you could work up the Gaby and Viv thing. Have a real murder. One of the students gets bumped off – no? No, well maybe not. I can see that's not the kind of thing you'd want to do. But a novel about Crackenthorpe, or a set-up very much like it – it's an idea, isn't it? Isn't it Serena? Are you excited by it? I think you are. You could be. And you could do it.'

And, indeed, she did look as if she might be excited, though a little nervously, as if she scarcely dared to believe that she could attempt it.

Slowly she nodded. 'I'll think about it,' she said.

'You'll *do* it. You see if you don't. It'll be a knock-out.'

She said, 'I don't want this coffee. It's cold anyway. Let's go to bed.'

'Okay. but you won't ditch the novel idea, will you? Promise?'

She smiled at him and he thought he saw in her eyes the affection they had not shown for some time.

'No. I promise.'

They got up and, leaving the cups on the table, went into the bedroom. Serena used the bathroom first and when Chris came out of it she was already in bed but sitting up, looking at him as he appeared.

He said, 'Why are you staring at me like that?'

'Like what?'

'I don't know. Sort of thoughtful. Got something on your mind?'

'I was thinking about you.'

'Not bad thoughts, I hope. What about me?'

'Your painting. You haven't touched a brush or done any sketching for a month at least. And there you were, worrying about me and my writing and stuff. I've been a selfish little bitch, haven't I?'

'No. Of course you haven't. My painting doesn't matter.' He held up one hand, the palm facing her, to forestall the objection she was about to offer. 'I'm not being unselfish or noble or anything like that. You know me too well for that. I truly mean it. It really isn't important to me and certainly not to anyone else. I scrapped all ideas of ever doing anything worthwhile years ago.

'Yes, I know I put on a bit of an act when we first got together. Tried to make you think I was the real thing, the Picasso of Kingston-on-Thames. But I've always known – well, ever since I was twenty or so at art school – I've always known I'm not really up to much. I mean I'm a fair draughtsman and can knock you up a reasonable landscape or still life but they wouldn't be any better or worse than a hundred other kids' work just out of college, or wherever. And things'll never be any different. I know that. And it doesn't worry me. I enjoy doing a bit sometimes, when I'm in the mood, but it's not important, it really isn't.

'If or when we leave here maybe I'll go back to advertising. I'm not bad at the kind of thing they want but it's only a way of making a crust. I'm not an artist, not one of the real ones, the big boys. And, like I said, it doesn't worry me.'

She continued to gaze at him. then she said, 'Come on. Get into bed,' and he climbed in beside her and put his arms about her and drew her close to him.

He said, 'I love you Serena. I really do love you.'

She made a little murmuring sound and snuggled close.

'Well, just you keep it that way Buster.'


Joan sat on the edge of her bed holding Gordon's *Selected Poems* unopened on her lap. Although the only sound in the room was the muted, silvery nail-tapping of the rain at the window, she was aware of echoes in her head of the noise of the party, the talk and laughter, the small exclamations of assent or disagreement, and something else, less easy to define, the sense of an ending, of events turning into memories, a nascent nostalgia.

She looked at her watch and saw that it was almost half past eleven but she did not feel at all sleepy. The two glasses of punch and one of wine that she had drunk had not had any soporific effect; indeed she felt very much awake and in need of diversion.

She opened the book and saw, for the first time, the inscription on the flyleaf: *To Joan with love and best wishes from Gordon.* Her reaction was probably intensified by the mood induced by alcohol and the still resonating party atmosphere, but she was surprised by the sudden warmth of feeling that seemed to rise from her heart and climb to a fullness and sweetness in the throat. The total sensation was only momentary but its evanescence left behind a shadow, like a scent or lingering flavour, and she found that she was smiling fondly and, perhaps, a little foolishly as she thought of Gordon writing those words.

She knew that if Viv were here, or almost any of the other women on the course, she would have been content to talk about the happenings of the week and of the evening and, perhaps, covertly or not, introduce references to Gordon and her increasing liking for him. But she was sure she would not see Viv until much later, if at all, that night, and all the other women would be back in their rooms by now.

After a while she began to turn the pages of the book, but her mind was not sufficiently focused for her to read with understanding and quite soon she turned back to Gordon's inscription, gazing at the words and wondering if the writing of *love* had been quite casual and thoughtless or whether – as she rather suspected, or hoped – it had been used after some reflection.

She had not really had the chance to thank him for the gift, for she had correctly sensed that he had not wished George to know of its presentation, and the old soldier had not left them alone together after Gordon had handed over the poems. She would be able to thank him in the morning, she thought, but the morning seemed a great distance away and it would be a time of hurried arrangements for departure, for practical decisions and actions, inhospitable to such sentiments as she was now experiencing which, in any case, would almost certainly have disappeared or grown faint by then.

When the party had begun to disperse, she, George and Gordon had left the library and made their way up the stairs, pausing on the first landing to exchange a few final observations and their good-nights. She recalled now that she had felt a small twinge of impatient frustration at George's constant proximity and what seemed to her his almost protective watchfulness over Gordon, and, as she left them both to go up to her room, she had glanced back to see that Gordon, too, had turned his head for a last look towards her which might have carried some message.

If she were now to go down to his room, she told herself, she would be able to thank him for the book and, perhaps, if he were as unprepared for sleep as she was, they would be able to enjoy at least a few minutes of private, uninterrupted conversation. She wished that she had something to offer him in return for the *Selected Poems*, but could think of nothing. Unless . . . but the brief, quickly aborted giggle, that reminded her that she was still less than strictly sober, was dismissed along with the idea that had provoked it.

She stood up, paused for a moment of irresolution then, dropping the book on to the bed, she went swiftly out of the room and down both flights of stairs to the hall, where she knew that a list of all the course members with their room numbers was posted on the notice-board. In the dim light she could just make out that Gordon was in number five. Her resolve was now beginning to weaken a little.

She thought, 'I'll go up to the room and if there's a light showing under the door I'll give a knock. If not, not.'

She went back up the stairs and, feeling tense and slightly breathless with a curiously childish kind of excitement, she tiptoed along the twilit corridor, peering at the numbers on the doors and praying that no one would emerge from any of the rooms to find her skulking there. She came to room number four, which betrayed neither light nor sound from within, but she could already see the thin strip of light from beneath the next door. Gordon had not yet gone to bed or, at least, he had not yet put out his light.

She hesitated, almost afraid, and then she slowly raised her right hand and was about to tap on the door when she was startled to hear voices coming from inside the room, the gruff chuckle of George Barnes and then the lighter sound of some remark from Gordon. She heard, too, the clink of glasses as she was turning away in panic and setting off, at a fast trot, back to her room.

When she arrived there she closed the door and leaned with her back against it, breathing quickly, as though she had been pursued by enemies. But soon her breathing became restored to normal and she was aware only of a sense of relief, as if she had truly escaped from hunters intent on her capture and destruction. Then she slowly shook her head, smiling at her own folly and moved away from the door into the room. She picked up the book from the bed and put it into the drawer where she kept the work she had done on the course. Then she got undressed and went to bed where, almost immediately, she relapsed into a deep and undisturbed sleep.

# SATURDAY

EVEN WITH A JACKET over Chris's heavy sweater, Serena was hugging herself against the sharp malice of the wind that whistled through the yard as Chris climbed into the minibus and started the engine. She could see the faces of the passengers all turned towards her and, less distinctly, the pale fluttering of valedictory hands. She waved as the vehicle moved off and out of sight. Then she turned back to the house and was hurrying towards the door when, on an impulse, or perhaps prompted by a peripheral half-sight of movement above her head, she looked up and saw, at one of the upper windows, the curtain fall back, but not before she had caught a glimpse of someone staring down at her.

She saw nothing of the watcher's features and could not, with confidence, have said whether it was a man or a woman. All she had seen was the pallid blur of the face and the small dark cavities of eyes before whoever it was had replaced the curtain and retreated from the window. For a couple of seconds she stayed outside, looking up to see if there would be a reappearance; then she went into the house.

The window, she was sure, had been that of the room which Gordon had occupied and he had just left with Chris and the minibus party. Whoever was in the building, it could not be Sludgens, whom she had seen a moment ago in the hen-run behind the lodge, nor could it be Ivy, who had not yet reported for work. Yet, as far as she knew, all members of the course had departed.

Tony had been one of the first to leave, roaring off on his motorcycle after taking a quick cup of tea and a single slice of toast for his breakfast. Then, during the next hour or so, the others had left in their cars – Gaby travelling mysteriously with Viv in the Ford Fiesta – until only the train-catchers were left for Chris to ferry to the station. So who could be up there? she wondered. Only one thing for it and that was to go and investigate.

She climbed the stairs to the first floor and made her way to room number five. When she got there she found that she was a little reluctant to open the door and enter. She stood in the corridor and realised that she was listening for a possible sound from inside the room and she was conscious of a growing sense of quite inexplicable unease. Of course no sound came to her ears for, as she knew, there could be no one in there. But still she waited. Then, with an impatient shake of her head, she reached out, grasped and turned the door-handle and stepped into the room.

The curtains were almost completely closed and what daylight spilled through the window was murky and comfortless. Serena shivered as if a current of cold air had touched her skin. She was quite sure that she had seen from the yard someone at the window but no one was there now. Gordon's bed was unmade and she saw on the table beneath the window an empty whisky bottle and two glasses. The place looked slightly squalid, drab, forsaken.

It was then that she was assailed by a strange unnerving feeling of isolation, of great loneliness. She was heavily conscious of the vast house being somehow populous with absences, with shades, revenants, memories, and again she felt the cold shiver as she turned to go.

At the open door she paused before leaving and looked back into the room almost fearfully. Then she frowned and sniffed the air, her eyes puzzled, wondering. She could smell something unfamiliar, a slightly bitter, perhaps earthy scent that she could not quite identify. It stayed, lingering in her nostrils like a half-captured memory or almost recalled tune from long ago as she went out of the room, closing the door behind her, and descended the stairs.

She knew that what she wanted at that moment more than anything else in the world was the presence of Chris, his strength and practicality, his common sense and his kindness. She went out of the building into the yard again, to wait, in spite of the bitter wind, for his return.

Gordon looked out of the train window at the grizzled landscape streaming past and felt relief that the Crackenthorpe Hall party had not been able to find seats together in the crowded carriage. The prospect of prolonged conversation with Arthur, Bernard and the three ladies would not have been an enticing one at any time, but this morning he felt particularly ill-equipped for such an ordeal. He had a hangover. It was not a vicious, mauling one, but bad enough to send him into retreat from all avoidable commerce with other people.

He and George had drunk the remaining half of the last bottle of *Famous Grouse* after quite a few glasses of red wine at the party, and Gordon had no very clear recollection of going to bed. He was now paying the price, a mouth that felt rather like the inside of an old carpet-slipper, eyes hot and gritty, and a nagging thirst for something cold and sparkling. He had bought copies of the *Guardian* and *Spectator* from the newsagent on the station but had not, so far, opened either of them.

He had seen Joan Palmer when he had gone down to the kitchen for a cup of coffee, which was all he could face for his breakfast, and he thought he had sensed a reserve, almost a shyness, between them when she had thanked him for the *Selected Poems* and said goodbye before leaving to drive to Bradford. Now, as the train rattled and shimmied on its journey South, he recalled her face, the hint of strength and mildly ironic humour beneath neat and regular features, the warmth and sweetness of her smile, and he felt a small but not really very painful stab of regret.

Well, he wouldn't be seeing her again, he told himself, or for that matter anyone like her, because he didn't think he'd be teaching at Crackenthorpe Hall in the future, not there or anywhere else. And that was no bad thing. He was too old and out of touch for younger students and the older ones, or most of them, weren't teachable. If, indeed, the writing of poetry was a teachable activity.

Some time later he unfolded his *Guardian* and saw, without properly absorbing the information, that a man had been arrested and was being questioned in connection with the murderous attacks on young women, reports of which had recently been in the news. He turned the pages and continued browsing.

Half an hour or so had passed when a steward came round offering sandwiches and drinks from a trolley. Gordon asked for and received a gin and tonic with ice and lemon and, after he had drunk it, he felt slightly better. He finished reading his newspaper and turned to the *Spectator*. He found he was able to focus a little better on a rather well-written and informative article about Government subsidies for the Arts and it was only when he reached the end of it that he realised that the author was someone whom he had taught at prep school, a quiet and self-contained boy with reddish hair and a quite pleasant though secretive smile.

'My God,' Gordon thought, 'that boy must be about fifty now!'

He dropped the magazine on to his lap and went back to staring out of the window but he saw little of the speeding landscape as he fell into a reverie that was not far from sleep. Images of his own school-days were interwoven with recollections of his time as a prep-school teacher and the early times of his marriage to Susan, the days when summer was the longest season in the year and each day dawned with thrilling possibilities.

He was jolted into full wakefulness by the train coming to a halt and the woman who had been sitting next to him getting up and reaching above his head to retrieve her luggage from the rack. Before he could do more than make an ineffectual move to help her, a young man who was making his way down the carriage had swung her two bags down with a brisk and, Gordon thought, unnecessary 'There you go!'

The woman left and the train proceeded on its journey. Gordon watched the procession of fields and ponds and reservoirs, viaducts, farms and warehouses, breakers' yards where the broken, crumpled automobiles were piled like the victims of some terrible disaster, the small derelict platforms and signal-boxes and then the tunnels and the high walls decorated with oddly professional-looking graffiti, giving way to huddled, squinting dwellings and the small backyards with washing on clothes-lines, the poorer suburbs of the metropolis.

At King's Cross Gordon decided to take a taxi to his home in Notting Hill Gate, even though it meant queueing outside the station. Once he was settled in the rear of the cab he became conscious of a small and pleasurable feeling of anticipation, a very faint echo of the kind of excitement he had experienced as a boy when coming home for the school holidays or as a young soldier on leave after months of the unlovely bleakness of military quarters and training. It would be good to be in his own environment, among his books, pictures, CDs and tapes, in his familiar welcoming armchair, good to sprawl in his own bath and his own bed, good to be home. Good also, of course, to see Susan and tell her about Crackenthorpe Hall and the odd mix of would-be poets who had congregated there.

The taxi took a left turn into Campden Hill Road and, a minute later, it pulled up outside the tall terrace house which was divided into two flats, one of which belonged to Gordon. He paid the driver, found his key and let himself into the house.

From the hall he shouted, 'Hullo! I'm back!'

Then he picked up the three envelopes that lay on the mat beneath the letter-box and pushed open the living-room door.

Again he called, 'I'm back!' as he went through to the kitchen.

There was no one there.

He threw the three envelopes on to the small pile of mail on the top of the fridge and went back into the living-room. Everything looked perfectly normal. His books, row upon row, signalled their genial and orderly welcome. Yet the place seemed to be gently shuddering with its emptiness. He could hear from beyond the window the usual noise of passing traffic and the faint tapping of footsteps and, now and then, distant voices.

Suddenly he was aware of a tiny flicker of, if not alarm, then an embryonic uncertainty. He was about to call 'Susan!' but he swallowed the sound and turned to go into the hall and, from there, to their bedroom when he stopped as something on the dining-table caught his attention. In the centre, propped against a small blue vase, was a piece of notepaper and he knew at once that it was a message from his wife.

He picked it up and read: *I have gone. I gave you until Thursday morning to phone me which is longer than you deserved. You could not be bothered. So don't bother trying to find me.*

There was no signature but none was necessary.

His first reaction was utter bewilderment. What did she mean? Where had she gone? How could she have gone? Who was she with? Why? Then, for the briefest of self-deluding moments, he tried to believe that it was a joke, that she would suddenly appear, laughing, teasing him for being so gullible, but sheer anxiety and outrage flooded back and he hurried to the bedroom to see what clothes and other possessions she had taken.

He looked into the wardrobe and saw that, though not all of her things had gone from the hangers, the ones still there he suspected were regarded by her as disposable. A rapid inspection of the various drawers she used conveyed the same message and he saw that their largest suitcase was missing. She had gone all right.

Disbelief pressed, but only feebly, for admittance, then anger, a nervous, uncertain anger began to churn, but this soon turned to a petulant self-pity. What had he done to deserve this treatment? He had been away in that God-forsaken place in the North, slogging away at teaching troublesome adults, working to earn a bit of much-needed cash. And he *had* telephoned, and it was *she* who'd failed to answer.

It was true he could have called earlier in the week, and made a little more effort later on, but the days at Crackenthorpe were filled with demanding tasks and demanding people and, in any case, she knew where he was and what he was doing. There was no real need for him to be reporting back to base.

He took off his coat and went back to the living-room and poured himself a small scotch. When he had drunk this he telephoned Pauline in Ealing. He held the instrument to his ear and listened to the repeated, mocking sounds of the unanswered summons. Then he tried the number of his son, Anthony, and this time it was answered by his daughter-in-law.

He said, trying to sound casual, 'Hullo Ursula. Is Anthony there?'

She said that he was and that she would get him.

'Anthony?'

'Yes. . . Hullo Dad. How are you? Been away, haven't you?'

'Yes, I'm all right. Been up North. Listen . . . er . . . have you heard or seen anything of your mother?'

There was a very small pause. 'What?'

'Have you – '

'What do you mean? Where is she? Why should *I* have seen her?'

Gordon made a big effort to sound relaxed and unconcerned. 'Oh, it's nothing to worry about. You see, I've just got back and there's nobody here. She must have gone out to the shops or somewhere. Expect she'll be here any moment now.'

'Oh . . . yes . . . But why are you phoning me?'

'Just for a chat. And I thought maybe when I was away she might have popped over to see you and Ursula or you might have met for lunch or something. I was just wondering how you found her. I mean if she was looking well and so on.'

'Why shouldn't she be?' Anthony sounded suspicious.

'No reason at all. That's not what I meant.'

'Has she been ill?'

'No, no. There's nothing to worry about. Just thought I'd give you a call. It's been too long since we saw you and Ursula. I thought we might make a date. Have dinner, either here or we could go out somewhere. What about it?'

'Oh . . . yes. Well, all right . . . When?'

'Next week?'

'Ah. . . wait a minute. I think we're pretty well booked up all next week. . . . I think it'll have to be the week after.'

'That's fine,' Gordon said. 'I'll ring you again when I've talked to Mum and we can fix a day.'

After he had put the telephone down he looked up June's number and tried to call her but all he heard was the answerphone's chirpy request to leave his name and number. He hung up without speaking and then tried to get Pauline again, but with the same result.

He went over to the sideboard and poured himself another scotch which he carried into the kitchen and added water to it from the tap. Then he returned to the living-room and switched on the television. At once the hideous rasping howl of racing-car engines made him wince and he quickly flicked over to another channel which was showing an old black-and-white movie. He sat down in his armchair with his drink and stared at the screen.

The film was set during the First World War and dealt with the adventures of young men in the Royal Flying Corps. The actors, one of whom looked very familiar, though Gordon could not remember his name, all spoke with the clipped accents of the period or, more accurately, of actors imitating what they believed was the speech of the time and place. They called each other 'old chep' and smoked a lot of cigarettes which they tapped on silver cases before lighting them. Gordon took a sip of his drink and put the glass down on the carpet at the side of his chair. Within three minutes he was soundly sleeping.

When he awoke the room was in darkness except for the light from the television screen which was now showing a football match. For a couple of seconds he was completely bewildered but then he remembered where he was and why, on coming to consciousness, he had almost instantly felt the descent of a dark weight of dejection and anxiety.

He got up, drew the curtains and switched on the light. He looked at his watch and saw that it was now a little before seven o'clock. He must have been asleep for about three hours. There was a great roar of voices from the television set and he glanced at it to see the goal-scorer performing what looked like a primitive fertility dance before he was leapt upon by his team-mates, hugged and kissed. Gordon switched the set off, picked up his drink from the carpet and swallowed it. Then he telephoned Pauline again and this time she answered almost at once.

He said, 'Hullo Pauline.'

'Dad! How are you? How did the trip go?'

'Fine. How are the children?'

'They're fine. We've been to the theatre. A matinée. *Doctor Doolittle*. They absolutely loved it.'

'Good . . . how nice . . . and – who went? I mean just you and Luke and Sarah?'

'Yes.'

'Didn't Martin go with you?'

'No. He's in Birmingham until tomorrow night. Some conference. I don't think he'd have fancied going anyway. Not really Martin's kind of thing.'

'No. I suppose not.'

'And how did your week go?'

'All right. Quite well really.'

'Good.'

'Yes, it was . . . and . . . er . . . have you . . . ah . . .'

'What did you say, Dad?'

'Did Mum come over while I was away?'

'Yes. She was here on Wednesday.'

'Not since?'

'No. That's only a day or two ago. Why?'

'I just wondered.'

'Why don't you ask her? She's there isn't she?'

'Yes . . . well, no. Not at the moment. I think she's . . . I mean she's gone shopping.'

'Shopping! This time of night?'

'Ah . . . yes. In the West End. I expect she'll be back in a minute. She's probably . . . I think she said something about meeting a friend.'

'What friend?'

'I don't know. It doesn't matter. I must go now Pauline . . . 'bye darling. I'll see you all soon . . . 'bye.'

Gordon stood wondering what to do next; then he went to the cabinet where he kept his CDs and cassettes and, after a little thought, selected Schubert's String Quintet in C Major and placed it in the disc compartment of the player. Next, he pulled the small coffee-table ·close to the side of his chair and then he went into the kitchen and filled a jug with water which he brought back to the living-room and placed with his glass and whisky bottle on the coffee-table.

The music began and he sat with his glass in his hand, in no hurry to drink, waiting for the patterns of sound to work their soothing enchantment. But the first movement seemed to lack, for once, its usual dramatic tension and even the adagio did not quite reach with its long caressing strokes to the centre of his unease but remained apart, voicing its own beautiful and melancholy preoccupations which somehow excluded him. But he let it play on and he stayed in his chair, occasionally taking a drink of his whisky and water, while the B Flat Trio succeeded the Quintet, and still consolation was withheld.

He thought, 'Where can she have gone?' And, for the first time since he had read her farewell note, he felt a stab of real concern for her well-being rather than for his own misery, and he groaned aloud.

'My God,' he said. 'I don't know what to do.'

But what he did was pour himself another drink and then he slumped deeper into his chair and waited for the alcohol to supply the temporary mercy that music had failed to deliver.


Susan Napier said, 'You were marvellous, Pauline. I was sure you'd burst into giggles and give the game away. What did he say exactly?'

Pauline said, 'Just a minute. I'll get us a drink and then I'll tell you.'

She brought two glasses of sherry to the table and sat down opposite her mother. 'He said you'd gone shopping.'

'Shopping! At seven o'clock at night!'

'Yes, I think I registered a certain amount of surprise. Then he muttered something about going to the West End and meeting a friend. All very implausible. I think he'd had a drink or two. Didn't sound drunk. Just a bit blurred, if you know what I mean.'

'Oh dear.'

'Now you mustn't weaken, Mother! Remember. He didn't call you for the best part of a week. It was very naughty. Very selfish. He deserves a lesson.'

Susan nodded. 'Yes, you're right.'

They both sipped some sherry.

'What we've got to decide is how long you're going to make him sweat it out,' Pauline said.

'Yes.' Susan spoke slowly and thoughtfully, stretching the word out.

'Well . . . how long?'

'How long do you think?'

'I'd say at least two or three days.'

'But what will he do? You know what he's like. The flat'll get in a terrible mess.'

'That's not important.'

'No . . . but . . . '

'But what?'

'I don't know.'

'Mother. It was your idea to teach him a lesson. I agreed with you he deserves one. He's been selfish and inconsiderate. Too much trouble to pick up the phone and give you a call. I bet he's been having a good time all week. People telling him what a clever chap he is. Mopping up flattery and, if I know Dad, mopping up the booze as well. So don't weaken now. Let him stew for a day or two. Right?'

'Yes. All right.'

'How long then?'

'Well . . . I thought perhaps a whole night and part of tomorrow would be long enough for – '

'No Mum! No! When you first talked about it you said a week!'

'I couldn't. That would be cruel. In any case, you don't want me here for a week. And Martin certainly won't.'

'All right. Till Tuesday. That gives him three days to repent his sins.'

Susan pondered for a few seconds and then said, 'Monday.'

They gazed at each other across the table.

Then Pauline said, 'Okay. Monday. And you mustn't weaken, Mother.'

'I won't.'

They smiled with the slightly appalled smiles of justified wickedness and, as they raised their glasses to toast their decision, the two women looked more like sisters than mother and daughter.

'Here's looking at you kid,' Pauline said and, in unison, they tossed back the rest of their sherry.